The

Four nights. Three days. The human son of two powerful vampires has been taken from his home, and if Carwyn and Brigid can't find him, the delicate balance of power in an immortal haven might just go up in flames.

Las Vegas holds a special appeal in the immortal world. It's a city of darkness, debauchery, and vice; a city where inhibitions are low and blood runs hot.

Rose Di Marco and Agnes Wong have been running Sin City as immortal bosses for nearly a century, but when their son is kidnapped, they turn to their neighbors for help.

Carwyn and Brigid know how to find the lost, but what they don't know is why Zasha Sokholov, a Siberian fire vampire and offshoot of an old crime family, became fixated on them. Carwyn has his suspicions, but all Brigid can think about is a fifteen-year-old boy who's been taken as bait. She'll need a clear head and the help of some unexpected allies to find him.

Bishop's Flight is the fourth book in the Elemental Covenant series by Elizabeth Hunter, ten-time USA Today Bestselling author of the Irin Chronicles and the Elemental Mysteries.

"We may try to run from our past, but it finds us. We can put continents—even millennia—between us, but in the end, the sins of the fathers will come back to visit."

PRAISE FOR THE ELEMENTAL COVENANT

An atmospheric paranormal romance adventure that will grip you to the last page.

KYLIE SCOTT, NYT BESTSELLING AUTHOR

Elizabeth Hunter has mastered the paranormal, urban fantasy suspense novel like no one else I've read.

BEAUTIFUL CHAOS REVIEWS

This story had heart pounding intensity and sweet harmony written in flawless execution.

THIS LITERARY LIFE

This book took me on a suspense filled journey that once I started I didn't want to stop... a must read.

BOURBON, BOOKS, AND BRENDA

A beautiful combination of mystery, romance, and survival.

NORMA'S NOOK

BISHOP'S FLIGHT

ELEMENTAL COVENANT
BOOK 4

ELIZABETH HUNTER

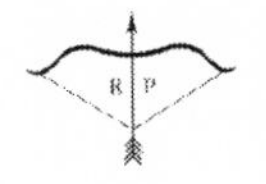

ISBN: 978-1-959590-30-9

Cover: Damonza.com
Content Editor: Amy Cissell, Cissell Ink
Content Editor: Bee Stevens
Line Editor: Anne Victory, Victory Editing
Proofreader: Linda, Victory Editing

Recurve Press LLC
PO Box 4034
Visalia, California 93278
USA

For Bee Stevens
who is the craic

ONE

Rebecca Garcia O'Hara exited the freeway onto Flamingo Drive and headed west, her trusty minivan joining the last dregs of revelers early on Monday. The roads near the Strip were mostly clear. After all, it was eight in the morning, not at night.

"Mama?" Her two-year-old daughter Anna spoke from her car seat in the back. "Anis and Wose?"

"Yes, baby, we're going to Aunt Agnes and Aunt Rose's house today. You're going to work with Mommy because Cece has the week off, remember?"

"Dey wake up?"

Lucas piped up to answer her question. "They aren't awake during the day, remember, Anna? They're asleep because they're different from us."

Rebecca smiled. Her children understood as much about vampires as was safe for them to know. It was hard for her not to explain everything to bright and curious Lucas, but Anna was still a baby. She accepted what her mama told her even if it meant missing out on her two favorite people... vampires. People. They were people first.

It had been a shock and a process she'd had to work through when she first discovered the truth while working at the casino. She'd been nothing more than a housekeeper until she'd stumbled onto Rose feeding on a problem guest in a room she'd been sent to clean.

Rebecca had been certain she was going to die until the vampire with blood dripping down her chin noticed her seven-months-pregnant belly. Rose's eyes had lit up and she'd cooed. "Ohhhh! When are you due?"

Life for the past six years had been one surprise after another.

Rebecca's minivan wound through the sleepy streets until it went into the hills and reached the guard gate of the exclusive community where Agnes Wong and Rose Di Marco made their home.

Or rather, Rebecca made it for them and they enjoyed it.

Felix the guard stepped out of the guardhouse and peeked at the kids. "Hey, guys! You going to work with mom today? Hey, Rebecca."

"Hey, Felix." She waited for the gate to slowly open. "How's Tiffany?"

"She's good!" Felix bent down to Rebecca's window. "I heard that you and the kids were going to be moving in with Agnes and Rose—is that right?"

Rebecca put a finger to her lips and nodded to Lucas. "It's possible they finally convinced me." She kept her voice low. "There are some empty rooms on the second floor that might be occupied soon."

"I feel like you already live here." Felix laughed.

"That could be how they convinced me." She smiled. "They kept adding hours to my day."

It was partly true.

Felix waved her through, and Lucas and Anna waved their little hands.

"See you later, Felix!"

"Bye, guys!" The friendly guard grew smaller in her side mirror as Rebecca pulled into the lush and private gated community where Agnes and Rose lived. Where she would live soon. They were the last house in the corner of the neighborhood, butting up to the edge of Red Rock Canyon National Conservation Area.

Agnes had told her once that it was important for her and Rose to be near open space. Rebecca wasn't quite sure why, but she didn't question it. She knew as much as she needed to about the vampire world of Las Vegas that Agnes and Rose managed, and she didn't really want to know more.

Rebecca turned in to the side street next to the walled estate and hit the button for the automatic gate. She waited for the gate to close behind her, as Agnes had instructed, then pulled into her parking spot and got the kids out of the car.

"Mom, can I go play in the game room? I want to play chess."

"By yourself?"

"Agnes probably made her moves on the boards."

"Oh right; go ahead."

Rose had made it clear that nothing in the house was off-limits for the kids except the usual things that would be unsafe for a child. The indoor pool, the sauna, and places like that. But her employers gave her the run of the house and made her children welcome too.

Once Agnes had taught Lucas chess, the game room was his favorite place to be. They had half a dozen chessboards set up on the game table, and they took turns making moves on each.

"Mama, I stay wit you." Anna was wearing her pink backpack, but she'd already taken her stuffed yellow duck out to hold. "Me and Wack."

"Oh good." She picked Anna up and smooched her chubby cheek. "I was hoping you and Quack were going to keep me company."

She started by checking any messages left that morning on the household line. There was one from the electrician about the dead outlets in Rose's bathroom—a semiregular problem with vampires—and another one from the tree trimmer. She made notes to return both calls when the house cleaners arrived.

"Anis and Wose?" Anna was tugging on her leg.

"Yes, baby, we're going to Agnes and Rose's room now." She grabbed her cleaning supplies from the utility room off the kitchen, put on her apron, and let Anna lead the way.

While Rose and Agnes employed a team of cleaners to keep up their nearly ten-thousand-square-foot mansion, only Rebecca was allowed to clean their rooms while they slept for the day. It was a trust that Rebecca honored. She felt protective toward both the women; while they were deadly predators at night, during the day they were as vulnerable as Anna or Lucas.

She let the fingerprint scanner and retina scanner unlock the room, then poked her head in, being quiet even though she knew the women were essentially in a vampire coma.

Anna scurried into the room and immediately climbed up on the bed between the two women, Rose in an elaborate chiffon dressing gown and Agnes wearing what looked like a smoking jacket and a pair of velvet trousers.

Rebecca's heart jumped for a moment, but then she took a breath.

"Hi, Anis." The little girl kissed Agnes's cold cheek; then she turned to Rose and lay down next to her. "Wose, I have Wack!" The little girl pressed the duck's fuzzy face to the sleeping vampire's cheek, and Rose's hand moved with ghostly languor to stroke Anna's soft brown hair.

Rebecca's heart settled and she let out her breath.

It had happened the first time by accident. Anna had toddled into the room when her mother had been distracted, not understanding that her two doting vampire aunties were asleep. Rebecca had come from cleaning the second bathroom to find her daughter snuggled up with two vampires, Rose's hand resting on Anna's forehead.

She'd been horrified until Rose had told her she sensed Anna's presence and it was comforting.

She set to cleaning the two bathrooms, the floor of the room, the dressers and dressing area, making sure to sort Rose's delicate dresses and lingerie for the laundry maid to take care of.

There were three maids who cleaned the house from top to bottom every day, a gardener, and a cook. The full-time cook was new, and Rebecca suspected she had been part of the plan to lure her into living with them since Agnes and Rose ate very little besides blood.

Rebecca managed all the household staff, but Agnes and Rose had been trying to convince her to move in since Jason had died when she was pregnant with Anna.

Her late husband had been Rebecca's childhood sweetheart, and he'd been working on his contractor's license when he collapsed on a job site, his heart giving out from a previously unknown genetic defect.

Jason and Rebecca had both grown up in foster care. They were disconnected from any living family, so they were each other's everything. They'd been kids on their own, in love and determined to make it without any help. It had been rough, but they'd been making progress. They got jobs and a shitty apartment. Then they got a better apartment. Then they got married. Then Lucas came and they were a little family of three.

Losing Jason had been devastating in a way that robbed Rebecca of words.

After his death, it had been Agnes and Rose who took care of her and Lucas, not the other way round.

Still, she hadn't wanted to make any big changes right away. She'd stayed in their little two-bedroom condo in Henderson, the first place that had felt like her own home. She'd found a babysitter in the complex and had been promoted by Agnes and Rose to manage their house instead of clean at the casino.

Now she was making a salary she'd never even dreamed of and was going to live in a mansion.

Lucas popped his head in the bedroom just as Rebecca was finishing up and Anna was snoozing next to Rose.

"Mom, I think the cleaners are here."

"Good," she whispered even though she couldn't wake the vampires. "I'll grab Anna. Can you get my cleaning caddy?"

Always happy to have a job to do, Lucas perked up. "Sure!" He picked up her cleaning caddy with both hands while Rebecca went to get Anna from the bed.

"See you later," she whispered to the sleeping vampires. "Anna, time to go. Let Agnes and Rose sleep."

"Mama?" She lifted her arms, and Rebecca picked up her daughter and buried her nose in Anna's sweet neck. Every now and then, she still smelled like a baby.

Or maybe that was Rose's powdery perfume.

Rebecca fluffed the pillows on the couch one more time, then set the automatic lights to begin their cycle at dusk, simulating dawn for the waking vampires.

"Okay, baby, let's go get you some breakfast from Mrs. Scott."

"Okay."

REBECCA WAS EXHAUSTED. It was almost nine by the time she loaded Lucas and Anna in the minivan. The cleaners had finished at six, Agnes and Rose had woken a little after, and they'd had dinner together that Mrs. Scott prepared.

Agnes and Rebecca had made a schedule for the move, and then Rebecca had finally announced it to the kids, who were both ecstatic when they found out they were getting their own rooms.

Then it was movies and ice cream. Rebecca was desperate to go home, but she didn't want to spoil the kids' time with their favorite aunts or their excitement exploring the rooms that Agnes and Rose had set aside for them.

It wasn't just three bedrooms—it was three bedrooms with a small kitchenette, two bathrooms, and a living room that was private. It was like a small apartment within the house, and Rebecca knew she and the kids would be comfortable.

It was just a big change.

She was yawning and Anna was asleep in her car seat by the time they pulled onto Flamingo Drive and headed back to Henderson.

"Mom, are we going to learn how to swim when we live in Agnes and Rose's house?"

"That will be one of the first things we do because you and your sister both need to be pool safe even though there's a lock on the pool-house door."

"Will I have chores like I do at home?"

"Of course."

"What?" He sounded shocked. "I can't empty all those trash cans!"

Rebecca laughed. "You won't have to empty all the trash cans in the whole house, baby. Just the ones in our little house."

"Oh. Okay." Lucas yawned too. "Are Agnes and Rose our real aunts?"

"They're real aunts because they care about you and love you," Rebecca said. "But your daddy and I didn't have any brothers or sisters, so you don't have any aunts or uncles like that."

"Why didn't you and dad have any brothers or sisters?"

Because my mother was a drug addict and killed my baby brother and I couldn't save him.

The blackness threatened to leap into her mind. She focused on the road. Lucas was too young to understand anything about that. If she could help it, he would never know about her mother in prison. She had no idea who her father was.

"We just didn't, honey. We weren't lucky like you and Anna."

"I'm not lucky because she takes my toys and doesn't put them back."

Lucas was naturally tidy like Rebecca, but she could already tell that Anna took after Jason and his chaotic love of clutter.

She turned onto the highway and merged into southbound traffic, which was scattered.

"Anna is little, so she doesn't really understand the difference between your things and her things, baby. She just thinks you share everything."

"But I'm going to have my own room soon."

She saw him smile in the rearview mirror. "Are you excited?"

"Yes. Agnes and I can play chess every night."

Rebecca laughed. "So you're most excited about the chess?"

"Yes, I think—"

The sound of Lucas's voice was cut off by the screech of tires and a rush of air. The road in front of her didn't make sense. There were headlights coming right at her, blinding her from seeing what was happening.

"Mom!"

Her breath caught and she jerked her wheel to the right, trying to avoid the oncoming headlights. The impact hit the car on the front edge of the minivan, and there was a popping sound in her ears as the airbags exploded and the car began to spin. She tried to right it, but everything was happening too fast.

No! Her babies! God, please no!

"Mommy?" Lucas was shrieking.

"It's gonna be okay, baby!" It wasn't going to be okay. "Mommy is here."

Time seemed to slow. Rebecca felt someone grab her hand and looked over to see Jason sitting next to her in the car. "Jason?"

He squeezed her hand and smiled. "It's going to be okay, Becca."

The car was spinning, spinning, spinning. "The kids."

"They're going to be okay. I promise you." He kept his hand in hers as the baby started to cry and Lucas's voice grew panicked.

"Mommy!"

"It's okay, baby!"

"Agnes and Rose will take care of them. They're going to be safe."

"Jason." The darkness was approaching. She could see the wall of black as the car spun inevitably toward the overpass. "Jason."

"It's okay, Becca." He was whispering. "I promise they're going to be okay."

"I love you so much."

Everything went black.

TWO

The old Volkswagen might not rattle when it drove down the highway, but it still bounced. The last pothole had nearly driven Brigid's fangs through her lip.

"Mother of Divine Jaysis, will ya please slow down?" She glanced at her mate, who was hunched over the wheel of the old van, his back arched because he had to duck his head. "Carwyn, we need a new—"

"No." He didn't even let her finish. "I love this car."

"You may have love for this car, but this car does not have love for you, my darling man."

Brigid looked over her shoulder at Lee Whitehorn, their new chief of information security, who was sitting in the far back of the Volkswagen camper with a table folded out and his computer resting on it.

"Lee, don't you think we need a new vehicle?"

"Switzerland."

Brigid frowned. "What does that mean?"

"I'm Switzerland back here. It's your car; I do not have an opinion as long as it has Wi-Fi."

"Are you still working?"

"No, I'm gaming."

Brigid had no idea how to speak to the man at times. It was as if he lived in an entirely different world. She didn't speak code or gaming, and she had no idea what Discord was or why he liked it. It sounded stressful by the name alone.

"Oh my Christ, I'm becoming a crusty old vamp," she muttered.

Carwyn glanced at her with a smile. "Join the club, darling girl."

She might be a crusty old vampire, but his attachment to the 1974 customized van was completely illogical. He barely fit in it. The windows had to be blacked out during the day. Sleeping in the thing was cramped for Brigid, which meant it had to be suffocating for her gargantuan mate.

"I've heard tell they're making an electric Hummer thing now," she said. "It's quite large. And friendly toward the planet."

Lee piped up. "Electric cars are the way to go for humans, but you'd short that whole thing out in five seconds and it'd be a brick, Brigid."

She turned and glared at him. "So *now* you have an opinion?"

He wasn't wrong, of course. As a vampire who drew energy from the element of fire, Brigid was particularly... sparky. All vampires lived with natural electricity, of course; a current of energy ran beneath their skin that many called *amnis*. It enlivened them. It allowed them to manipulate their body heat and even manipulate humans.

It also shorted out almost all modern electronic equipment.

"You guys should get an old camper," Lee said. "Like a seventies-era Winnebago or something. You could bling that out and have more room."

"See!" Brigid pointed at him. "Lee thinks the van is too small."

"Betrayer!" Carwyn yelled. "I thought you loved this van, Lee."

"I do." The man closed his computer. "I can't play when you guys are yelling."

The man had been manipulated, abused, and stalked by one of their own kind, and Brigid sometimes forgot to tread carefully. "Apologies, Lee. We're not truly fightin' or being aggressive, and I'm sorry if we've made ya uncomfortable."

Lee raised an eyebrow. "I just meant that you're loud and your accents get stronger when you're pissed off."

She blinked. "Oh. Right."

"But I do love this car, which is why you need a bigger camper. So then you can sell it to me." He gave her a toothy grin. "See? I'm conniving, not traumatized."

Carwyn peered in the rearview mirror, and the corner of his mouth turned up. "Indeed you are."

"Lee, could you do an internet search for classic Winnebagos?" She turned to Carwyn. "Did I say that right? Winnebago?"

"You did, but I make no promises." He patted the wheel of the van. "Lucille and I have bonded." In fact, Lucille had just received a bright new paint job that was the color of the turquoise-blue stone common in the American Southwest.

It was, she had to admit, ridiculously pretty, but that didn't mean she was wrong. "I'm sure you'd bond with a fancy, restored Winnebunko too."

"Winnebago," Lee said.

"Aye, that's what I meant."

THE DRIVE to Las Vegas from their home base in the forests of Humboldt County was long and had taken them across the state, through the city of Reno, and down along the eastern side of the Sierra Nevada mountain range. Along the way, the land had grown flatter and drier, and the air had gone from the balmy cool mists of the redwood forest to the scrub brush and piñon trees of the desert.

While all climates suited her earth vampire husband, Brigid had a particular fondness for humidity because it allowed her to easily control the static electricity that was drawn to her. The desert was not her favorite place.

"Tell me more about these women." She opened her notebook, trying to distract herself.

"Rose Di Marco is the only one I've met, and that was about a hundred years ago when she was in a cabaret show in Chicago."

Lee piped up. "Uh-oh. The priest revealing his sordid past?"

Carwyn grinned, and Brigid didn't try to hide her laugh.

"Remember," Carwyn said. "I never claimed to be a *good* priest. And the Americans had restricted whiskey, for the love of Christ. More than one priest found himself at a cabaret just to get a decent drink after a Friday confession."

"Was Giovanni with you?"

"He had been, but he'd moved on and I was visiting some other old friends. There was a promoter—earth vampire like me —who'd left France before the wars came. Erik, his name was. Erik had organized the cabaret, catered to our kind with all sorts of immortal performers, a few humans in the group, but Rose..." He sighed. "Rose was the star. Her voice was like an angel's. I don't know who trained her as a human, but she was a stunning vampire."

"And Erik was her sire?"

Carwyn nodded. "He had two children, Agnes Wong and Rose Di Marco. I don't know who came first, Rose or Agnes, but they've been mated for over a hundred years now, and they've been running Las Vegas since Erik was killed."

"I thought Vegas was known to be pretty well-run," Lee said. "Small permanent immortal population, holiday escape for the mortal and the undead. Really safe, right?"

Brigid turned. "Ya know, some vampires are offended by the term *undead?*"

"Have you seen what you guys look like when you sleep?"

"Fair dues." She turned back to the road. "I've heard the same things about Las Vegas. The vampire population there rarely causes trouble because no one wants to upset the status quo."

"And they'd be correct," Carwyn said. "A city that comes alive at night? Plentiful humans who are regularly intoxicated and rarely stay in the city for long? It's the perfect feeding ground for vampires."

"So who killed Erik?" Brigid asked. "Who killed Agnes and Rose's sire?"

Carwyn smiled. "Agnes and Rose, of course."

THE DEL MARCO CASINO was one of the last remaining old establishments in a city that rarely valued the past. Newness was the lifeblood of Las Vegas, with old casinos and dated hotels razed to make room for bigger and better every year.

Brigid walked down Fremont Street, trying to get a feel for the history of the older part of town, but it was hard to put a finger on the undercurrents she was feeling.

Glee, debauchery, and suspicion. It was as if a glossy, superficial energy had been layered over a simmering underbelly of grime and addiction. As a human, heroin had controlled Brigid's life, so she could easily recognize the frantic energy driven by craving. Here it was everywhere.

Sex, booze, and more than anything the incessant ringing of

coins that signaled the ubiquitous presence of the casino. Slot machines were everywhere. In the petrol station, in the hairdressers, even in the loo.

"What is this place?" She swept her eyes from side to side. "I don't understand it."

"It's..." Carwyn spread his arms. "It's the Roman bacchanal. It's Berlin before the war. It's—"

"Spring break for grown-ups?" Lee looked around, nodding as he took it all in. "It's interesting."

Brigid watched a woman in a pink veil with a string of pink plastic penises run toward a public rubbish bin and vomit something that was also pink. "*Interesting* is one word for it."

"Come on." Carwyn tugged her along. "The Del Marco is just a couple of blocks away."

The farther they walked from the bright lights and the deeper they retreated into the shadows, the more comfortable Brigid felt. The glossy was stripped away and the seedy came out to play.

Seedy she could deal with.

"We're going to the service entrance of the casino?" She spotted delivery trucks parked in the alley behind a tower with bright gold letters emblazoned across the top. "Really rolling out the welcome, are they?"

Del Marco.

"This is the family door." Carwyn kept one hand at the small of her back. "I was told to go this direction."

Brigid knew Carwyn was correct when the blocky silhouette of a black Bentley rounded the corner and pulled up at the back. A guard hopped out of the passenger side and walked around to open the doors. Out of the sleek vehicle, an elegant man stood, sweeping his eyes around the alley and pausing when they got to Carwyn and Brigid.

The stranger took them both in, from Brigid's black combat

boots and black leggings to Carwyn's cargo pants and flowered shirt.

Her mate lifted a hand and waved. "How'r'ye?"

Without a word, the vampire looked away and followed his guards inside the building.

"He's right posh, isn't he?" Brigid sniffed. "We're lucky his eyes lingered upon us."

"Very lucky indeed." Carwyn was stifling laughter. "Come on, let's go meet the ladies of Las Vegas."

THE RECEPTION ROOM of Agnes Wong and Rose Di Marco's office looked like any other office space Brigid had ever seen, except the color scheme was distinctly more boudoir.

There were red velvet sofas and gold-leafed wallpaper. A hostess in a tight-fitting burgundy dress offered them their choice of blood, blood-wine, or cocktails. The secretary typing silently on her computer was wearing a black corset and an elaborately sculpted hairdo.

Dominating the space, a portrait of Rose hung on a wall. In the painting, she was wearing nothing but her long blond hair and a few artfully draped satin sheets.

Brigid, Carwyn, and Lee settled in to wait with three glasses of water, no ice.

Lee leaned over. "Do you think they'll keep us waiting—?"

A set of double doors cracked open, and a stern man stepped through them. "Are you the detectives?"

Carwyn and Brigid exchanged a look.

"I suppose some folks might call us that," Carwyn said. "We came at the ladies' request. The message was passed through Katya Grigorieva's office, as we live in her territory."

The man examined them carefully. He was a vampire, and

he'd been turned in middle age. Silver touched the temples of his dark hair, and if Brigid had to place his severe features, she would guess he was Latin American.

"Very well," the man said. "I'm Bernard. Come with me."

Carwyn, Brigid, and Lee stood.

"Not the human."

Brigid said, "That's fine for the initial meeting, but he will need access to information as he's our tech consultant."

"You can take that up with Miss Wong and Miss Di Marco."

Brigid turned to Lee and nodded.

"Okay." He sat down and pulled out his smartphone. "I'll keep myself busy."

Carwyn and Brigid followed Bernard through the double doors, down a long hallway with offices on either side, and through another set of double doors that closed with a thud behind them.

She wasn't nervous; she was a fire vampire whose fire burned away from her, which meant she could get out of nearly any situation when the air was as dry as it was.

And Carwyn? She glanced at her carefree mate. Carwyn never worried about anything.

The room they entered was dim and looked like a dressing room from the 1930s. There was more velvet furniture and lush throw rugs that covered a black-and-white marble-tiled floor.

On the far end of the room were three people—an elegant Asian woman in a tailored pin-striped suit, a confection of blond wrapped in pink silk and feather trim, and lying in the blonde's lap was a dark-haired preteen girl petting a white Persian cat.

Brigid froze and immediately switched to Irish so the women couldn't understand. "Carwyn, cad é sin?" *What is this?*

"Iníon." *Daughter*. He answered in the same language. "Is é iníon siad." *She's their daughter.* "It's nothing untoward."

The cold dread in Brigid's chest eased, and she looked again.

The blond vampire was stroking the girl's hair and murmuring something that Brigid couldn't hear. The girl was comforted, not fearful.

The woman in the suit rose. "Carwyn ap Bryn and Brigid Connor? Thank you for coming quickly. My name is Agnes Wong."

Carwyn bowed his head slightly. "Miss Wong. We haven't had the pleasure of meeting."

"Please call me Agnes."

"And I'm Carwyn. This is my mate, Brigid Connor."

Agnes nodded. "Miss Connor, my thanks to you as well. Your reputation precedes you."

As always, Brigid was slightly confused and somewhat concerned that she had a reputation in the vampire world, but as long as people were afraid of her, she didn't mind.

Carwyn continued. "I had the pleasure of meeting your mate nearly one hundred years ago, and I've never forgotten her voice."

The woman on the couch raised her voice. "Carwyn, darling, how are you?"

"I'm grand, Miss Rose." He turned to the couches. "It's good to see you well."

"But we're not well at all." Rose swung her legs to the floor and gently set her daughter's head on a pillow. Her blue eyes shimmered with blood-tinged tears that matched her pink satin robe. "It's been three days, and we're running out of time."

Brigid looked at Agnes, then at the little girl, who was staring into nothing and petting the cat. Her hand never stopped moving, and her eyes were unfocused.

"Something's wrong." Brigid met Agnes's eyes. "What's happened?"

"Three days ago, we received a ransom note from Zasha Sokholov." Agnes drew a picture from inside her jacket pocket.

"They sent us this picture." She handed over a photograph of a teenage boy, blindfolded and holding a newspaper. "Proof of life for our son, Lucas."

Carwyn's normally jovial expression fled; she saw his jaw tighten and his chest expand.

Her husband knew what it meant to have a child taken.

Brigid touched Carwyn's arm and reached for the picture. "What are their terms?"

Rose walked over. "They want our city." There was fire in her eyes. "We leave Las Vegas and turn over our operations to Zasha, or they kill our son."

"But that's not going to happen." A small voice spoke from behind Rose. Every eye in the room swung toward her.

The little girl was sitting up on the couch, her huge brown eyes turned to Carwyn. "You're going to find Lucas. Rose told me."

He walked over and knelt beside the girl. "My name is Carwyn. What's your name?"

"Anna."

"I am going to do everything I can to find your brother." His eyes were locked with Anna's. "Do you trust me?"

"Yes." She crossed her legs and dragged her cat into her lap. The animal purred as the little girl began to stroke its fur. "You're going to find my brother, and then Rose is going to cut off the head of the vampire who took him."

THREE

Lucas stared at the wall across from the narrow bed where he'd woken up the day before.

You haven't spent much time on boats.

The thought entered his mind; he examined it, then filed it away like Agnes had taught him. He took in as much of his surroundings as he could. Small room, mild rocking, but not enough to make him ill. There was fresh air coming in from the vents.

What does the air smell like? Agnes's voice whispered in his mind.

It smells like... nothing.

It smelled like any other air he would smell waking up in the morning and walking out to the garden. It was dry and a little dusty.

What does that mean?

I'm in a boat but not on the ocean.

They're keeping you from us.

Agnes and Rose were both earth vampires, so the boat made sense. If he was anywhere on land, they'd be able to track him. When he was a child, they'd pricked his fingers, tasted his blood, and told him it was for his own safety.

At the time Lucas had been terrified, but he'd looked at Anna and his sister had smiled. She held out her hand and watched Rose intently as the blood welled and her vampire mother tasted her little finger.

Once we've tasted your blood, if you're ever lost, we'll be able to find you.

Agnes had told him that, but he wasn't really sure if it was true. Could Agnes and Rose really find him? Maybe if he'd been on land they could, but not when he was in water.

He'd been raised his entire life by two vampires, and he knew that sometimes they lied to themselves and others to make their life easier or more manageable or less stressed. All adults did that, human adults too. They didn't realize that kids knew.

Maybe kids knew better than grown-ups.

Life was a game. It was a really complicated game sometimes, but it was still a game. There were winners and losers. You could move ahead or fall back. You could come from behind and win when no one expected you to, and you didn't always have to be the smartest or the best at the game to win.

A lot of it was just luck.

You play with the hand you're dealt, kid. That's all we got.

Lucas wished Miguel was here. Miguel had taught him cards. He'd taught Lucas how to curse and how to ride a bike and helped him with his homework when he was younger. Later he taught Lucas how to shoot and how to take out a vampire's eyes with his thumbs if he needed to get away from one.

He knew Miguel had been hired to guard him, but he felt like—not a dad, because Lucas's dad had died a long time ago—maybe a cool uncle. Lucas knew Miguel cared about him; he looked out for Lucas.

I hope Rose doesn't kill Miguel for losing me.

She might, and if she did, Lucas would have that on his conscience forever.

Probably Agnes would stop her. Agnes would know it was his own fault.

He'd been stupid to run away; that was obvious now. He should have known better than to go meet Angel when she asked him to ditch school. It was daytime, he'd thought.

All the real monsters came out at night.

Agnes rarely played cards. She played poker occasionally, she said blackjack wasn't fair because she could easily count the cards, and she didn't like statistics enough to play craps. She never gambled anything, and she never played games of chance. Agnes had taught Lucas chess before he could remember, and that was how they spent time together.

This didn't feel like a card game, like so many of the games in high school where hundreds of kids his own age scrambled for attention and admiration based on things they had no control over like how tall they were or how much money their parents had or whether they were good at sports.

This game felt more like a game of chess, and in this game? Lucas was a pawn.

His opponent was smart, but so was Lucas.

He glanced to the right. There was a small refrigerator with wrapped sandwiches inside and some sodas. Water bottles lined the small desk across from the bed. The bathroom was tiny, but there was a toilet and a sink and a small shower. There was an ancient desk clock on a shelf with the kind of numbers that flipped over as minutes passed, so he knew what time it was.

On top of the fridge was the newspaper they'd forced him to hold when he was blindfolded. It was from the day after he ditched school. Did that mean they'd come back today and take another picture of him with a new newspaper?

Proof of life.

That's what they called it the movies, but he didn't know if that was accurate or just Hollywood stuff.

His fingers itched for his mobile phone. He felt disconnected and edgy, as if someone had taken away one of his senses like sound or sight.

He reached for the newspaper, opened it, and started to read.

For now there was nothing to do. For now all he could do was wait.

FOUR

Carwyn scanned the closet of the teenage boy they were looking for. He was searching for a shoebox or a dusty backpack or any place a young man might stash secrets. Brigid was looking through the extensive bookcases filled with fantasy and sci-fi novels while Lee tried to hack the boy's computer.

"He's not an idiot, I can tell you that much." The computer was proving harder than Lee had expected. "He's followed guidelines on security, so it's probably random." He snapped the laptop shut and stood. "I'm going to need to take this somewhere that I can get it hooked up to my computer if I want to try something different. Also, I'm not a vampire, and I will need sleep before you guys. I'll probably be up until midnight if you need anything."

Carwyn glanced at Lee. "Agnes and Rose said we could take anything we want and the house is already set up."

Getting secure lodging in foreign territory could be laden with complications. Since Carwyn and Brigid lived in Katya Grigorieva's territory—even though they weren't under her aegis —she'd been able to arrange a house via her diplomatic relations with Agnes and Rose. The house was light safe, secure, and Brigid had already checked it over.

"If you want to head out, take the van," Brigid said. "I'm sure their driver can bring us back."

"Cool." Lee tucked Lucas's laptop under his arm. "How much time are we working with here?"

"Four days." Brigid never took her eyes off the books. "This kid is obsessed with Japanese animation."

"His mom's Japanese, right?"

"I believe Miss Wong is Chinese," Carwyn said. "Lots of kids love manga."

Brigid scanned his books. "He also loves chess."

Lee leaned against the doorjamb. "So the life of the party for a high school kid, huh?"

"It's hard to tell." Carwyn noticed most of Lucas's clothes were casual. He wore very few dress clothes except for three obvious suits that hung in garment bags and had probably been purchased by his adoptive mothers for formal events. He stepped out of the closet. "Brigid, do we know if there's a vampire-friendly school in the area?"

"No, I checked. Not enough permanent residents. The few immortal families in the area tend to use private tutors."

Carwyn nodded. "The little girl has a private tutor, yes?"

Lee pointed at the wall. "The kid's got stuff from a high school here though."

"It could be they gave him the choice when he was old enough to be trusted." Carwyn was guessing isolation wouldn't be something the average teenage boy would choose.

Lee wandered over to a corkboard filled with notes, a couple of pictures, and some papers that appeared to be school certificates. "Captain of the chess club. Awards for math league. Looks like he was active. He probably wouldn't have been popular, but—"

"He might've had a core group of friends at the school who'd know more about his life," Brigid said. "We might need you to go to the school and find out."

Lee blinked. "You want a thirty-year-old man to hang around a high school and talk to kids who don't know me about their missing friend who hasn't officially been reported missing? Do you know teenagers? Or cops?"

"Right. Feck." Brigid frowned. "Focus on the computer, I'll figure out how to contact his friends. He's fifteen and probably lives on his phone. Text messages, location trackers, anything that might be backed up to the network or the server or the..." She waved a hand. "Clouds or something."

Lee smiled indulgently. "You're so funny when you try to speak technology." He turned to go. "I'll crack it. Is it really that important though? They know who took the kid, right?"

"We know who took the lad," Carwyn said, "but finding out where he was taken might give us a clue to where he is, and in order to know where he was taken, we need to track his movements, and in order to do that—"

"Got it." Lee waved at Carwyn. "I'll get on it, boss."

Lee left the room, and Brigid sat on the edge of the bed, flipping through a notebook that looked like it was full of sketches like the posters on his walls.

Carwyn turned in a circle, staring at the jumbled detritus of an active teenager.

Proof of life.

Lucas O'Hara's proof of life was all around him. Despite being raised by two vampires, he'd had a full and active childhood. There were pictures and notebooks, evidence of friends and school activities.

And this seemingly happy, active child had been caught in the cross fire of a simmering battle he had nothing to do with.

"Lee's right," Brigid muttered.

"About your ignorance of technology? Yes, but don't take it personally. I still find automobiles jarring at times." He walked to Lucas's desk and sat in the chair, which groaned under his weight.

"No. We know who took the boy, and we know what to do to get him back." She kept her voice low. "Should we be pressuring Agnes and Rose to leave their city and get their kid back?"

Carwyn turned. "Do you actually think that Zasha Sokholov will leave that child alive, no matter what the boy's mothers choose?"

Brigid's face was stone. "No."

It was a truth that no one wanted to say aloud. Unless they found Lucas, the boy would die. Handing over the city would mean nothing. The moment Zasha Sokholov obtained control, Agnes, Rose, and their children would be fair game.

"This vampire does not play by any accepted rules of engagement. They backed human hunts in Northern California. They encouraged Lee's abuse in New Orleans and attempted to undermine Marie-Hélène's rule. They've attacked vampire rulers across the United States and overseas and broken taboo after taboo. They don't respect aegis of territorial loyalty."

Brigid ran a hand over her face. "I thought the human trafficking was bad."

"There is the Sokholov family, and then there is Zasha. I don't think that they're really connected anymore. At one point? Probably. But now?" Carwyn shook his head. "They're not following anyone's orders."

Brigid curled her lip. "Could they be allies? Zasha shares a name with the organization, but they're not faithful to that."

Carwyn shook his head. "I don't know, and it's a dangerous game. Perhaps, but is that an alliance we want to form?"

"Definitely not." She closed her eyes and closed the notebook. "I don't understand any of this."

"For some reason, Zasha has fixated on you. You think it's a coincidence that they're targeting someone in our backyard?"

Brigid pursed her lips. "Katya's too powerful to take on. Her network is widespread, and she controls territory from the edge of Russia to Northern California."

"And Ernesto Alvarez controls all of Southern California, and he's spreading into Northern Mexico since Ivan was killed," Carwyn said. "Which we also had a hand in."

"You think Zasha gave a fuck about Ivan's life?"

"I don't know." He came to sit beside her. "But I think they cared that their child died and we helped to kill him."

"But why Agnes and Rose? Why Las Vegas? Compared to Ernesto or Katya, their territory is ridiculously small."

Carwyn looked around the room of a boy who was clearly loved. There weren't just fancy gaming systems, computers, and large closets. He had multiple family photos with his sister and Rose in different locations. There was a photograph of Lucas and Agnes standing next to a massive trophy with a chess piece at the top. There was a portrait of a human couple with a little boy. The mother was pregnant, and the father was red-cheeked and beaming.

"They loved him," Carwyn said. "Agnes and Rose love their children. They may be predators—I know they are—but they had a weakness for these children, and Zasha saw it for the vulnerability it was."

AGNES SAT BEHIND A MASSIVE DESK, smoking a thin cigarette and sharing a whiskey with Carwyn. Her lieutenant, Bernard, stood behind her and to the right, his rigid posture never easing and his face set in stern lines.

"We never wanted much." Ash lingered on the glowing tip of

her cigarette. "Just a safe place for those we valued, a comfortable life, and independence."

Carwyn sipped his drink and examined the three photographs that Agnes had handed him. They were pictures of Lucas with that day's newspaper, sitting on the ground in a featureless room with a black floor and white walls.

"For now it appears he's safe." Carwyn glanced up. "At least there's that."

"Is that supposed to be comforting?" Agnes flicked an ash off the sleeve of her coat. "Safety. Comfort. Independence. My son doesn't have any of those things right now. I'm holding Rose off from executing his bodyguard, but if we don't find him soon..."

Brigid had left the hotel with a list of Lucas's friends that Rose had provided along with their parents' phone numbers. She'd do her best to interview them that night, but she wanted to do some quick research, and she was hoping Lee would help her.

Carwyn sipped whiskey in Agnes's plush office. It was an aged Irish blend that he had tasted before. "Brigid and I have family too. Not young children—"

"The children were Rose's idea." Agnes's stern face softened. "She'd always wanted a child. Their mother was our housekeeper; she died in a car crash."

"No family?" He looked around an office that spoke of backroom deals and ruthless business. There were no family pictures. There was no frivolity.

There was, however, a chessboard set up on the coffee table in the sitting area and cat hair on the leather sofa.

Agnes took a slow drag on her cigarette and tapped the ash meticulously into a crystal ashtray. "Both of Lucas and Anna's parents grew up in the foster-care system. They didn't have any family. Nothing had ever been given to them, but they were succeeding, making a real home and life together; we had to honor that. We couldn't let Rebecca's children end up in a system she'd worked so hard to leave behind."

Carwyn suspected that Agnes Wong was a vampire who understood and respected grit. "Do you have any idea why Zasha Sokholov would be targeting you?"

"Because they're greedy?" Agnes shrugged. "We have a small but highly lucrative territory. Because it's small, it's easier to manage. Not much happens in the city without us knowing."

"How did Zasha come to the city?"

Agnes shrugged. "How else? They came as a tourist."

"You invited them?" Carwyn glanced at Bernard, and the tension in the man's jaw made Carwyn suspect his fangs had come down.

"Inasmuch as we invite thousands of vampires every year? Yes," Agnes said. "Zasha Sokholov came to Las Vegas to visit, as nearly every immortal in the world eventually does." Agnes drew on her cigarette. "We had no idea they had ulterior motives."

"When did they arrive?"

Agnes glanced at Bernard.

"Three weeks ago," the man replied. "Staying at a vampire suite on-site. They gambled at the high roller's table, took advantage of the in-house donors, though not often."

"Which isn't unusual," Agnes said. "Part of the draw of Las Vegas is the variety of feeding establishments. There are at least a dozen in town; they range in size from very intimate to large clubs that humans frequent."

"And Zasha?"

Agnes looked at Bernard again.

"Sokholov seemed to frequent the smaller clubs."

"And you kept your eye on them."

The man shrugged. "They were new; they have a reputation for causing trouble."

Carwyn turned back to Agnes. "But they were welcome in your city?"

"We don't judge vampires, Father." Agnes smirked. "What happens in Vegas and all that. Our kind come here to revel in the night city, not be faced with their past or their responsibilities."

"And that philosophy works for you?"

The lingering ash fell from the tip of her cigarette. "It has until now."

"And if we can't get Lucas back in four days?"

Agnes flicked her hand at Bernard, who walked out of Agnes's office and shut the doors behind him.

Agnes's rage was palpable. "You and I both know that Zasha Sokholov has no intention of letting our boy go." She stubbed out her cigarette in the ashtray. "Rose won't admit it, and Anna obviously can't be told the truth, but handing over the city to Zasha would mean the end for me, my mate, and *both* our children."

"So you're saying that Brigid and I can't fail."

"You will be given every resource you need." Agnes's dark eyes were wide and piercing. "You have full authority to question anyone in my city in whatever way you deem necessary. My people now answer to you. Do you understand?"

"You don't know me."

The corner of her mouth turned up. "I know you. I know your kind. And you're not going to do this job because of what we'll pay you or because you care about political stability like Katya or Ernesto. You're going to do it because you're a man who protects the innocent."

She wasn't wrong. "Why Lucas? Why not the girl?"

"Anna is rarely out of Rose's sight. She's guarded and pampered. Even the cat has better security than most presidents."

"And the lad?"

A flicker of regret. "He used to have that level of security and he chafed under it. He wanted the things all young men crave. Freedom. Independence."

"And you understood that."

"We were losing him." She closed her eyes. "He might have run away; he was smart enough for it."

"So you loosened the reins a bit."

"I told Rose we had to." She took out another cigarette and lit it. "I'm the one who allowed him that freedom, and I had to fight my mate for it. His security was lessened. He was allowed to go to a private high school. He was allowed to visit friends."

"No guards?"

"Of course guards, but it was reduced to his primary bodyguard, Miguel, and one other rotating human."

"How did they lose him?"

"Because he's smarter than both of them." She took a long drag on the cigarette. "He's probably smarter than you, me, and Rose put together. The boy slipped away from them—probably to go somewhere he wasn't allowed—and three hours later the ransom note was delivered from Zasha."

"During the day or the night?"

"Day."

"Zasha had humans waiting."

"Clearly. We've had a new picture delivered by bike messenger every night since he's been gone. Same pose. Same place. Fresh newspaper."

"And you've looked?"

"I've tunneled around the city and so has Rose. She can sense the children better than I can. Wherever they're keeping him, we can't feel his energy or smell his scent."

"What about human surveillance?"

"What do you mean?"

"Zasha had humans waiting, so those humans might have been captured on security footage," Carwyn said. "There might be a vehicle we can track."

"Whatever you need, you will have it." Agnes narrowed her eyes and stared at the glowing ember of her cigarette. "Every casino owner in this town owes me in some way. There's nowhere in the city Zasha Sokholov will be able to hide for long."

"They don't have to hide for long; they have to hide for four days."

Agnes moved her eyes from the ash to Carwyn's eyes. "It's not me you have to worry about. It's not even Zasha. Rose hasn't slept since Lucas was taken. She's becoming less stable by the day." There was a tremor in Agnes's right thumb. "It's not good for Rose to be unstable."

Despite Agnes's severe expression and ruthless demeanor, Carwyn had a feeling that if a vampire bloodbath were to happen in Las Vegas, at the heart of that neon melee would be Rose Di Marco.

FIVE

What are we getting pulled into?

Brigid was staring at three large computer screens sitting on the large conference table where Lee was working.

This boy's life is in your hands, Brigid.

And she had no idea why.

What wrong had she done in a previous life to garner the fixation of Zasha Sokholov? Who had she crossed in her short vampire life? She wasn't particularly powerful or influential; in fact, she and Carwyn worked their hardest to remain neutral in a quickly shifting world. They were friendly, but only close with few. They had no formal alliances except to those in their immediate family.

They were under no aegis.

"Okay, what are we looking for?"

Lee's question knocked her back to the present problem. "There are two prongs to the investigation." Brigid sat behind Lee and to the right, watching as he worked. "We know who took Lucas, so we look for any connection, any trace, any trail that Zasha Sokholov has to Las Vegas. They're keeping the lad somewhere. Are there secret properties they own? Do they have relationships with residents? They came as a visitor, but clearly there's humans working with them. Who are they? We've four days to find where they're keeping Lucas."

"If he's still alive."

Brigid scanned the screens where half a dozen video feeds from around the casino were running. "Lucas will be safe until Zasha gets what they want."

"Why not just kill him?"

Why not?

She could almost hear Zasha's taunting voice in her mind. *Why would I do that? Where's the fun in killing the boy right away? Far better to watch you scurry around the desert like beetles on hot sand.*

She glanced at Lee. "Whatever game or plan Zasha is playing, they need Lucas alive."

"So he's safe for now?" Lee was tapping around, using some kind of program to search for Lucas's face in all the frames.

"If Zasha wants control of the city, yeah."

"And trading their kid for their city is... what? Is that even legal in the vampire world? That's how you take over territory?"

"We're vampires. Legal and illegal are loose concepts. Power makes legality."

"Lucas is a kid. Isn't he supposed to be, like, under aegis?"

"Zasha can always claim that Lucas went with them willingly. They can lie. What's to stop them?"

"It's clearly kidnapping! He's fifteen years old."

"In my experience, most vampires, especially older ones, will assign adult motives to any human past puberty. Before then? Children. Past that? Essentially young adults."

"Fucking messed up, man." Lee shook his head. "That's so uncool."

"Agreed, but power makes the rules." Brigid leaned in. "What are we looking at?"

"I'm trying to find any trace of Zasha Sokholov in the casino footage. Supposedly they were staying here, but other than one little glimpse, I got nothing. They're very good at avoiding cameras."

"You're wondering who Zasha talked to?"

"Who they talked to, who they worked with, any employees who seemed particularly interested in them as a guest." Lee shrugged. "Hopefully we can get a handle on any ties they have to the city. What's the second prong? You said there were two prongs to the investigation."

"Lucas. We look into Lucas's pals. How did they spend time? How might Zasha have lured him away from his security? Or was it another vampire? Or another human?"

"Oh." Lee sat back and blinked. "Uh... so most vampires see like a fifteen-year-old kid as an adult?"

"Older ones like Zasha? Yes."

Lee closed some screens and opened others. "What about this one?"

Brigid leaned in but kept her distance; this wasn't vampire-approved equipment. "Who is that?" There was a pixie-looking girl on the screen with a heart-shaped face, curvy round hips, and a black ball cap. Her eyes were hidden by the brim of the cap, but blond hair stuck out around her neck, and her tight black shorts barely covered her backside. "She looks like a comic-book drawing."

"She's pretty easy to spot moving around in the vampire floors of the casino, so she's either immortal or she's with a vampire guest," Lee said. "But this caught my attention; I already noted it in the log. It was about a week ago."

He sped up the tape and Brigid saw the curvy blond girl—Brigid was near certain she was a human—walk into an elevator with...

Brigid blinked. "Is that Lucas at the back of that lift?"

"Yeah." Lee backed it up and paused.

The young man was flanked by two extremely noticeable bodyguards, but he had a slight smile when he looked at the woman entering the elevator.

"Look at her. Look at his face." She leaned in and lifted her finger, but the screen went fuzzy.

"Back." Lee slapped her hand. "Yeah, he knows her or he wants to. Can hardly blame the kid. She looks like a character from one of his mangas."

Brigid glanced at Lee. "I knew you were into those."

"Of course I was. Especially at his age." He pointed at the woman. "And if a vampire-woman-girl came on to me at that age, I'd have been putty in her hands."

"Stop looking for Zasha for now. Start looking for this girl." She lifted her hand, then dropped it when Lee gave her a dirty look.

"On it." He started doing things on the screen. "You know, she could be, like, two hundred years old."

"I think she's human, but you're right that she's probably older than she looks. Doesn't matter. To Lucas she's a teenager. As much as he's grown up around our kind, he probably still has the human instinct to go with appearances." She sat back. "I want to know where she went and who she met with. Keep an eye on Del Marco employees especially. Zasha has a tendency to plant people inside or turn them."

"Really?" Lee batted his eyes at Brigid. "How shocking. I had no idea."

"Smartarse." She bumped his shoulder as she stood. "I'm focusing on Lucas's friends for now. Hoping a few calls to parents might get me some meetings with the kids Lucas hung out with."

Lee grimaced. "Good luck. High school kids." He shuddered.

"I'm counting on 'em being more scared than loyal at this

point. Gimme a frightened teenager, and I can get them to spill their guts."

The amusement fled Lee's face. "How? With amnis?"

He'd been manipulated by a vampire by the same means, so Brigid understood why he was sensitive about it.

If it came down to getting answers and saving a boy's life by manipulating a human mind, she'd do it. But she'd try old-fashioned methods first.

"No, not with amnis," Brigid said. "Just ordinary old teenage fear."

"What are they going to be afraid of?"

"Me." She winked at him. "I have this canny preternatural ability to smell bullshit."

BRIGID SAT ACROSS from a young man in jeans and an oversize T-shirt with a Japanese animation character emblazoned on the front. He was Black and his hair was clipped close to his head in a neatly trimmed cut. His jeans fit well, but his shirt was baggy. His shoes were designer, just like his mother's.

Peter Anthony was slumped on the couch, clearly irritated to be talking with Brigid; his mother was sitting beside him.

"Mrs. Anthony, thank you so much for taking the time to speak with me, especially when it's so late. I know you understand time is important here."

"Of course. If there's anything we can do, please just tell us."

Brigid turned her attention to the boy. "Pete, thank you especially. I'm sure you're adult enough to understand how serious this is."

The boy sat up a little straighter. "Well... I mean yeah."

Joy Anthony was a prominent attorney in Las Vegas, and Rose had identified her son Peter as Lucas's closest friend.

"When Rose called me and told me what happened..." Joy shook her head. "I mean, you hear about these things happening to wealthy families, but not in Las Vegas."

"Unfortunately, it can happen anywhere, and the more publicity there is, the more likely copycats are to take advantage. So ya understand why we're tryin' to keep this from the media?" Brigid spoke to the mother, but she kept her eyes on the son.

"Oh, of course." The woman looked distraught. "It's terrifying. I don't know how Rose and Agnes are holding themselves together. And poor Anna! I know how close they were."

Brigid didn't have time to waste on niceties. "Pete, I know you and Lucas were close."

The boy shrugged.

"Lemme guess, you thought his security meant his parents were overreacting?"

He didn't say anything.

"Was Lucas the only one at school with security?"

The young man sighed and leaned forward. "No. Not the only one. I mean, there are, like, superrich families at my school, okay? The money we have? The money Lucas's parents have? It's like, minor compared to some of them."

"So there was other security."

He narrowed his eyes and sneered. "I mean, kinda. Lucas was the only one whose security, like, followed him to class and stuff."

The mother wanted to be part of the conversation too. "My husband, Rod, and I were always welcoming to his security guards whenever Lucas came over. Our house was one of the few houses where Rose and Agnes allowed Lucas to spend time."

"Oh my God, Mom." Pete winced. "Whatever."

Joy Anthony looked confused. "What?"

Brigid needed the conversation back on track. "Did other kids at school tease him for having visible security?"

Pete snorted. "Obvious, man."

"I'm not a man." Brigid leaned forward and allowed her amnis to leak into the room. Nothing specific or pointed, but the electrical charge could create a low level of anxiety that humans perceived on a subconscious level. "And it's not obvious to me. Did he hate it?"

Pete dropped the cocky look on his face. "Yeah. He hated it, but he didn't complain or anything. I think he knew his moms were involved in some dangerous stuff, you know?"

Brigid looked at the boy's mother. "Did you know?"

The woman looked uncomfortable, but she nodded slightly. "I don't have any specific knowledge and I don't work in criminal law, but there were rumors." She quickly added, "Children aren't responsible for their parents. Lucas is a nice boy, and he was welcome in our home. That's all that we cared about. Do you think someone in that world—the criminal world—took him?"

Brigid leaned back and kept her eyes on Pete. "My partner and I were hired to find out."

"Shouldn't you call the police?"

"If you want Lucas dead, you should do that." Brigid looked at the mother. "Do ya want the boy to die?"

The woman gripped her son's arm so hard her knuckles turned white. She shook her head.

Brigid turned back to Pete. "Did Lucas have a girlfriend?"

Pete was slowly realizing that his friend was in very serious trouble. "I don't think so. I mean, he said there was someone he was talking to online, but he showed me a pic and..." The young man shrugged, clearly uncomfortable. "I mean, guys like us don't get girls like that, you know? She was a complete catfish."

"What do ya mean?"

"She was superhot. She looked like one of those girls video

game companies hire for conventions, you know? It was probably just someone using a picture."

"Was the woman in the picture blond?"

"Like, dyed blond maybe? It was hard to tell in the picture, but I think she was part Asian? I'm not sure."

Brigid pulled out a screenshot Lee had printed for her. "Is this the woman in the picture?"

Pete leaned forward and frowned. "Yeah. You mean she was real?"

Brigid showed the picture to the boy's mother. "Have you seen her? Do ya recognize her? She might've been around the school or in the neighborhood at night."

Joy Anthony shook her head. "I don't remember ever seeing her. How old is she?"

Possibly far older than Lucas. "We don't know who she is. This picture was taken from casino security."

She glanced at her son. "Is she a... a predator?"

"We think she may have been used to lure Lucas away from his guards." Brigid put the picture away. "If you see her, call us. Don't confront her. Don't attempt to speak to her. Keep your distance 'cause she could easily be dangerous."

"Holy shit. She's like, real isn't she?" Pete's eyes were the size of tea saucers. "Like, he wasn't making her up."

"What did he say about her? Be specific."

"Uh..." The boy furrowed his brow. "He said he met her on Discord and they liked a lot of the same games and stuff. He said she was really into chess." Pete rolled his eyes. "Lucas was like, really into chess. Everything in life was about chess. He actually used to say that to people, you know? Life was a chess game and most people didn't have a clue about the rules."

That sounded like a young man raised around vampires. Brigid remembered feeling similar things when she left the comfort of her childhood home and moved to university. She'd been astonished at all the humans living around her in ignorance.

"So she liked chess and he met her on Discord?" Brigid was sure Lee had mentioned something about that. "Did they ever meet? Did he mention having plans to meet her?"

Pete blinked. "I think maybe so. Last week he was all... I don't know. He was, like, goofy or something. I asked him what his deal was, and he said something about that weekend changing his life or something. I don't know what he was talking about, but maybe he was going to meet this girl."

"Did he mention where she said she was from?"

"Overseas." Pete grimaced. "He said she was a model for car shows, which is why I thought she wasn't real. He said she traveled to a lot of shows because her dad owned the company or something."

"Pete! How old was this girl?" Joy Anthony looked horrified. "Lucas is fifteen and so are you!"

"She wasn't that much older." He shrugged. "Like seventeen or something."

Mrs. Anthony looked at Brigid, who shook her head silently. The woman took a deep breath and gripped her son's hand. "Pete, tell Ms. Connor everything you know."

Pete slumped in his seat again. "She said her name was Angel."

SIX

"Angel?" Carwyn scoffed. "Leave it to teenage boys to buy that one."

"Hey, Angel is an actual name in America." Lee piped up from across the room. "Especially in the southwest. It's pretty common in Spanish."

"This girl told Lucas she was born in Japan."

"Okay, so that's probably fake."

Carwyn was staring at the picture. Heart-shaped face. Wide blue eyes with a bit of an angle. The young woman was a blend of East and West if he'd ever seen one. "I'd bet Central Asian, which is probably how Zasha recruited her. They were based in Siberia for centuries."

"Do ya think she's one of ours?"

Carwyn shook his head. "I don't think so. Zasha knows Lucas grew up around vampires; he'd be suspicious of a vampire in ways he wouldn't suspect a girl he saw as a teenager."

"Agreed. I think she's in thrall to Zasha somehow, and he used her to lure Lucas away."

"Agnes said he disappeared from school."

Lee asked, "How did his guards lose him?"

"The oldest trick in the book," Carwyn said. "He snuck out a bathroom window."

Lee muttered, "It's a classic 'cause it works." He stood. "Okay, I'm going to be useless in another ten minutes. Leave me a task list for the morning and I'll get it done, but right now I gotta go pass out."

"Thank you, Lee." Carwyn walked across the room and sat next to Brigid, who was staring at the screens where Lee had frozen them.

"The idiocy of teenage boys," Brigid muttered. "Did he think the guards were there to make him look cool?"

"I'm sure he thought his mothers were overprotective." Carwyn stared at the girl's picture. "His bad luck that a predator was waiting."

But was the predator Zasha, Angel, or both?

It was their first night looking, but the clock was ticking in Carwyn's brain like a persistent drumbeat. Lucas's disappearance was in the front of his mind, and Agnes's warning about Rose was lurking at the back.

Carwyn glanced at Brigid. "What are our next steps?"

"If the girl is human, she'll have a trail. Uncovering it might narrow down where Lucas is being kept." She was paging through a folder with all the screenshots of Angel that Lee had printed out from the casino footage. "It's gonna be somewhere close enough that they've access to local papers but far enough away that they can't sense him." She glanced at Carwyn. "They're earth vampires, both of them?"

"Correct."

"If you were looking for a kid, how would you look?"

Carwyn put himself in Agnes and Rose's shoes. "I'd do what they've done. Tunnel and search with my amnis. Look for clues in the human world. Try to pick up on their scent and energy."

"But in a city like Las Vegas, with all this concrete and building, he could be anywhere."

"Yes." Four more nights. Three more days. "We don't have much time."

"We have to split up," Brigid said. "I'll keep talking with the lad's friends and work the other casinos. Luckily this place runs on a twenty-four-hour clock. Lucas's guard Miguel is gonna take me to the casino where the car show was held last weekend."

"You think the lies she told might be grounded in some truth?" Carwyn nodded. "Very possible. I'm going to call Gavin and find out what clubs in Las Vegas Zasha Sokholov might find attractive. Bernard is coming with me."

"Does Gavin have a club here?"

"He has two." Carwyn tucked the photos of Lucas in Brigid's file next to the screenshots Lee printed out. "He'll know the atmosphere of the clubs here—it's a shortcut to figure out where Zasha might like to drink."

"Take a picture of the girl." Brigid shoved one in his front pocket. "Show it around the clubs. Zasha might have shown her off or even lent her out if they were feeling like an arsehole."

"Which they are."

"Exactly."

He caught her wrist as she started to stand. "How're you feeling? This is a lot of pressure."

"Four days."

He heard the despair in her voice.

"It's not enough time, Carwyn. Cause it's not really four days, is it? It's four nights. These are the times I hate being a vampire, because we're feckin' useless during the day. I can't be out and about searching for him, and he deserves that."

"Agnes and Rose have people who will search during the day. And Lee will search as well. We can only do what we can do."

Brigid stared into nothing. "Did I bring Zasha here? Am I the reason that this kid might die?"

"You can't think that way. We have no idea why—"

"Exactly!" She stood and started pacing. "I don't know why this vampire has fixated on me. I'm worried about our family."

Carwyn stood and reached out, but she dodged his hand. "I've already told all my children, and I've warned Deirdre especially."

"I know that, and I know their security is good, but I'm not going to be easy with this until this vampire is dead." She shook her head. "Zasha Sokholov needs to end. I don't know what it's going to take to do that, because they're more powerful than me. I have no illusions about that. I need to kill them, and I don't know how. So right now I'm focusing on this boy." She lifted his picture. "I can find *him*. I'm just worried he won't be alive when I do."

He caught her chin between his fingers and pulled her closer to kiss her mouth. She hooked one arm over his shoulders and pulled him tight, threading her fingers through the thick hair at the base of his neck.

At her touch, his amnis went on alert. *Mate*. He could feel his amnis alive in her, just as hers threaded his veins. She held him close for a long moment, anchoring herself.

He needed this and so did she. They'd been traveling for days with others, and they hadn't taken a moment for themselves.

"Come to the bedroom."

"We don't have time."

"We need this." He kissed her mouth. "You need this, Brigid."

He bent down, hooked his arms under her thighs, and lifted her in one movement. He carried her to the light-safe bedroom they hadn't even visited and tossed her on the bed before he closed and locked the door.

"I think you need..." He reached down, unbuttoned her pants, tugged off her shoes, and stripped her naked below the waist. "A bit of a bite to clear your mind, Brigid Connor."

She raised one eyebrow. "And where do ya intend to bite me?"

The corner of his mouth lifted up as he knelt at the base of the bed. "Don't worry, darling girl. I'll kiss it and make it better."

Without another word, he spread her legs and bent his mouth to taste her. She was already wet for him, and the taste of her body made his fangs fall. He scraped them along the inside of her thigh and heard her panting.

"Not just yet." He wanted to make her come first. He needed her to get out of her own mind for a moment. He wanted to make her scream.

His mouth was on the sweet center of her body, licking and kissing her sex until he felt the tension rise. Her amnis reached out to his, and he reached up to grab her hands and placed them on his head.

"Fuck me, fuck me, fuck me," she muttered under her breath.

That was definitely the plan, but he needed her to come first.

The tension in her body rose, crested, and snapped with a burst of pleasure that made her cry out and grip his head with her thighs.

He reached up, pulled her thighs apart, and pressed deeper, wrenching a deeper orgasm from her before he turned his head and sank his fangs into her right thigh. He pulled hard for a second, drinking deeply of her blood, then turned to the left and gave her another bite on the other side, the fang marks welling with blood that he licked up and took into his body.

He reached down, unbuttoned his pants, and freed his aching erection.

"In me," she whispered, pulling at his shoulders. "Carwyn—"

He slid up her body and into her in one movement, driving himself to the hilt as he joined his bloody mouth to hers.

She purred when she tasted the mix of her blood and arousal on his mouth. The kiss felt endless. She bit his tongue and drank him in as he moved in her like a heartbeat, the gentle rhythm slowly building until he felt his pleasure draw up and explode in an orgasm so intense he felt like he flew.

He looked down as Brigid reached up, tore his shirt down the center, and sank her teeth into the muscle that rose below his collarbone. His body shook as another orgasm ran like a shiver up his backbone. His back arched and her teeth tore his skin a little, but the pleasure and pain combined in a rush of sensation, amnis, and electricity that had the hairs over his body standing on end.

A shudder ran through the room, and the bed slammed to the floor.

Carwyn rolled over, pulling Brigid to his chest. "Sorry about the earthquake."

"It wasn't so bad."

A voice called from the other side of the house. "For fuck's sake, you guys. Stop breaking the house!"

Brigid stretched over his chest, licking the fang marks she'd put there. "Lee's still not used to the earthquakes."

"They're not common where he's from." He ran a hand over the shorn hair at her neck. "How's your head?"

"Better." She propped her chin on his chest. "I need to meet Lucas's guard. I need to figure out the boy's habits and see if the guard knows anything about this girl who was flirting with him. Figure out if Angel was at that car show."

"Okay, but when you need me," he said, "call. Don't wait. Call."

She pressed her forehead into his cheek and held it there. "I will."

SEVEN

Miguel was an average height, average weight, human bodyguard who specialized in two things as far as Brigid could tell in their short time together.

Lucas O'Hara.

And chess.

"You want to talk to the kid, you have to learn chess. It's his thing." He piloted the dark car through the thick traffic on the Las Vegas Strip just before midnight. "He and Agnes have at least a half dozen matches going at any given time."

"Would you say Lucas is closer to Agnes than Rose?"

"Eh." Miguel shrugged. "They're both his parents, but yeah, I'd say that he and Agnes are pretty damn close. Sometimes I'll hear them on the phone or something, and all they do is speak in chess, you know?"

Brigid frowned. "I have no idea what that means."

"Ya know, knight to D4 and all that stuff. About half the games they run are verbal only. I heard Agnes tell him it's the best way to build his memory."

"Gotcha." Brigid wasn't experienced in chess. She'd been

taught the basic rules as a child, but she wasn't competitive. "Did you ever play with Lucas?"

"Oh yeah. The kid beats me every time." Miguel smiled; then it faded. "I'm still kicking my own ass, Miss Connor."

"Please call me Brigid, and in my experience as someone who grew up around vampires, if a kid wants to escape protection, they usually find a way to do so. It's impossible to guard someone who doesn't want to be guarded unless you put them in confinement, and that's not possible with a teenager like that."

It was one of the reasons many children who grew up under vampire aegis learned fighting and evasion skills early in life.

"Does Lucas have any survival skills? Martial arts? Knife fighting? Evasion?"

"He took martial arts, but he didn't enjoy it. He's not really a sports kid. Except swimming. He likes to swim."

Brigid nodded. "Good to know." She stared at the passing traffic from the back of the black sedan. "I'm not trying to be antisocial, so ya know."

"Nah, it's cool. Agnes said you're a fire vampire." He glanced over his shoulder. "Never met one of you guys before."

"You might've and not known it. We don't tend to advertise our element."

"Why?"

Because vampires could only be killed in two ways, a blade that severed the spinal cord at the neck and fire.

"We're not the most popular in the immortal world," she said. "We can get a bit explosive."

"This vampire who took Lucas," Miguel said. "Rose said they were a fire vampire, yeah?"

"That's correct."

"Someone you know?"

Brigid frowned. "Unfortunately and unwillingly, yes."

Miguel was silent a long time, changing lanes as they approached the neon-bedecked edifice where the car show had taken place.

"So it's good you're here," he said. "Sounds like you and your husband are the best people to find the kid."

"I for sure hope so, Miguel." The car turned in to the long driveway. "I definitely pray that's the case."

THEY WALKED through the mazelike expanse of the casino to reach the convention headquarters, following the general manager who oversaw special events.

"The car show was sponsored by a consortium of owners from the Middle East and Asia," the man said. "I could not possibly tell you names, though there were several crates that were... I'd say unusual in nature?"

"How so?"

The man frowned. "Keep in mind, I'm only sharing this because I received instruction that you were to have all access to our records. There were three crates in particular that were definitely not automobiles."

"And how would you know?"

"They weren't on the manifest we were given, and their weights were a gross mismatch."

Brigid and Miguel exchanged a look.

"Were they light safe?" Brigid asked. "Any vents or open screens?"

"No." The man shook his head. "Absolutely impenetrable. I cannot lie—I did try to peek inside, but from the moment they arrived to the moment they left, the consortium's guards had possession of the show materials."

"Was it just cars and stuff?" Miguel asked.

"Cars, memorabilia, some exhibitions and trophies from road races, things of that nature." The man turned right through a large set of double doors. "The casino's security and the convention center's security are overseen by the same team, but they exist in different locations. If you'll just go through here." He motioned to a pair of steel doors secured with a thumbprint lock. "Follow me please."

The minute Brigid walked inside, she realized it was going to be a problem. The room was awash in technology, from panels of television screens to sensors for security, touch panels, and more.

She tried to stay as far away from the screens as possible, but she could feel her amnis reacting to the dry cold air, the surrounding electricity, and her own tension at being around so many electronic devices.

Brigid leaned closer to Miguel. "I won't be able to stay in here long," she murmured. "Can you get the footage from the car show without me? You have the picture of the girl, right?"

Miguel looked around the room and his eyes went wide. "Ohhh, right." He nodded. "I'll make an excuse for you. Go, and I'll see if they can send it over or something, right?"

"I'm gonna wander 'round, see if I can question some of the staff."

Miguel nodded. "Sounds good."

"I'll meet you by the valet station in an hour?"

"Sure thing."

Brigid waved at the manager. "I'm very sorry, but I need to make a call. Miguel has all the information that Agnes and Rose requested. Would it be okay if I step out?"

"Of course." He showed her to the door, and Brigid saw a monitor go black when she bumped into it. "Not quite sure what's happening with that, but I assure you our technology and surveillance system is state-of-the-art."

"I'm sure it is." She pulled out her picture of the girl. "We're looking for this young woman in particular. Our information says she may have been traveling with the auto show. Miguel has the details."

He nodded. "I'll make sure our screeners are aware." He paused. "Is she dangerous?"

"Only to teenage boys. Probably." Brigid smiled a little, then backed out of the room and walked back toward the front of the convention center.

She had a bartender to find.

BRIGID HADN'T BEEN to many conventions when she was human, but the one thing that she remembered was that most conversations and socializing happened at the bar. She searched for a watering hole in the casino nearest to the convention center and found herself wandering under a pair of arches just off a large stage where a colorful wheel was spinning.

Inside the bar, screens plastered the walls, set high up to remain visible throughout the bar. Sports of every type were playing on different televisions, and on the largest one that hung over the bar, a European football match was in full swing.

This was definitely the kind of place automotive convention-goers would congregate.

She sat at the bar and leaned on it, purposefully allowing her amnis to spark and short out the video poker game under the glass.

"Oh!" A girl rushed over in a black-and-white checkered apron. "I'm so sorry about that. Do you want to pick another seat?"

"No worries. I wasn't going to play."

The girl drew a paper napkin from under the bar and set it in front of her. "What can I get you?"

A group of men in red-and-yellow-striped jerseys erupted into shouts and applause as one of the teams scored a goal on the big screen.

Brigid smiled. "Soccer fans, are they?"

The girl leaned closer. "Don't let them hear you call it that. They get a little touchy about it. It's *football*."

Brigid smiled. "I'll have a whiskey and soda please." She wouldn't drink much of it, but it was always good to pay the bartender. "D'ya work here all the time?"

The girl glanced at her, possibly trying to judge if Brigid was hitting on her. "I work here pretty regularly. My boyfriend works nights, so it's nice to be on the same schedule, you know?"

Clever boyfriend insert.

"My husband is a night owl too." *See? We're just two heterosexual ladies shooting the breeze.* "My name's Brigid."

"Sierra." The girl tapped her name badge. "So is it your first time in Vegas?" She set the drink in front of Brigid. "Let me get your receipt."

"Or I can start a tab." She pointed toward the convention center. "I'm waiting for my partner. He's inquiring about the convention security. Our boss is thinking about hosting an event next year. You get much convention traffic here?"

"Oh, for sure." She took the hundred in cash that Brigid held out. "What kind of convention is it?"

"Motorbikes and motorbike accessories," Brigid said. "Motorcycles they call them here, yeah? We work for a European company, and our boss has a collection of old Triumphs and Indians. Thinking about arranging some kind of show with his buddies here in the States."

"We had this huge car show just a couple of weeks ago, and it got a ton of traffic, so this is probably a good place for that kind of thing."

"I heard about that." Brigid waited for Sierra to tend to two men who sat themselves halfway between her and the football watchers.

"Bikers." Sierra wandered back over to Brigid. "I could probably even get my boyfriend to come out for that one. He's always wanted one, but his mom's a nurse, and you know what they call them?"

Brigid feigned ignorance. "What's that?"

"Donor-cycles." Her eyebrows went up. "Like organ donors?"

"Ah." Brigid nodded. "I won't tell my boss."

Sierra laughed. The woman seemed more than happy to chat with Brigid. They were the only two women in the bar, and most of the men were in a midnight stupor, shouting at the screen, drinking their beers, and ignoring everything else unless they were hooked to a video poker machine.

"So were you working the auto show convention?"

Sierra nodded. "Lots of high rollers, and there was a match from like Turkey or something on one of the nights? That night was packed in here. There were three bartenders working, and we could barely keep up."

Bartenders. They always had the news. "So I've a random question that may seem odd." She pulled the picture of "Angel" out of her jacket pocket. "But do you happen to remember this girl wandering around the car show? She might've been a hanger-on with some of the high rollers. That kinda thing."

Sierra squinted at the picture, and then her eyes went wide. "Oh my God, she didn't have that hat, but she was totally there. I do remember her. She had, like, these huge blue eyes. I remember wondering whether they had some kind of cosmetic surgery to make your eyes look bigger in Russia because they didn't even look real." Sierra shook her head. "That's so weird that I remember that. She stood out though. She was pale, like *really* white, and her hair was this icy, snowy blond. Russian accent, big pouty lips." Sierra smirked. "She was definitely getting a lot of attention, that's for sure."

Brigid mentally recorded everything Sierra was saying. "What else do you remember?"

The bartender cocked her head. "Okay, so it's kind of weird that you're asking that. Do you, like, know her?"

"Uh..." She thought up a quick excuse. "It's kind of awkward to mention, but this girl goes by a few different names. And she tends to hook up with older, wealthy men at collector events like this. Someone mentioned they'd seen her at the recent show, and my boss wanted to know if she was a regular here. To be honest, I think he might avoid the place if she is."

"That's so weird." The woman frowned, still staring at the picture. "I don't think I've ever seen her before that weekend, so I don't think she's a regular. I mean, there are a lot of those types —the male version too, if you know what I mean—but I don't remember seeing her before."

"D'ya remember anyone in particular that she was with? Any regulars maybe?"

"Um..." Sierra took a deep breath and let it out slowly. "I mean, it was mostly people passing through. Regulars are not very common in places like this." She closed her eyes for a second; then someone called her at the end of the bar. "Give me a sec."

Brigid watched her walk away and come back. So Angel had been at the convention, and it was entirely possible that was how she'd entered the country. She had a Russian accent, which might fit with Carwyn's guess that she was Central Asian.

But how did that relate to Lucas?

Sierra came back. "So what's up with this girl? You trying to find her or something? I mean, it's not illegal."

Brigid needed to convince Sierra to give her whatever information she knew about a girl that was just passing through and hadn't really done anything wrong in the bartender's eyes. On the surface, it was gossip, but Angel wasn't a criminal and Brigid wasn't a cop.

Brigid sighed. "Okay, it's kind of embarrassing, but here's the deal. My boss's son... he was kinda taken in by this girl. She took advantage of him and she took something pretty valuable from him. Family heirloom kind of thing."

Sierra's eyes lit up. This was the kind of gossip that reached beyond the mundane. "Oh shit. That sucks."

"It really does. My boss could call the cops, but honestly, he'd really like to avoid the public embarrassment. He's a fairly prominent person, and he likes to remain as private as possible."

She was all the way in. "So he's like a celebrity or something?"

"He's fairly well known in England, and he doesn't want this to be a big deal, but if I could find the girl and just..." Brigid put on her exhausted face. "I don't know, I'll probably just pay her to get the necklace back, but I don't even care. That'll clear the way for this convention to move forward, the family gets the jewelry back, and this girl won't be in trouble for taking advantage of a fifteen-year-old kid."

Sierra's jaw dropped. "Fifteen? You're kidding me."

"Poor kid was head over heels. This girl completely scammed him."

"Oh, that *sucks*." She was clearly thinking it over. "Okay, I don't know for sure because I wasn't here that night, but I know one of my friends mentioned this blond girl too because there is a regular we get in here for any San Diego State games—pretty sure he's an alumnus—and the car show coincided with March Madness finals." She pulled out a receipt and scrawled a number on it. "So my friend was saying that the weird blond girl was taking the attention from her regular and she was kinda pissed because he's a really good tipper."

"Sounds like exactly the kind of man she'd be interested in."

"Oh yeah, he's got money. He's like a real estate developer or something." She wrote a name under the number. "Try asking her what the developer guy's name is. I don't know. My friend's name is Savannah. She'll probably know the rich guy's name."

Brigid took the paper and folded it neatly. "Sierra, you're a lifesaver. Thank you."

"Hey, I hope it works out to bring that motorcycle show here. I'd love to get tickets for my boyfriend."

Brigid held up the paper. "For this? I'll find a few to comp you if the show happens. Thanks a million." She walked away from the bar, and Sierra was beaming as she cleared her drink.

EIGHT

Lucas was halfway through reading the newspaper from the second night when he heard someone at the door.

He glanced up and saw the dead bolt in the door slide back. He got to his feet. No way was he going to be on the ground—helpless—when his captors walked in. When they'd come in the night before, he'd been sleeping, groggy, and they'd been able to cut the lights, blindfold him, and shove a newspaper in his hands before he could gather any information.

That wasn't going to happen again.

The ancient desk clock had an alarm, so he'd taken a nap that afternoon and woken at nightfall. If he was going to be held by vampires, it was better to be on their schedule.

There was a gentle tap, and then the doorknob turned and the strangest person Lucas had ever seen walked into the room, which was saying something since he'd grown up in Las Vegas.

The vampire—it had to be a vampire—gracefully bent its head, giving Lucas a formal nod totally at odds with their surroundings. "Mr. O'Hara," the vampire said. "I apologize that we must meet in this way."

Their voice was oddly musical, and Lucas felt both

discomfort and confusion when he realized he couldn't tell if the vampire was a man or a woman. There were nonbinary kids at school, but he'd never met a vampire who was, and everything about the creature was disconcerting. They were tall with very pale skin—that was typical for a vampire —and hair the color of fire. Their eyes were black and their lips full and deep red, almost as if they were wearing lipstick.

Or if they'd just fed.

"Uh..." Lucas swallowed. "Hi. I'd like to go home please."

The vampire put a hand on their chest. "I am sorry, but that's not possible." They walked into the room, and the guards in the blackness behind the creature closed the door, leaving Lucas alone with the predator. They folded themselves gracefully into the desk chair that barely looked able to hold Lucas's weight, much less a grown adult.

It wasn't just their appearance that was throwing Lucas off—their clothes were stark white. They looked like hospital clothes, or maybe priests wore things like that. The pants were wide and loose, and the vampire wore a tunic that hung off one shoulder, exposing a crawling black tattoo.

"Sit." The vampire gestured to the bed. "We should get to know each other."

Lucas decided to sit. If the vampire was going to kill him, he probably would have already. She? Their hair was also at odds with his appearance because it was long and flowing, giving the vampire a feminine air, but their height and the breadth of their chest felt masculine.

Maybe if he pissed the vampire off, he'd get some more information. It might be a stupid idea, but so was sitting there doing nothing.

Attacking is defending. Agnes's voice was back.

Lucas leaned against the wall and examined the vampire just

the way the vampire was examining him. "So are you a girl or a boy or what?"

He was being rude. If Agnes and Rose heard him, he'd be in trouble, but maybe you were allowed to be rude to the vampire who had kidnapped you.

The red lips curled in amusement. "I have been both when it suited me. Sometimes neither. What are you?"

A boy. A man. Neither. "I'm Lucas."

"Yes, I know."

"So are you really old?" He'd been taught never to ask about vampire ages too. He was checking off all the buttons tonight.

"I'm old." The vampire shrugged their bare shoulder. "Others are older than me. Others are younger. You're fifteen."

"I'm sure that seems like a little kid to you."

The vampire cocked their head. "On the contrary, I find myself impressed by you, Lucas O'Hara. You have not panicked. You have not cried. I come in your room at nightfall and find you calmly reading the newspaper. Most impressive."

The vampire was trying to lure him into thinking they were a friend.

"Thanks. What's your name?"

"Zasha. Do you like being called Lucas or Luke?"

Lucas blinked. He hadn't expected them to answer. "Lucas."

"Why not Luke?"

"When I was little, there was this really obnoxious kid on my soccer team who was named Luke. I hated him. My name is Lucas."

"Very good. My name is Zasha, and that is my real name. I think it's silly to hide who you are. Many vampires do, but that's because they think secrets make them look impressive."

"I don't think secrets are impressive." Secrets were onerous, which was one of his favorite words. Secrets were heavy and intruded on life and friendship.

Lucas hated secrets.

"I agree." They leaned forward. "Keeping secrets about yourself makes it look like you want to be impressive."

"Which automatically makes you less impressive."

"Correct." The vampire smiled a little. "You're a very clever young man."

How the hell do I accept compliments from my kidnapper?

"I'm not going to be friends with you or have Stockholm syndrome or any of that shit." Lucas sniffed. "I don't want to be here, and you're keeping me against my will."

"Do you know why?"

"I'm assuming it has something to do with my mothers."

"They're not your mothers."

It was something Lucas thought about a lot, especially because Agnes and Rose had never asked or expected Anna and him to call them mother. Sometimes he was resentful of that. Sometimes he was grateful.

"They're my mothers," Lucas said. "Isn't that why you took me? Because they love me and you can use me for leverage?"

Zasha's smile was indulgent. "Pets are loved and pampered, but they're still pets."

"What kind of vampire are you?" Another taboo question, but this Zasha person was making Lucas mad.

Don't reveal your thoughts to an enemy. He kept hearing Agnes's voice in his mind. *Don't give them the gift of insight.*

"I'm a fire vampire." They snapped their fingers, and a ball of yellow fire floated in their palm. "Have you met a fire vampire before?"

"No." Lucas was trying to hide his fear, but he knew Zasha could sense the minute changes in his body scent and his heartbeat. They were a predator.

"I'm not going to burn you," Zasha said. "None of this is your fault."

"So let me go."

Zasha sighed. "I didn't want to take you, but my partners thought it was the best way to get what they wanted, and I admit that they're probably correct. I can be somewhat sentimental."

OH YEAH, the sentimentality was dripping off the redheaded crazy. Lucas thought it but he didn't say it. "What do your partners want?"

"They want something from your guardians."

"Obviously. What do *you* want?"

"To spend more time with an enemy who intrigues me."

"Agnes or Rose?"

"Neither, though it's amusing that you think they would interest me."

Lucas felt oddly offended on behalf of Agnes and Rose. "So you needed to kidnap me so you could spend time with your enemy?" Lucas scoffed. "That's dumb. Who wants to spend time with their enemy?"

"You think I'm dumb?" Zasha was amused again. "I try to think of it as quality time with someone new and intriguing."

"You couldn't just ask them to be friends or something?"

They curled their lip. "It's just not as fun to be friends with someone. Much more entertaining to be enemies."

"What's wrong with you?"

"I was probably twisted at a young age by trauma; then my vampire mate was killed." Zasha blinked their large black eyes. "I suppose I became less... civilized after that."

"Both of those sound like a you problem, not a me problem. You should find a good therapist and let me go."

Zasha smiled. "I know it's bravado because I can hear your heart and smell your fear, but I am intensely amused by you. Maybe I'll keep you after all. You could be Angel's companion."

He blinked.

"Oh! You hadn't realized that she was the one who led you to me?" Zasha smiled. "She's quite besotted with me, you know."

"Angel's your pet?"

"She enjoys my bite." Zasha smiled widely, running their tongue along one fang. "An amusing little thing. I think she's somewhat fond of you."

Lucas couldn't stop his face from burning.

"She went on and on about how you like chess, which she found peculiar but I find interesting. Young humans usually don't appreciate war games unless they're on a screen and they can blast things with pretend guns."

Lucas wanted a real gun. So much. He would aim for Zasha's head like Miguel had taught him.

"Shall I get you a chessboard?" Zasha asked. "Would you enjoy that?"

"I don't need one."

Their eyes lit up. "I see. Shall we start a game, you and I?"

"No." Lucas glanced at the door. "Are they waiting to take my picture? Why don't you just take my picture and leave me alone?"

"I wanted to be civilized."

Lucas met their eyes and held them. "You're not civilized."

Zasha leaned forward and smiled. "It's good that you know that."

NINE

"Zasha Sokholov again?" Gavin's voice echoed through the speaker of Carwyn's voice-activated mobile phone. It had an unwieldy case and tinny speakers, but it worked and he couldn't complain. "Why is Zasha in Las Vegas?"

"They've taken Agnes and Rose's son, and I'd appreciate your discretion."

There was a long silence on the phone.

Gavin Wallace was a wealthy wind vampire with clubs, bars, and drinking establishments all over the world, including two in Las Vegas. He was Lee's former employer, the CEO of a new vampire technology start-up, and he owed Carwyn more than a few favors.

"How is Rose?" Gavin asked.

"Agnes is watching her, and she has her other child but...." Carwyn pictured the brown-eyed girl and her bloodthirsty pronouncement.

"You're going to find my brother, and then Rose is going to cut off the head of the vampire who took him."

"I think the daughter is keeping her grounded for now, but things will turn bad quickly if Zasha harms this child." Carwyn decided to probe Gavin's business mind. "Why would Zasha want Las Vegas?"

"Is that why he took Lucas? Money is the immediate thought. Agnes and Rose are far wealthier than they pretend. I know how profitable my clubs there are, and I know what I pay in tribute. It's substantial, but it's worth it because the money that rolls into that city is obscene."

"Have any Sokholovs visited your clubs in Vegas?"

"Of course."

Carwyn snorted.

"The organization pays their member fees like everyone else, and they use the city to meet. Would you rather they hide in the shadows so you don't know what they're plotting? Not Zasha. Not that I know of. But the rest of them use the clubs."

"So Zasha isn't on good terms with the rest of their clan?"

"*Clan* is a very... loose word to describe the vampire offspring of Old Sokholov, but that's a long story and I don't think it will help the current situation. I can put you in touch with my manager. Her name is Justine and I'll give her a call when I hang up with you."

"Good. I'm with Agnes's second and we're headed to all the vampire clubs in town. Hoping to get an idea of where Zasha has been."

"I don't know if Justine has seen them, but if they've been around, she'll tell you. I'm in New Orleans at the moment but heading back to New York in two days. Would my presence be helpful? I wouldn't consider Agnes and Rose friends, but we're friendly."

"Not as yet, and we only have four days. I'll call you if I think you can help."

"You know I have no love for Sokholov."

Zasha Sokholov had been responsible for the death of some

of Gavin's employees, the rift in his mentor's organization, and the scarring of several others.

"This vampire has fixated on Brigid for some reason." Carwyn frowned and tugged on his pant seam. "I don't like it."

"You're growling, Father."

Carwyn's better angels couldn't overcome his instincts as a mate. "I'm worried she's going to take chances I don't want her to take. She's gifted, she's smart, and she's dangerous, but she's still young." At the end of the day, Brigid was barely over a decade in vampire life while Carwyn had over a millennium behind him. "I want to bury Sokholov and put this challenge behind us."

"And the worst part seems to be that whatever strange rivalry this vampire has created has pulled in two vampires I like quite a lot and their completely innocent son."

"We'll find the boy." They had to. Brigid would never forgive herself if an innocent child was killed because a vampire held a grudge against her. "Send me your manager's information, and I'm going to send you a picture of a woman. We think she's human, and I want to know if you recognize her."

"I'll get her picture to Raj and see what we have in our system. How's Lee?"

"He's excellent, and he likes working for us more than you. He says you were cheap and your personal grooming habits were a more than a little lacking."

"Fuck all the way back to Dublin, you glorified gopher. And tell your wife I said hello." Carwyn was smiling when he got off the phone. He tapped on the divider, and the window rolled down. "Wallace is letting his manager know we're coming and has instructed her to cooperate."

Bernard turned and looked through the window. "We'll head to the... less reputable clubs first. It's more likely that Zasha fed there. We can ask about the girl at the nicer clubs. There are two in particular that human pets tend to frequent when they want to be bitten."

The girl Lucas knew as Angel was definitely human according to his guards. She'd tried to strike up a conversation with the boy a few times at the casino, which put the guards on alert.

"They'd been talking before he slipped his guards," Carwyn said. "She planned this."

"I'm sure they did. Lucas is a very bright young man." Bernard looked grim. "Guarding him has been a challenge since he was a child."

"I'm surprised Rose ever let him leave the house."

Bernard had nothing to say. Carwyn had met the type before and could spot loyalty in the man's carriage. He'd worked for Agnes and Rose for decades. Nothing could convince him to say a cross word about his mistresses.

"Vampires with power produce enemies no matter who they are," Carwyn said. "Human family members are always targets."

"This enemy was unprovoked."

"Surely this isn't the first challenge to their power."

He'd bet that the two women had suffered more than their share of opportunists who underestimated them. They were young in the vampire world and relatively inexperienced.

"This is the first challenge that has violated their aegis like this."

Carwyn frowned. "Zasha Sokholov doesn't follow any accepted rules of combat."

"Apparently not."

They pulled into a strip mall where neon lights flickered in the window and a crooked beer sign pointed to the entrance of the club. The cars in the parking lot were a mix of rusted beaters and discreet luxury sedans.

"Feeding club?"

"We'll start with the seediest" —Bernard got out of the car and straightened his suit— "and work our way up. I hope you fed before you joined me, because I would not advise tasting anything on the menu here."

Carwyn glanced at the sign over the awning. DESERT CRAVING. It was made of cracked vinyl, and there were at least three lights out, leaving the sign looking more like DESE T RAVIN.

"They don't even clear enough to fix the sign?" Profitability was usually a given in a vampire club. Humans craved the bite, and vampires were happy to pay for it. It was as much of a no-brainer as humans and casinos.

"Oh, they clear plenty." Bernard slid on a pair of blue mirrored sunglasses. "They just like this place exactly the way it is."

THEY WENT to three clubs before they had any success, and they got their first hit at Tequila Chaser, Gavin's country-and-western establishment near Fremont Street.

"Oh, this girl." Gavin's manager Justine was cooperative. "Yeah, I've seen her. She likes the older ones, but she hasn't caused any issues here. I told her no feeding was allowed in the club except from designated donors, but she just picks them up and takes them other places." She shrugged. "You know how bite addicts are."

There was country-and-western music blaring over the speakers in the club, and a mechanical bull was tossing pretty young men and women off its back as the crowd whooped and hollered.

It was hardly the atmosphere Gavin cultivated in most of his clubs, but Carwyn had to admit the place was packed. It was a caricature of a cowboy bar, and many vampires were dressed the part. Carwyn had even seen a pair of chaps with fringe down the side.

"How long has she been coming around?" Bernard asked.

"Maybe two or three weeks? I don't notice all the bite bunnies, but she stood out with that hair and that skin. I thought she was your kind at first."

"Why?"

"I mean, most people around here aren't that pale, and..." Justine shrugged. "Just her manners, I guess. She felt older than she looked. That's usually a clue."

It might also indicate the young woman had been raised by vampires.

"Did you get a name?"

"I didn't, but it would probably have been fake if I had. You can check with the security guys if you want. If she had an out-of-country ID or something, it might have stood out."

"Did she have an accent?"

"Yes, Russian," Justine said. "We get enough of them here that I can recognize it."

Bernard asked, "Do you remember who she was spending time with?"

"Mostly old rich vamps looking for blood and sex. She seemed to like men and women equally." Justine frowned. "Actually, there *was* someone who caught my attention because it seemed like they were going to have a problem but they ended up just talking." She snapped her fingers. "Sokholov."

"Zasha Sokholov?"

Justine frowned. "I don't know who that is, but this was one of the clan soldiers. I don't know his name. Dark hair and a cross tattoo right in the center of his neck. Kind of the typical look for that crowd."

"Do they come here a lot?"

"Not a lot, but when one of the bosses is in town, they'll

usually go to Gavin's other place" —Justine smiled— "the one *without* the bull, if you know what I mean. The bosses go there to talk business, and some of the soldiers hang out here. They like girls in tight outfits and cowboy hats." She put on a Russian accent. "Very, very *American*."

Bernard smirked. "Thanks, Justine."

"Anytime, Bernie." She winked at him. "Gavin tells me Rose and Agnes need a favor, we're always happy to help. We like things nice and boring here in our little corner of the desert." The crowd whooped as another person went flying off the bull. "Our version of boring anyway."

"You said something about the door guards?" Carwyn asked.

"Sure." She slid out of the booth and held out her hand. "Let me take you over."

"OH YEAH, I REMEMBER HER." The guard was a burly human with a thick neck and tattoos on his neck, but these reminded Carwyn of the designs he'd seen among Latino men in Los Angeles, not Russian gang tattoos. "Anna something?"

"Not Anna," his partner said. "Alina but call her *Angel*." The man smirked. "Typical bite bunny. They usually pick some kind of name that's going to sound more exotic. Like the vamps care."

Bernard glared at the man and growled.

The human stepped back and his puffed-out chest deflated a bit. "I just mean the girls who want a vampire to notice them, they don't want to go by Suzy, you know?"

Carwyn put on his soothing voice. "I understand your meaning, but I'll bet she stood out anyway, didn't she?"

"I thought maybe she was albino because of the skin and the hair, but her eyes were really blue."

"And she had roots." The other guard handed the picture

back. "I noticed them the last time she came in. She definitely dyed her hair."

"Contacts?"

Both men shook their head. "No idea. Her ID was Russian; we could read the birthday. That's all we care about."

"Passport?"

"Yeah, but I noticed she had a US license too, so I don't know if she's been here for a while or it could have been a fake license."

"State?"

The men exchanged a glance.

"Not Nevada," one said. "Not California or Arizona either."

The other man snapped his fingers. "It was the one with the red, white, and blue flag in the corner."

"The United States?" his friend asked.

"No, dumbass, a *state*."

"Texas," Bernard said. "Was it Texas?"

"Yeah," the first guard said. "That was the one. She had a Texas ID."

Carwyn immediately stepped away and turned on his phone.

Lee answered, and he had clearly been sleeping. "Carwyn, I told you—"

"Alina," he said. "Look for Alinas with Texas driver's licenses. There can't be that many of them. There's not a huge Russian community in Texas."

"Alina's a pretty common name." The man sighed. "I will start on it first thing in the morning. I can hack into the Texas DMV no problem. Their security is shit."

"Good. Go back to sleep."

"This could have been a text, Carwyn."

"My fingers are too big for the little keyboard." He snapped the cover back on the phone and walked back to Bernard. "Did they give you anything else?"

"They knew the name of the man Justine mentioned, the soldier from the Sokholov clan." Bernard looked angry.

"That's excellent." That was a lead. "Who was it?"

"His name is Mika Arakas, and I know him because he's Oleg Sokolov's enforcer. He always brings Mika when he's in town."

Carwyn cocked his head. "Is Oleg in town right now?"

"He got in a week ago." Bernard's face was stony. "And Mika was definitely with him."

TEN

Brigid fought against the dawn, but it was inevitable. Whether she wanted it or not, she and Carwyn were in their day chamber when the sun rose and still had two leads to follow at nightfall.

She fell asleep in Carwyn's arms and woke at dusk knowing that their first night was gone.

One down. Three left.

"What do we know about Oleg Sokolov?" Brigid asked. "I know Murphy hates him, but that's 'cause Anne and Oleg are friends and get together a couple of times a year."

Anne O'Dea was the mate of Brigid's old boss and the only vampire therapist that Brigid knew of. She'd always wondered if Oleg was a friend or a client, but Anne was tight-lipped about the Russian.

"Well, he's not a sociopath, because Anne wouldn't be friends with a sociopath," Carwyn said. "He's a complicated figure who lives in a brutal world. His sire was a madman, and the scattered remnants of his extended family tend to feed into the worst stereotypes about Russian vampires, so you can imagine he's cranky about Zasha."

Oleg Sokolov.

The difference in spelling was intentional. Oleg had spent centuries distancing himself from the more brutal family he shared a sire with.

That sire was dead, and rumors said that Oleg had been the one to finally kill the old man.

"Two fire vampires from the same sire?" Brigid said. "That's unusual."

"I've heard Russians say something along the lines of 'The smoke of hate hides the fire of fear.'" Carwyn's arm came around Brigid. "Old Sokholov's children were sired in fear. He cultivated it among his offspring. It's no wonder that two of his children were sired to fire."

"Could Oleg have anything to do with this?" Brigid asked. "Do ya think he knows what shite Zasha is up to?"

"I doubt it, but there's only one way to find out." He kissed her forehead. "Time to go ask for an audience with the Russian."

But before they met with the Russian, they needed to update Agnes and Rose and find out what Lee had discovered about Alina during the day.

They dressed in haste, both wearing black to blend in with the Las Vegas crowds. As much as Carwyn could ever blend in.

"Tell me something good," Brigid said to Lee when they exited their day chamber.

"Alina Oorzhak, and you're welcome." He pulled up a file with a picture, a birth certificate, and a passport. "Born in 1997, she's twenty-six years old, and she was surrendered to the state when she was seven. Parents both died in a car accident."

"Horrible," Brigid muttered. "She's young. When does she pop up again?"

"No school records that I could find, but she applied for a passport when she turned eighteen, and since then she's traveled pretty extensively. No employment on record, so someone else is paying the bills."

"Zasha?"

"Definitely could be." Lee turned his chair toward them. "She entered the US for the first time three years ago on a tourist visa and has been hopping in and out of the country since."

"Interesting."

"She got an ID in Dallas using a forged birth certificate, uses that for getting around in the States."

"Does she have an address in Dallas?"

"Only real address on record is an apartment in Moscow that seems abandoned and a mailing address here in the States." He turned and clicked to the next screen. "A public mailbox in San Francisco." There was video on the screen of a dark-haired Alina going into a storefront with sunglasses and a hoodie on. She gathered a bunch of mail from a small box, tossed most of it, then walked out of the store with a few items clutched under her arm. "That's all, folks."

"That's a lot," Carwyn said. "Good job, Lee."

"And Brigid, I tracked down that server you got the phone number for last night. Her name is Savannah Smith, and she's a part-time dancer at a club here in town in addition to her job serving at the hotel. I called and she's working tonight."

"A dancer?" Brigid asked. "Like for one of those fancy casino shows?"

"Uh..." Lee looked uncomfortable. "No, a dancer as in she takes off her clothes and spins around on a pole at the Pink Daiquiri nightclub in Henderson."

"Oh right." Brigid blinked. "Well, at least it's not cold."

Carwyn was trying to hide his smile. "Indeed."

"Okay, let's head to the Del Marco and update Agnes and Rose."

"We may need to use them to contact the Russian too."

Lee's eyebrows went up. "Anytime I hear a nickname that's just a nationality, I'm wary."

"You should be." Carwyn put his hand on the small of Brigid's back and ushered her to the door. "Keep your phone on."

AGNES WAS STONY FACED, and Rose was mildly frantic. The girl, luckily, was not in the room.

"We got another photo today." Agnes handed it over to Carwyn. "Three nights."

Brigid took the photo and examined it. Unlike previous photographs, in this one the young man was not blindfolded and he stared straight at the camera without a single sign of fear.

Rose was pacing in the office. "He's not blindfolded. That means he's seen their faces. That means they're going to kill him."

"I'm sure they might think they will," Brigid said. "But we've already made progress. We found a young woman Lucas was talking with and messaging. We suspect she's the reason he ditched school and his guards. We've identified her, and we'd like your help setting up a meeting with Oleg Sokolov. Bernard mentioned he was in town."

Agnes and Rose exchanged a look.

"Does Oleg have something to do with Zasha?" Rose's lower lip was trembling. "We always assumed they weren't connected even though they had that same nasty man as a sire." Her fangs dropped down and she bared her teeth. "Bring him to me!"

"Rose." Agnes's voice was sharp. "Let them speak."

"We don't know that he's connected to Zasha, but his enforcer—"

"Mika Arakas," muttered Agnes.

Carwyn took over. "Arakas was seen arguing with the young woman who was messaging Lucas. We think the young woman is connected to Zasha, but Arakas seemed to know who she was."

"The Russian has a house here in town that he keeps for his people to use," Agnes said. "I'll have Bernard call them and tell them you need a meeting."

"Give my name first," Brigid said.

Carwyn stared at her.

"I've a connection to Anne, and Oleg and Anne are friends. He won't consider me a threat, and he won't wanna piss off Murphy."

"Two fire vampires in the same room?"

"I'm too young for him to consider me a threat."

"Fine." Carwyn clearly wasn't happy. "But don't think you're going alone."

"We have two leads," Brigid said quietly. "And limited time. I'll take Bernard. You and Miguel should go find Savannah and see if she knows who the businessman is."

He raised an eyebrow. "My darling girl, are you forcing me to go to a strip club in Henderson?"

She smirked. "Better you than me."

BRIGID SAT IN the back with Bernard as their driver was waved through the gates of a large compound in a gated neighborhood along the shores of Lake Las Vegas. There were thick walls around the property, and shaded walkways, stark landscaping, and bubbling fountains decorated the grounds.

The house itself was a brutal concrete facade with very few windows and broad balconies stacked on three levels. Ornate tiles decorated the front of the house, which was painted a stark white.

"So warm and cozy," Brigid muttered.

"Oh yes, when Oleg Sokolov comes to mind, the first word I always think of is *cozy*."

Guards were everywhere, nearly all of them with the heavy black tattoos on their neck and face that characterized Russian organized crime.

Scattered among the human guards, the vampire lieutenants were conspicuous for their clear complexions and neat suits. The humans might be wearing the uniform of a gangster, but Oleg's own men looked like business professionals.

"He was cooperative about us comin'?"

"More than cooperative—he seemed happy on the phone." Bernard pursed his lips. "Damn near jolly."

"Why is that more frightening?"

"I don't know, but I agree."

They drove up to the main gate, and a man in a suit opened the car door. Brigid and Bernard slid out, nodding at the collection of vampires around them.

"Brigid Connor." A tall man appeared at the top of the steps and spread his arms. "Dear friend of my friend Anne."

Oleg Sokolov was tall and barrel-chested with a thick brown beard and closely cropped dark brown hair cut to military precision. His face was angular and handsome with high cheekbones and a honed jaw marked by a vicious scar that crawled down his neck to his collarbone. His eyes were a smudged grey, and his lips were sensuously full.

Rumors in the vampire world cast him as a lover of many women, but there were none in view that night. His rumored relationships read like a who's who of powerful women in the vampire world.

He wasn't wearing a suit like most of the men around him

but a Cuban-style embroidered shirt and a pair of linen pants, suitable for the warm spring weather in the desert.

"Oleg Sokolov." Brigid walked up the steps with Bernard behind her. "It's been years since I've seen you. How are you?"

"I am doing well." He ushered them into the house. "Can I take your coats and weapons please?"

"Of course." It made Brigid nervous to remove her coat, then her 9mm, then the two daggers strapped to her chest. The ankle holster was the last to be removed; then she stood in Oleg's front room, utterly naked except for her clothes and her fangs.

"My friend." Oleg leaned down and hugged her. "How is Anne? It has been too long since I have seen her." Oleg smelled like pine and woodsmoke. It was a more-than-pleasant scent.

"I video chatted with Anne last month. She's doing well. Spending more time at the country house in Galway these days, I think."

"It's a beautiful refuge; I cannot blame her."

"And you've met Bernard of course?" Brigid turned to introduce the taller vampire. "Agnes's first lieutenant. Bernard, did you have the…?"

"Of course." Bernard turned to the driver, who was following them with a large pink box from the Del Marco bakery. He took the box and handed it to Oleg. "We brought something for tea."

It had been Brigid's suggestion, based on her experience working with Katya, and the gesture was obviously taken well.

"So thoughtful." Oleg snapped his fingers, and a tattooed human rushed forward to take the pink box. "I will have the cook add it to the tea service. Come, join me in the sitting room. It's most beautiful this time of night."

The sitting room where he led them was a glass-paneled wonder with a glass roof and walls that overlooked the glittering lakeshore and the hills in the distance. The lights of the Strip lit up the night sky, casting the desert black in a deep blue velvet with only a few scattered stars.

"Is that a dock?" Brigid looked down the hill to a square house that seemed to hover over the water. "You have a boathouse too?"

"And a boat for the boathouse." Oleg smiled. "I confess I do not use it much, but visitors seem to enjoy this little... body of water." He waved at the lake. "It's man-made, but it's suitable for a holiday home."

"I imagine you have much bigger lakes in your home region."

"We do." He smiled a secret smile. "There is no place as beautiful as my home. I freely admit that I miss the stars there, but Las Vegas is an excellent place to do business, especially due to the current political situation." Oleg glanced at Bernard. "Your mistresses run the city well. I give them my thanks."

"I will be glad to share that with them."

"Please do." His expression was solemn. "When I got your message, Brigid, it was vague but it mentioned my associate Mika. I do hope there has been no trouble. He's typically a very disciplined employee."

"No trouble at all," Brigid said. "We were actually hoping to speak to him about someone he met at a bar in town about a week ago."

Oleg raised an eyebrow. "Perhaps it is someone I know as well?"

"Do you know a young woman named Alina Oorzhak? She may be working for a very distant family member of your clan."

Oleg's eye twitched. It was barely perceptible, but she caught it. "You're speaking of Zasha."

"I am."

"Has there been some trouble?" Oleg looked at Brigid and narrowed his gaze as if he knew she wouldn't have been in the city if everything was A-OK. "If Alina is around, so is Zasha. She's their pet."

Brigid looked at Bernard. It was up to him how much he wanted to share.

"There is an isolated situation that has come up regarding Zasha Sokholov," Bernard said. "We understand that you and Zasha have different organizations. We would not want to trouble you with the details, but we were hoping to locate Alina and wondered if Mr. Arakas might know her whereabouts."

"Of course." Oleg waved someone over and muttered something low in Russian. "We will fetch him, but I hope you have time to join me for tea."

"Of course," Brigid said. "We would love that."

Within seconds, an elaborately decorated samovar was brought out along with a steaming pot of tea and plate after plate of sweets and pastries, among them the petits fours that the baker at the Del Marco had made.

"Tell me, Brigid, what kind of trouble has Zasha been making?" Oleg snapped his fingers, barked something in Russian, and as fast as the servants and guards had appeared, they disappeared, leaving Oleg, Brigid, and Bernard alone. "I have called for Mika, but please, you must tell me. What has Zasha done?"

Brigid glanced at Bernard.

"I trust your judgment," he murmured.

How could she make Oleg understand the seriousness of the situation without revealing the threat against Agnes and Rose?

Brigid turned to Oleg. "A couple of years ago, my husband and I were part of a team that Katya Grigorieva sent to the forest in Mendocino County. She'd discovered that Ivan Sokholov had been holding unauthorized hunts in the region and needed to be dealt with."

Oleg poured dark tea concentrate into a teacup, added water, and handed the delicate cup to Brigid. "I see. You and Carwyn were part of this... team."

Brigid heard the unspoken question. Did she and Carwyn have political aspirations in California? "One of the humans taken was related to Carwyn's clan."

"An understandable intervention then." He poured another cup of tea for Bernard. "Continue."

"Ivan was killed, and though Carwyn and I were not directly responsible for the death, we encountered Zasha during the battle."

"Ivan's loving sire." Oleg's smile was humorless. "Zasha has always taken after our late sire. Both the cunning and the cruelty."

"They've become fixated on me," Brigid said. "I don't know if it's because I'm a fellow fire vampire or if it's because I was involved in Ivan's death—"

"Zasha had no real paternal feelings for Ivan, just like most of my extended family has only a loose connection to their kin. It wasn't a value we were taught."

"Then I have no idea why they have become obsessed, but they have stalked Carwyn and me across the country, going so far as to try to undermine Marie-Hélène Charmont in New Orleans."

Oleg poured his own cup of tea and sat with it for a moment, adding some sugar after he'd taken the first sip. "I see and I do not."

"We don't want to bring trouble to your door, Oleg. Does Mika know where this girl is? It's imperative that we ask her some questions."

Oleg took a deep breath, then let it out slowly. The corner of his mouth turned up in a rueful grimace. "Would that you had come to me with this question last week, my friend."

Brigid's heart sank. "What happened?"

"Two days ago, Mika discovered that Alina had been drugging one of the guards here at the compound to obtain information about our organization. We supposed it was for Zasha, of course. It was not the first time the girl had made unwise decisions for money." He shrugged. "She'd been warned before, and she ignored it. Alina Oorzhak is dead."

ELEVEN

Carwyn sat in the car in the parking lot of the Pink Daiquiri Gentleman's Club in Henderson, Nevada, only minutes from the Las Vegas Strip and light-years from the small parish he'd watched over for centuries.

Miguel was watching his obvious discomfort. "Not a fan of the strip clubs, eh?"

"I was a Catholic priest for about ten centuries."

The human guard blinked. "Oh yeah, I can see how that wouldn't be something you... Yeah."

"I'm not a prude." Carwyn stared at the flashing neon lights as men strode into the club, laughing and joking with their friends. "The human body is a beautiful thing, and I believe practicing modesty is more to do with living a humble life than covering up skin."

Miguel opened his door. "Hey. These girls gotta make a living, you know?"

"I don't judge them." Carwyn joined Miguel exiting the car, his eyes still watching the men entering the club. "I do judge *them*."

Miguel laughed. "I mean, it's just a little T and A, Father."

"Exactly. And to most of the men entering this place, that's all these women are. Tits and ass." Carwyn followed Miguel through the double doors. "I believe all human beings are far more than their physical selves, but you are entitled to believe as you will."

They paid the cover in cash and walked into the club, then Carwyn waited for Miguel to speak to the bouncer watching the bar. The man nodded and pointed to a stool where a middle-aged woman with short blond hair was watching the stage and talking on the phone.

"That's Cheryl. She's the owner," Miguel said. "Bouncer said we need to talk to her first."

"Does she know Agnes and Rose?"

"Everyone knows the Del Marco." Miguel turned. "I have a private investigator's license too. That helps."

There were two women dancing on the stage, both topless and wearing G-strings as they performed. Carwyn glanced at them but watched the crowd more.

Was the high roller the bartender had mentioned to Brigid in the room? Was Savannah a favorite?

Any number of the men could fit the description of the guy Alina had been trying to lure.

Miguel reached the bar and greeted Cheryl. "Miss Scarsdale?"

The woman turned to Miguel and Carwyn. "Just call me Cheryl, honey. You need something?"

"My name is Miguel Cerritos, and this is my associate Carwyn."

Carwyn nodded. "Madam."

Her eyebrows went up. "You're a cute one. Where you from?"

"I'm originally from North Wales, but I currently live in California."

"Cutie." She seemed pleased to make their acquaintance. "I love your accent."

"And I like yours." Carwyn turned on the charm. "You're the owner of the bar, yes?"

"Yeah." She smiled. "You like it?"

Carwyn looked at the stage where the two women were now sitting on chairs and performing a seductive routine. He turned back to Cheryl. "I have mixed feelings about the commodification of the female body for the pleasure of the male gaze."

Cheryl lit a cigarette. "Don't we all?"

"But your dancers are clearly very talented."

"Thanks." She blew out the smoke and looked at Miguel. "Who do you work for?"

"I'm a private investigator working for the Di Marcos. Are you familiar?"

"Sweetie, everyone knows Rose Di Marco. What do you need from me?"

"We were hoping to speak with one of your dancers. Savannah? We're not sure of the last name."

"We only got one Savannah. She in trouble?" The woman's gaze turned sharp. "She's a good girl and she doesn't cause any trouble. Far as I know, she ain't got no vices or exes. You get me?"

Carwyn leaned in. "I appreciate that you're protective of your employees."

She narrowed her eyes. "When they deserve it, I am."

"She's not in any trouble. A friend of hers mentioned that she knew a certain gentleman we're trying to locate. He could be involved in a crime against a minor, and all we want is information from Savannah. If she could help us, Rose Di Marco would owe her a favor."

"Any blowback for Savannah?"

"There's absolutely no reason we'd even have to mention her name."

Cheryl considered it for a moment, then nodded. "She's in back. I can give you one of the private rooms to talk. It's early. No one's in 'em yet. If she wants to answer your questions, she can. If she doesn't, that's up to her. You'll still pay her for a private hour."

Miguel nodded. "Fair enough."

"We appreciate your cooperation and your protective nature toward Savannah," Carwyn said.

The woman didn't seem to know what to make of him. "Right. Follow me. I'll point you to one of the rooms, then I'll get Savannah for you."

"Appreciate it," Miguel said.

They followed Cheryl down a pink-lit hallway with mirrors on the walls and four doors that were upholstered in pink leather with black buttons. She opened one, waved them inside, then shut the door behind them.

Miguel sat on one of the black leather couches that lined the walls. "So you have problems with the commodification of the female body, huh?"

"Mixed feelings." Carwyn sat down as well, trying not to think of the many human asses that had sat on the couch before him. "Do you think they clean these?"

"I'm pretty sure they'd have to. So how do these mixed feelings come into play when it comes to blood donors, huh?"

"Fair question." Carwyn looked around the room, immediately spotting the two cameras that were watching them. "I'll have to get back to you on that one." He nodded to the cameras.

"Right." Miguel stretched his arm across the back of the couch. "I mean, I get it. I wouldn't want my sister being a stripper, but it's not because of her, you know? She wants to do... whatever. That's up to her. I just know the mentality of the guys who go to these places, you know?"

"Exactly. You can't erase the context of the interaction."

"No one's forcing them to do it though. They make good money."

"As they should. And some of them could be forced or coerced. You don't know their whole story."

"But you'd like it better if they were on the stage dancing and presenting a paper on literature or archaeology or something instead of taking their clothes off?"

"You have to admit that would be the absolute best way to listen to a presentation on archaeology."

Miguel pursed his lips and nodded. "You're not wrong."

SAVANNAH WAS a statuesque young woman nearly as tall as Miguel. She had thrown on a robe and was wearing something glittery underneath. She sat across from Miguel and Carwyn, holding her robe closed at the neck. "I don't know. I see a lot of people when I bartend."

"We have a picture." Miguel showed her the picture of Alina.

"Oh my God, I do remember her." She tapped a short pink nail on the picture. "She was something else. Just a guy magnet, you know? She had that sexy baby thing going on but with a Russian accent." Savannah rolled her eyes. "Probably fake, but whatever."

"She is Russian, and she's been making the rounds of the casinos. She was seen at the Del Marco a few days before a young man went missing from the casino," Carwyn said. "Sierra said there was a particular man this girl was flirting with."

"Hard-core, yeah. He's usually one of my best tippers, which is why I always schedule work on nights when San Diego State is playing."

"Do you know his name?"

"I remember his credit card. Gary Preston, Summit Mountain Development. Pretty sure he was a real estate guy, that kind of development, you know?"

"That's helpful," Miguel said. "Thank you so much."

"She was flirting with a couple of guys, but Gary was the only one I remember clearly." She narrowed her eyes. "But there were so many guys in there that night, and then there was the weirdo."

Carwyn leaned forward. "Weirdo?"

"I mean, you see a lot working in a casino, so not much fazes me, but this guy had to be six foot, flaming red hair down to his shoulders, and he was wearing something that looked like an oversized bathrobe. He just appears out of the convention area, barks something at the blond girl when she was practically in Gary's lap one night, and she runs after him like he's her dad or something." She wrinkled her nose. "Was he her dad? I have this vivid impression of this guy, but I could not have told you how old he was, you know? He seemed really old somehow, but his face was young. And pretty. Like, ridiculously pretty."

So Zasha was at the casino? Carwyn hadn't been expecting that.

"Was anyone with the redhead?"

Savannah's mouth dropped open. "Oh my God, you have red hair too. Are you like, related? He wasn't as tall or as built as you, but—"

"Not related," Carwyn said. "Not Russian. But we are interested if anyone was with them."

"Uh..." She huffed out a breath. "I don't think so, but like, he was really striking, so I might not have noticed. It was the March Madness finals and the bar was crazy busy."

"Thank you so much, Savannah." Miguel handed over a card. "This card has my personal cell phone number on it, so if you remember anything else, just call me. Or if you see either of these two people again, please call."

"Yeah sure." She smiled. "The girl had been hanging out for a few days, but I haven't seen her recently. She kind of disappeared after the car show, so she was maybe working with one of the vendors or something."

"That's possible."

Carwyn smiled. "Thank you. Can I ask, are you going to school or does working take all your time? You're quite young."

"I'm trying to do online classes right now, but it's hard. The good thing is, I'm a saver, so I figure about three more years here, then I can just do bartending and go to school-full-time."

"Brilliant. What do you want to study?"

"I've been thinking about teaching, but I also really love history. I don't know. Maybe archaeology or something, but I don't know how practical that is."

Carwyn's eyes lit up. "I think you'd be a brilliant archaeologist."

A broad smile spread across her face. "Thanks!"

THEY WALKED BACK out to the car, Miguel smirking at Carwyn. "So when she gets her archaeology degree, you going to come back and convince Cheryl to change the format of the club?"

"If you think there isn't a market for beautiful women lecturing men, you clearly haven't spent much time on the internet. Then again, I could be biased, coming from Great Britain."

Miguel shook his head. "I do not understand you, but hey, at least we got a name."

"Indeed."

Miguel got behind the wheel of the car. "Where to?"

"We need to find out where Gary Preston lives," Carwyn said. "I'll call Lee."

The phone rang and Lee picked up. "I'm here. What do you need?"

"Gary Preston."

"Uh...?"

"Gary Preston is the name of the man Alina was trying to seduce at the car show. Summit Mountain Development. Can you see what information there is about him online?"

"You've given me more than enough. What do you want?"

"Address, financials. Any ties to Russia in particular. Clients maybe. Oleg owns a house here, why not Zasha?"

"Address shouldn't take long." Lee was already tapping keys. "Brigid came in and went out again. She looked stormy."

Uh-oh. "Thanks, Lee."

"No problem. I'll text you when I get an address. Should be only a few minutes."

He hung up the phone and called his wife. "Hello, my darling wife, this is your husband."

"Carwyn." She let out a sigh. "Alina Oorzhak is dead."

Damn. Not that it was a total surprise, but it was still a blow. "The meeting with the Russian?"

"He ordered it. She'd been drugging one of their guards and it sounded like it wasn't the first time. That one is ruthless when it comes to Zasha."

"No love lost?"

"Oleg doesn't want a hint of Zasha's volatility rubbing off on his operation, that's my read." She took a breath. "Where are you?"

"At the Pink Daiquiri. The drinks are amazing!"

He could hear her smile through the phone. "Are they? Just the drinks then?"

"We spoke to Savannah, and she gave us a name. Lovely girl. She'd like to study archaeology."

"Fascinating." It sounded like Brigid was in the middle of something. "What's the name?"

"What are you doing?"

"I'm maybe meeting Mika Arakas for a drink."

"Mika Arakas? The most lethal Estonian vampire in history?"

"Is that a difficult title for Estonian vampires to achieve though? I always thought of Estonians as being fairly chilled. Great musicians. Not particularly bloody."

"Mika Arakas is an assassin, Brigid."

"And I'm a fire vampire, mo ghrá. I'll be fine."

"Are you going behind Oleg's back?"

"Not... exactly."

"Brigid." He took a deep breath and let it out. "What are you doing?"

"Three nights, Carwyn."

It hit him again.

Three nights. Two days. Lucas O'Hara's life hung in the balance, and Brigid was being aggressive. He couldn't blame her.

"Be careful," he said. "Call me when you can."

TWELVE

Brigid didn't meet Mika at the cowboy bar but at the quieter establishment that Gavin owned on the top floor of a very fancy casino. She walked through the hushed lobby after getting off the private elevator and was immediately struck by the quiet scent of blood-wine and money.

Mika was already sitting at a table with a woman wearing a low-cut black dress and a ruby necklace around her neck.

Brigid glanced around and saw other demure donors wearing ruby-encrusted jewelry and assumed they were the paid donors. This was a drinking club, but it also had the air of the social club that Murphy ran in Dublin. There were bookcases and low tables, small clutches of men and women speaking in hushed voices. It was the exact opposite of the cowboy bar Carwyn had told her about.

Brigid kind of wished Mika had picked the cowboy bar. People with money made her itch.

A hostess approached her. She wasn't wearing a ruby necklace, but she was human. "Miss Connor, welcome to the Enclave."

"Thank you. I'm meeting—"

"Mr. Arakas is already waiting for you. He asked for a table by a window. We employ sound-dampening technology to ensure the privacy of all our guests. Is that acceptable to you?"

"It is, thank you." Many of Gavin's clubs were the only places that vampires could safely and securely conduct business. They were tiny oases of neutrality, and there was good reason vampires paid the hefty dues needed to belong to them.

Brigid had never paid Gavin money, but she'd been added as an elite member after a favor years ago, and she didn't take the gesture for granted.

Mika spotted her as she approached, leaned over to the donor, and whispered in her ear. The woman left the table with a smile and a satin clutch that was probably thicker than when she arrived.

As she passed, Brigid caught her lush scent and her fangs began to ache. She looked around the club, knowing that it would be a good idea to feed here before she continued in her mission. Gavin's clubs were always safe places to hire a blood donor even if they were expensive.

He gestured to the chair across from him. "I ordered a bottle of blood-wine. Portuguese. Thank you for meeting with me."

"Thanks to you as well. I appreciate your discretion." She sat down and examined the assassin across from her.

Mika Arakas was the kind of vampire who fit into the role of an assassin perfectly. He was tall—nearly unavoidable for an Estonian—with brown hair and blue eyes. He was handsome in a low-key way with even features and the ability to blend in to nearly any crowd, save for his height.

"I know about the boy." Mika's expression was blank. "So does Oleg. We didn't want to bring it up in front of Bernard because my employer wants to avoid the impression that he is searching for power or supports Zasha's attempts. Las Vegas is run well and discreetly under Agnes Wong and Rose Di Marco. A power shift serves no one's interests."

"Except Zasha's."

"Does it?" Mika's expression remained blank. "Has anyone asked themselves what the motivation for this is? Zasha has money, and frankly, they don't value it. It's not interesting to them."

"Power then."

"Las Vegas is not a seat of power, and that kind of power isn't the kind they crave. Fear. Intimidation. Zasha thrives on being the ghoul in the darkness not the emperor on the throne."

Brigid sat back as the server came to the table, uncorked the blood-wine, and poured two glasses. Mika reached for the goblet, tasted it, and gave the server a curt nod. The man left the table, but Mika still didn't speak.

"Me then."

Mika cocked his head.

"Zasha has fixated on me. They sought me out in New Orleans. They seemed… interested. I don't know why."

"That is not implausible. You're a young fire vampire, and your power is similar to theirs."

"How'd you know about my power?"

"It's my job to know those things." The corner of his mouth turned up. "Don't you know who I work for?"

"I've zero quarrel with Oleg. He's clearly older, more powerful, and more influential than me. I'm just trying to live my life, and Zasha Sokholov keeps poppin' in to fuck things up."

"You're a do-gooder, you and your husband, the priest." Mika looked amused. "Zasha would find that amusing."

"Why?"

"Because they believe as the old ones did." He spread his arms. "We are the gods of this world. Why not act like it?"

"Do you believe that?"

"I don't *believe* in anything. I do what Oleg tells me to do."

"Is he your sire?"

"None of your business." Mika smirked. "I enjoy your boldness. I don't think you've ever been truly afraid, have you? Sired into a powerful and respected clan. Not even your own dangerous element will touch you. It protects you, Brigid Connor." He sipped his wine again. "You don't understand fear as we do."

In the center of her stomach, Brigid remembered nights of terror in her childhood bedroom, waiting for the light to shine through the crack of the door. She remembered cold, sick dread; it was bitter on her tongue.

"You mistake my boldness for courage. I was born into fear, Mika. There's a reason fire claimed me."

The man's perceptive eyes locked with hers. After a few silent moments, he nodded. "That is it then. That is why Zasha is fascinated with you. I imagine they see your fear, and yet somehow you have not allowed hate to consume you."

"Do you know where Lucas is?"

"No." Mika shook his head. "I wish I did, because I dearly wish someone would defeat Zasha in their sick little games. They irritate me."

"So they do see it as a game?"

"Everything is a game to them." Mika looked around the room and leaned in. "I've told you that Zasha doesn't care about money."

"I believe that."

"That does not mean others around them don't."

"Others?"

"Who benefits if Zasha takes over Las Vegas?"

"Zasha."

Mika shook his head. "You're missing it."

"Who then?"

"The one who benefits from what Las Vegas has to offer."

"The only one campaigning for power here is Zasha."

"Openly? Correct."

Brigid sat back. "There's someone behind the scenes."

"There is always someone behind the scenes. That is usually how our kind works. But Oleg doesn't particularly want these people in power either."

"If your boss has something to tell me, I'd appreciate him being more direct."

"Direct isn't his way except when it comes to violence."

Brigid sat and waited. Mika clearly wanted to tell her something, so she could be patient. She wasn't going to guess at answers like an eager schoolgirl when the man called for the meeting and clearly had an agenda.

Mika threw back his blood-wine and set down the glass. "Sometimes we overlook an answer because it is too obvious. Because it's been the answer before."

Who had they battled before? Who had known ties to Zasha Sokholov?

"The Ankers?" She shook her head. "The Ankers don't trade in power; they deal in information. Their money comes from..." She blinked.

"Ah." Mika smiled. "You see now."

Brigid looked around at the hostess and the servers. They carried discreet card readers, tiny computers in their pockets.

The casinos had it all. Names, addresses, players' club information, credit card numbers, gambling habits, travel plans, everything.

Las Vegas wasn't just Sin City—it was a data gold mine.

"Zasha as the reluctant emperor," she muttered. "Reigning over a city of chaos."

"We both know they enjoy chaos. What do the computer people say?" Mika smiled. "Chaos is a feature, not a bug."

"With the Ankers holding the keys to the treasury."

Mika stood. "Zasha would never share power, but that's fine with the Ankers. They don't want to share power—they want to steal information."

It made sense. They had thwarted the Ankers' attempts to plant a data scraper in Gavin's new software devices, but in Las Vegas, not only vampire data but human data would flow like water from a spring.

"I don't know how this helps me find the boy."

"Sadly, I suspect it won't. If I had information to find him, I would give it to you. But know this—Zasha and the Ankers don't have the power to take over Las Vegas on their own; the vampires here are too loyal. Agnes and Rose would have to hand it over. And would handing over control of an entire city to a criminal enterprise such as the Ankers be worth it to save a single human life?"

Brigid wasn't going to answer that question.

Mika looked at her, shrugged, and poured another glass of blood-wine. "I suppose that is not your decision to make. I wish you luck with your search, Brigid Connor." Mika looked over his glass. "I would feed before you leave. Your eyes are hungry and your blood is young."

BRIGID WAITED FOR Agnes in her office after asking Bernard to summon her. She was flush with fresh blood and feeling fidgety. She wanted to be out searching the streets for Lucas, but she knew that was useless. She needed to wait on Carwyn for their current lead to pan out. She also needed to update Agnes and Rose.

She sat in front of the chess game set up on the coffee table, examining the pieces.

Whoever was playing was in the middle of a game. Pieces were in motion across the board, and several pieces were lined up on the side, having been taken out of play.

"He captured my queen."

Brigid turned to see Agnes standing in the doorway. "That's the most powerful piece on the board, right?"

"Undoubtedly yes." She came and sat across from Brigid, picking up the glossy black chess piece topped with a crown. "But taking the king is the only move that wins."

"I remember that part."

Agnes stared at the board. "He's a very gifted chess player."

"Was he good at other games?"

"Any games of strategy. Any games that depended on wit more than luck."

"You taught him that."

"Some people call the children our pets." Agnes leaned back against the couch. "I hear them. I ignore them. It's better that they don't realize how much Rose loves them."

And you. Brigid didn't need to say it aloud. "How is she?"

"I'm forcing her to spend as much time with Anna as possible. The girl keeps her steady." Agnes set down the chess piece. "What have you come here to tell me? Why aren't you out looking for Lucas?"

"Are you familiar with the Ankers?"

"The Dutch Ankers?"

"Yes."

Rose frowned. "They died. The brothers died years ago."

"They died, but their children lived."

"What does that have to do with Lucas?"

"Maybe nothing, but I believe that Zasha targeted you in cooperation with Otto Anker. The power and influence..." She grimaced. "That's not really the kind of motivation that Zasha craves. They prefer being feared but remaining in the shadows. Have any of the Ankers visited Las Vegas recently?"

"Not that I know of, but you'll have to ask Bernard. Look into aliases, look at face recognition, that sort of thing. If you have pictures, I'll set our team on it."

"I'll get pictures. And speaking of pictures...?"

Agnes handed over another envelope. Brigid opened it to find a single picture of Lucas looking much the same. Again, he was staring right at the camera, holding a newspaper from that day.

Brigid looked for any clues in the picture, but she was still disappointed. The walls were stark white. The floor was black. Lucas was sitting in a chair with no unique features.

They had to lead to *something*. "How are these being delivered?"

Agnes said, "They're dropped off in different places; then we get a call to go and fetch them. Parks. A bus station. None of the places have video surveillance. Bernard already checked."

"Give me the locations anyway. Lee might be able to find doorbell cameras or traffic cameras or some kind of surveillance that give us a face. It's a long shot, but we can try."

Agnes nodded.

"Carwyn got another name tonight. Gary Preston. Does that sound familiar? He was a man that Alina—the girl Lucas knew as Angel—was cozying up to at the car conference weekend before last."

Agnes shook her head. "Not familiar to me, but I'll have Bernard search the casino records."

"How about Summit Mountain Development? That was Preston's company."

Agnes frowned. "That does sound familiar."

She touched the intercom and a voice came back. "Yes, Miss Wong?"

"Call Bernard to my office."

"Yes, Miss Wong."

A few minutes later, Bernard entered the room. "Agnes, has there been—?"

"Gary Preston was a man connected to the girl who tricked Lucas into leaving his guards to meet her. He was the owner of Summit Mountain Development."

"They put a bid in for the planned community," Bernard said immediately. "They didn't place the winning bid, but it was in the top four."

"That's right." Agnes looked at Brigid. "Rose and I are building a planned community via a private LLC. It will be tightly controlled and cater to vampires and their people. Elemental considerations taken into account, of course. Summit put in a bid for the project. They had experience with the Lake Las Vegas development."

The lake where Oleg had his house. "Does Preston have property in Lake Las Vegas?"

"I have no idea, but I'm sure we can find an address."

"Our man is already working on it," Brigid said. "I imagine we'll have an address soon. Carwyn and Miguel are waiting for it."

"Good." Agnes rose and started to pace. "Bernard, leave."

"Yes, Miss Wong."

The man left the room and closed the door behind him.

"Tell me what your best guess is," Agnes said. "Are you going to be able to find Lucas?"

It was an impossible question. "We've made good progress so far, but there are no guarantees."

She continued pacing. "At what point do we evacuate our people and give this vampire the city?"

"I wouldn't advise doing that. The minute you hand over the city, they've no reason to keep Lucas alive."

"They say they'll return him if we leave."

"And you believe them?"

Agnes sank onto the couch and closed her eyes. "I never should have allowed Rose to get attached. We should have hidden them better. We've put the children in danger."

Brigid felt her phone buzzing in her jacket pocket. She pulled out the device and saw Carwyn's name on the screen, then tapped the button through the case. "I'm here."

"We have Gary Preston's address. It's a large compound south of town, and from what we can tell, his car isn't there but a bunch of other ones are. We're heading there now."

She tapped the couch to get Agnes's attention. "I'll have Agnes get her people and we'll meet you there. Text me the address."

"I will."

Brigid shut the phone off and set it to the side. "We have an address. It's out of town and appears to have some cars parked there, but no sign of Preston's. This could be it."

THIRTEEN

The house wasn't set on its own but within a large complex of sprawling estates with unnaturally green grass for a desert. Gary Preston's ranch consisted of a main house with a lavish swimming pool in front of it, horse stables on the hill, and several smaller guesthouses scattered around the ten-acre property.

Preston had two cars registered to his name, neither of which was visible. There were, however, five other cars and trucks on the property. They didn't spot anyone outside, and there were only two lights on in the house.

At the guardhouse, Miguel got the lone security guard to admit that the last time he'd seen Mr. Preston was four days ago. His guests had shown up right after him, but Mr. Preston had asked him not to record their names and the man had reluctantly agreed.

Miguel joined Carwyn in the car after he'd surveilled the house from the road. "No movement. It almost looks like they parked the cars here and took off on foot."

"If they're immortal, that's not improbable. Remember, we

can run much faster than humans and we don't tire. Some of us can fly."

"Agnes called me. Told me your wife is coming with a team of people. Bernard is with them."

"Good." He could wait. If the boy was in the house, he was safe for now. The moment they started an attack, he would be vulnerable.

"You never answered me about the donor thing." Miguel was staring at the house, tapping his fingers on the steering wheel.

"What about the donor thing?"

"At the strip club, you didn't want to answer me about how you justified the donor thing when you don't like objectifying humans."

"I have mixed feelings, and I don't actually feed from humans."

Miguel frowned. "How is that possible?"

"Vampires can feed from wild animals too. Any mammal actually. Probably other animals, but mammal blood is the most nourishing after humans."

"So you could just buy cow blood or pig blood and not feed from humans?"

"Yes. I suppose they don't taste as good. I imagine it's a little like eating meat replacements instead of a good steak. But it will keep you alive and strong."

"I had no idea."

Carwyn shifted in his seat. He was as eager to get into that house as Miguel was. "There are so many willing donors now, it's rare that a vampire would ever need to feed from an unwilling human unless that was part of the appeal." He looked at Miguel. "Make no mistake, the taste of fear is desirable to some of our kind."

"That doesn't surprise me. So does your wife—?"

"Miguel, is that house on a raised foundation or a slab?"

"Uh..." He squinted. "I'm honestly not sure."

"Either way, I'm going to tunnel around the house and see if I can hear anything." Carwyn jumped out of the car and stripped his shirt off. "Keep your lights off and wait for Brigid and Bernard."

"But Carwyn—"

The ground opened up the moment he took off his shoes.

Ahhh, hello my old friend.

This ground was new to him. His amnis reached out and greeted the living earth, stretching into the land in front of him. It was hard-packed earth, thick with metal and minerals, older than the new land closer to the city. This land had been sleeping for centuries, baking in the desert sun.

He moved slowly at first, letting the earth become accustomed to him. He could have tunneled directly to the house, but he didn't, instead moving around several large boulders so as not to displace the old stones.

The ground approved of that. It grew softer the closer he got to the house, greener with living things and roots and new life. He moved through the ground, reaching out for any trace of vampire amnis.

As he approached the house, he sensed the presence of immortals above him, but they weren't of his element. Zasha Sokholov was a fire vampire, but the Sokholov clan was mostly earth vampires. He was surprised to feel none of his element, but then again, he knew that Zasha didn't have many loyalists. They hired those of any element who were motivated by money.

He poked his head up in a flower bed on the side of the house. His face was crusted with dirt and his hair was thick with stones, so he was well camouflaged.

Carwyn listened for signs of life, but he heard nothing.

Except...

There was the stench of death in the soil.

He returned to the ground and followed the scent to an area behind the stables. Mixed with the manure and smell of composting hay, he smelled the familiar stink of decomposition. Impossible to tell if it was human or animal.

He rose from the ground, careful to keep out of the line of sight of the Preston house.

He walked around the stables, his amnis reaching into the ground to sense where the ground had been disturbed.

The earth wasn't concerned by the dead. To his element, death was just another form of life. The body made of earth returned to it to feed the plants that fed the animals above. The animal that had once lived in the sun rested in the dark, and the insects and fungus that recycled the dead were happy in the work of eternity.

Carwyn found three bodies in the ground and knew they were all adult humans. He pressed his palms to the ground and asked the earth to reveal their secrets.

The ground shifted and unfurled, slowly revealing three dead humans, a man and two women. One was Gary Preston, based on the file Lee had sent him. His face was bloated, but he was recognizable. The two women with him were wearing uniforms that appeared to be the same, so they were likely domestic workers.

"Thank you," Carwyn whispered. He asked the earth to cover them again, and the soil around the bodies settled and sighed.

In the distance, he felt his mate arrive, her amnis as familiar to him as his own.

Take me back. He returned to his element, returning to the spot where he'd first touched the ground on the edge of the mountain. He passed the old boulders in the ground again, brushing his palms against them and whispering a prayer for the dead as he passed.

He emerged from the earth to find Brigid looking down at him.

He smiled up and felt the grit between his teeth. "Hello, wife."

BRIGID RAN IN front of him, her feet so swift that he could barely keep track of her as she moved, clothed in all black, a tiny angel of justice in the night.

Carwyn had kept his shirt off and his feet bare, the better to use his element in the upcoming fight. Bernard had two wind vampires on the security staff, and the women had identified four vampires visible in the house and it was possible there were more they weren't seeing.

None of them had seen a sign of the boy.

There were a dozen vampires in Bernard's group along with Carwyn and Brigid. There were half a dozen humans waiting at the cars and more waiting on standby a few miles away.

Most of the vampires were earth vampires like Carwyn, who fought barefoot. All of them kept their distance from Brigid.

Bernard motioned for Carwyn and Brigid to fall back as he and his people ran forward.

They flooded the house in utter silence, save for the sound of breaking glass. Black shadows moved through the dark house, and the lights that had been burning went out.

"Feck this, I'm going in." Brigid ran into the house and Carwyn followed her, already suspecting that the boy wasn't there.

It was too easy. Too neat. This was a staging area, not a battleground.

They breached the front door with a single shove and found

Bernard and his people in the front room, dragging bodies from around the house.

"Only five." Bernard shook his head. "No sign of the humans or of Lucas."

"Damn." Carwyn had been hoping he was wrong. "The graves are behind the stables. I found Preston and two women buried behind there."

"No signs of Lucas?" Brigid proceeded to search the house from top to bottom. It was chock-full of electronics, luxury furnishings, and huge closets that were mostly empty. It appeared that Gary Preston had lived in the giant mansion by himself.

"Wait." Carwyn touched Brigid's shoulder. "Is there a basement? I feel like there's a basement."

"Let's go look."

There had to be something. Alina had focused on Preston for a reason. There had to be something about this house in particular that Zasha Sokholov wanted.

"Why this man?" Carwyn asked. "This house is remote. It's not convenient to the city. If the boy isn't hidden here, what is the point?"

Brigid walked down the stairs to find a luxuriously finished media room decorated in black and red dominating the space. It came complete with movie-theater seats, sports memorabilia in custom cabinets, and a bar.

Carwyn looked around. "If he had all this, why did he go to a sports bar on the Strip to watch all his college basketball games?"

"Maybe he fancied Savannah," Brigid said. "Or maybe he'd no friends."

"Possible." What a sad life, and to end it at the hand of vampires who disposed of you like a dead animal.

Why Gary Preston?

There had to be a reason.

"Let's get Lee to look through Preston's financials," Brigid said. "He had to have some connection to Zasha."

Bernard joined them in the basement. "There is a sizable classic car collection in the garage. It looks like several of them are missing."

Carwyn and Brigid exchanged a look. "Is that why?" Carwyn asked. "Because Zasha Sokholov wanted a car they could drive?"

Brigid muttered, "That makes as much sense as anythin' that vampire does."

"It appears they've been living at the ranch since they arrived," Bernard said. "We killed five vampires. It might take a few days to determine their element."

Vampires returned to their element a few days after death. Earth to earth. Wind to wind. Water to water.

The bodies of fire vampires spontaneously combusted, but Carwyn didn't like thinking about that.

Bernard asked, "What did the bodies look like? I'm going to call a contact in Las Vegas PD. He'll know who to alert since we're not within city limits."

"Four days he's been missing?" Carwyn nodded. "I'm not a decomposition expert, but that sounds about right. All three were pretty intact. Also, I don't think they were tortured."

"That's a mercy at least," Bernard muttered. "The vehicles on the property don't look like they've been moved. Miguel is getting the guardhouse video now."

"I don't think we're gonna learn anything useful from it," Brigid said. "Is there any sign that Lucas was ever here?"

"No. Not a backpack or bag or anything like that. None of the rooms appear to be the room in the photograph."

"I thought it would be a garage or a basement. It didn't look like residential flooring." Carwyn frowned. "Let me see one of the pictures again."

Brigid reached in her jacket and handed one to Carwyn.

He looked at the photo and focused on the flooring since that was the only part of the room that was even vaguely unique. “It’s black, so it’s hard to tell, but it looks textured to me. Not like carpet. I thought it was industrial, but it looks... I don’t know, softer somehow.”

Brigid grabbed the picture. “You’re right. Do you think Lee can isolate it and look closer?”

“If he can’t, my people can.” Bernard was already pulling out a phone in a heavy case. “Cara, call Bernice.” His scowl didn’t change. “My daughter runs the tech division for Agnes and Rose.”

Carwyn glanced at Brigid, trying not to laugh. Bernard and Bernice? He had so many questions. Was it Bernard’s human daughter? Vampire daughter? He was guessing vampire daughter since the steady earth vampire felt at least a century old. Did she change her name? Did he give her a vampire name that sounded like his own?

His eyes must have been dancing because Brigid reached up and tweaked his ear behind Bernard’s back.

“Behave,” Brigid whispered. “Not the time or the place. I’m going upstairs to call Lee.”

“Bernard and Bernice though.”

“When Lucas is back, we can joke. Until then, we focus on the job.”

FOURTEEN

Lucas drummed his fingers on the wall, his eyes closed, and pictured the chess pieces in his mind. He was replaying Bobby Fischer's famous win against International Master Donald Byrne in his head. He liked to replay that one when he was feeling like an underdog, imagining the pieces like real knights and pawns, bishops and chariots. That's what the little castle pieces were supposed to be. Not castles—chariots, which made a lot more sense.

Fischer versus Byrne was a brilliant game and one of Lucas's favorites. Bobby Fischer was an asshole—he'd watched enough YouTube to figure that out—but he was only thirteen when he decisively beat an international chess master.

Sometimes Lucas needed to remember that.

He'd gotten sick the night before and spent most of the night in the bathroom. He didn't know what they were feeding him, but it wasn't food like he got at home. It was mostly fast food with a little bit of truck stop sandwich thrown in.

Rose hated fast food. She wouldn't even let Anna get chicken nuggets. She and Agnes fought about it sometimes because Agnes didn't seem to think fast food was poison the way Rose did. One time Lucas convinced Miguel to sneak in some chicken nuggets for Anna because she saw them on the television, but luckily she thought they tasted nasty and asked for caviar after she'd tasted one.

Miguel was really relieved.

Lucas had no idea how his little sister was going to function in the normal world when she got to be older. Then again, if he could imagine a human destined to be a vampire, it would be Anna. She was ruthless in the same way Rose was. She wasn't as erratic, but Lucas kind of wondered if Rose's human life had been awful. He thought maybe so because sometimes Agnes let things slip and they weren't good.

He missed them. He'd spent the past year daydreaming about graduating from high school and going off to college and how awesome his life was going to be when he wasn't Rose and Agnes's kid anymore.

Now? He wanted nothing more than to sprawl on the giant sofa in the movie room and watch some stupid kid movie with Anna and Rose cuddled up and Agnes and him indulging them and playing a chess game in their heads.

He missed his family.

Lucas blinked back the tears when he heard the doorknob rattle. They weren't blindfolding him anymore, which meant that probably they were going to kill him. If he thought about it too much, he wanted to throw up.

So he thought about chess.

The redheaded vampire came into the room again. This time they looked down their nose at Lucas with an amused expression on their face. "Lucas."

"Zasha." He looked up. "Is that like another version of Sasha or a completely different name?"

"It's another version of Sasha."

"But *Z* names are cooler than *S* names."

Zasha smiled. "Exactly."

Lucas bounced his head against the wall. "No picture tonight?"

"Your mothers broke into my house and killed seven of my people." Zasha kept their unearthly eyes on Lucas.

He froze.

Lucas had seen a documentary about a leopard once. Some people got leopards and cheetahs confused because of the spots. Not Lucas. Leopard jaws were so strong they could crush a bowling ball. Their heads and bodies were massive and muscled. A leopard wasn't superfast, it hunted alone, and it wasn't afraid of much.

Zasha reminded Lucas of a leopard.

Calm the leopard.

"I'm sorry about your friends."

"They weren't my friends. They were my people."

"I don't know what that means."

Zasha took a deep breath, which made Lucas release his own lungs. Sometimes the vampire went a really long time without breathing, which he knew wasn't actually necessary for vampires, but it still freaked him out when they didn't breathe.

"My people work for me for money, which means that they assume some risk when they accept payment from me."

"So they're employees."

"Exactly."

"I guess... I'm still sorry?"

"You shouldn't be. You are not an employee of your mothers. You are their child. Children are different than employees."

"Do you have any children?"

"I did once. They're all dead."

"I'm sorry."

Zasha heaved another long breath. "Well, I killed some of them myself, so I don't think you should be sorry."

Lucas felt like throwing up again. He tried to keep the question in, but he blurted it anyway. "Why?"

"To be fair, two of them tried to kill me first." Zasha rolled their eyes. "And the last one disappointed me."

"All kids disappoint their parents."

"You certainly disappointed your parents when you ran away from your security." Zasha winked at him. "Worked out for me though."

He didn't want to think about Angel. Just thinking about her made him sad and angry at the same time. "What did you ask my mothers for? Money?"

"Oh no." Zasha picked at their voluminous robe. "Something far more valuable." He looked at Lucas. "I asked for their city."

I am going to die.

Lucas tried not to let the despair show on his face. "Well, that's too bad. Because they're not going to give you the city, and they shouldn't."

It wasn't logical, and Agnes was logical. Rose was more vicious and emotional, but Agnes would know that sacrificing the safety of an entire city to a crazy vampire like Zasha in exchange for one human life wasn't logical. It would put so many people at risk. It would put his sister at risk.

Despair grabbed him by the throat; then he took a deep breath, the fear released, and Lucas felt oddly calm. He remembered the car and the blackness and the spinning sensation before the crash.

"Mommy!"

"It's okay, baby!"

She'd said Jason before she died. She'd said it again after the car crashed into the overpass. Then his mother was silent because she died.

Lucas knew heaven existed because on the worst day of his

life, in the last moments before his mother died, she was talking with his dad.

He looked at Zasha with pity. "They're not going to give you the city. And I don't think you're strong enough to take it on your own, otherwise you would have done that instead of taking me."

Zasha stared at him intently.

"Checkmate." The corner of Lucas's mouth turned up. "I mean, the game is still going, but you've already lost."

FIFTEEN

It was near dawn when they finally wrapped up at Gary Preston's house. Agnes had arrived with a team of secretaries and clerks, packing up every scrap of paper from Preston's office they could find in hopes of discovering some tie or clue that would lead back to Zasha or the Ankers.

Brigid didn't have much faith. She suspected that Gary Preston's house had been chosen for a few reasons: easy access to vampire-friendly cars, isolation, and a large and comfortable basement. It was also likely that the man had a large stash of cash since they'd found an open, empty safe in a second-floor bedroom.

She sat on the edge of their borrowed bed and tried to imagine where Lucas was sleeping that night. Could he sleep? Was he too afraid? Brigid could imagine how the young man was feeling. He had to be terrified.

Putting herself in Lucas's shoes was easy enough. She might be a powerful vampire now, but the first years of her life had been spent sleeping fitfully, listening for a quiet footstep and watching for a narrow beam of light at her bedroom door. Even years later, she remembered that sliver of light, the pad of feet on plush carpet, and the near-imperceptible whine of door hinges that her stepfather was so careful to oil so her mother wouldn't know.

Can't have these old doors creaking all times of the day, Mammy.

Her mother knew; her mother had always known.

If Brigid closed her eyes, she could still see the unnatural angle of Richard's neck, hear the quiet pop of his spine snapping, his death coming at the hands of the very vampire she fell in love with decades later.

I'm not angry he died. I only wish he hadn't killed him because I wanted to do it.

Sometimes when she missed the rush of heroin in her veins, she thought about what Richard's blood would have tasted like —hot, sour, and dripping down her chin. She wouldn't have swallowed any part of that monster, not even to kill him. She would have spat his blood in his own face as he lay dying.

She sat on the edge of the bed, her elbows resting on her knees, and imagined his face. Imagined the terror and the delicious spite. Her skin heated as she ruminated on the idea of killing him over and over again. Maybe she should dig him up just to see if he was still dead. Hopefully he was rotting.

Her stepfather was laid to rest in a very respectable cemetery in the Southside of Dublin, his headstone reading BELOVED SON; LOVING HUSBAND.

Not father. Never father. Aunt Sinéad had put her foot down.

"Darlin' girl." Carwyn's hand fell on her shoulder, and she heard the sizzle as his skin touched her flesh.

"Carwyn!" She sat up and reached for his hand, pulling back when she realized what had happened. "I'm sorry." She stood and rushed to the bathroom. "Tá brón orm."

"Brigid, it's fine."

"No, it's not." She flipped on the tap and stuck her hands under the water. "I've scarred you for a year, dammit." She could feel the tears well up in her eyes, spill over, and sizzle as they reached her cheeks.

She took a deep breath, grabbed a washcloth, and brought it to Carwyn, pressing the cold cloth to his hand. "Should ya put it underwater? Maybe a bath. There's a shower—"

"What are you thinking?"

She shook her head and took a deep breath, trying to dissipate the heat. "Nothin'."

"Nothing doesn't make your skin sizzle." He grabbed her shoulder. "You're still burning up. Shower."

She shook her head. "I'll be fine."

Carwyn turned her around by the shoulders and pushed her toward the luxurious marble-clad bathroom in their rental house. "Shower."

"Carwyn—"

"I'm covered." He laughed. "Brigid, I've got rocks in my hair. Take a cold shower with me; you know I prefer it anyway, even when you aren't burnin' up."

Brigid stepped into the bathroom and tugged off her clothes, careful to lay them neatly in a pile on the counter. She stuck her arm in the shower and turned on one knob, then the other, finally figuring out how to get both showerheads working in the walk-in enclosure.

Carwyn walked into the bathroom behind her and flung his dirty pants and socks into a pile on the ground, gravel scattering across the floor.

"Jesus, Mary, Joseph and the wee donkey." She laughed as the turned to him. "You're filthy."

"I am." He stood before her stark naked, massive and grubby, his red hair sticking out in unholy directions. "Still devilishly handsome though."

Brigid blinked away her tears. "Do ya know how I adore you?"

His blue eyes softened. "Do ya?" His smile was soft and uncertain. "Get in the shower, Brigid Connor. I need to wash up so I can do sinful things to you, and I don't want to get my chest hair singed."

She stepped under the cold water and felt the bubbling sizzle as the water hit her skin. Within seconds, the bathroom was filled with steam.

Carwyn stepped in the bath behind her and stuck his head under the tap. "Oh, I'm gonna take two or three rounds with all this."

"If you'd gone and jumped in a lake, it would have washed out faster." As soon as she was cooled off, she grabbed a washcloth, soaped it up, and began to work on the streaks of mud across his back.

"Oi." He wiggled under the water. "Don't look, but I might be shitting rocks."

Brigid burst out laughing, and the tension from the previous three nights finally broke loose. She laughed and laughed as she squeezed water over Carwyn's back and arms, nearly pissing herself when he turned his back to the stream of water and attempted to rinse out the gravel from truly awkward places.

"You were wearing pants!" Her tears had turned to ones of hilarity. "How?"

"That ground hadn't felt an earth vampire in decades, my love. Maybe centuries. It loved me. And when I say it loved me..." He shifted his hips, and more gravel fell to the tiles. "It *really* loved me."

"You know, I don't mind sharing you with Mother Earth, but she's getting a wee bit handsy if you ask me." She held out a bottle of shampoo when the water was mostly running clear. "Bend down. Let's get your hair."

Carwyn kept his eyes on her as she poured shampoo into his hair and began to knead his scalp, scratching at the grit and caressing his nape and the sensitive places behind his ears that she loved to kiss.

"What were you thinking of to get you so heated, Brigid?"

She rubbed his scalp, pushed his head under the water to rinse, then poured more shampoo into her palm. She nearly slipped trying to reach the top of his head, so he knelt down, his knees hitting the tile floor and his head near her belly.

"Much better," she whispered. She rubbed the shampoo through his hair, the wavy red locks thick and a little coarse between her fingers. She loved her mate's hair. While she couldn't keep hers long to save her life—seeing as she burned it anytime her fire let loose—Brigid adored Carwyn's thick, wavy hair with its red and gold and brown streaks.

She ran her fingers through it, then tipped his head back to rinse it clean.

Carwyn had his hands warm and steady on her hips, but his eyes hadn't left her face for a second. "What were you thinking of, darling girl?"

She closed her eyes, the water around them starting to steam again. "I was remembering what it felt like to be afraid to fall asleep."

He wrapped his arm around her torso and pressed his cheek between her breasts, hugging her tightly as she allowed the pain of those memories to wash away with the stones.

SHE FELL ASLEEP WRAPPED around her mate, not caring that he'd have to unwind her dead weight in the early evening to free himself. He didn't need as much sleep as she did, which meant that he usually woke at least an hour before her.

Usually he rose and started with his evening, but that night he was still with her when she woke, stroking her hair and running his hand up and down her back.

They hadn't done any "sinful things" at dawn. She'd been too emotionally wrought and he knew it. Part of the reason Brigid was good at what she did was because she could empathize with victims.

She worried that sometimes that empathy blinded her.

Blinking her eyes awake, she looked up and saw Carwyn watching her.

"Evenin', wife."

"Good evening." It was only within the safety of a fortified room or with Carwyn next to her that Brigid slept without fear. "What are you thinking of?"

"Honestly?"

"Always."

"I was contemplating your arse."

She pressed her lips together to keep herself from smiling. "What about my arse?"

"Well." He rolled to his back, his giant frame taking the crisp cotton sheet with it, and plucked her from her position beside him, turning her and placing her on his lap with an enthusiastic erection right between her spread legs.

"Is this what they call the reverse cowgirl?" Brigid asked.

"We're talking about your arse, so I need a clear view." He patted her hips. "Now listen."

"All ears." She reached down and wrapped both her hands around his cock. "And hands."

"Oh, ya wicked..." He grunted. "So about your arse."

"Yes?" She idly began stroking him up and down.

He grabbed her bottom with both hands in retaliation. "It's no secret that you're a wee tiny bit of a woman, Brigid darlin'."

"Admittedly, I did not inherit any blood of the Northmen."

"You're a tiny, delightful Hibernian to the core."

She shifted over him. "Did you say *core*?"

He muttered something that would have made her blush if she could.

"You're a delicate bit of a minx, but then you have this..." He squeezed both her cheeks. "...this absolutely abundant arse."

"It's God makin' amends as he forgot to give me tits, Carwyn."

"I appreciate your tits too. Don't insult them. But my God, this arse is... Well, it's a work of art." He gripped her bottom with both hands. "A man might be starving, but if it came to eating a steak or taking a bite of this arse, he'd happily die with this arse between his teeth."

"Is that so?" She started rocking over him, her hands rubbing up and down his cock.

"You're goin' to kill me."

"That's not at all the idea." She knelt up and slowly guided him into her body, sliding down until he was seated inside, filling her up with delicious, decadent fullness. She leaned forward and braced herself on his thighs, starting to rock, playing her fingers along her sex to find her own pleasure as she drove her husband mad.

"That's right, ride me." He gripped her hips with both hands. "Ride me all you want." He guided her up and down his erection. "I'm yours. I've always been yours. Did you know that, Brigid? A thousand years, I was waiting for you."

"Carwyn?" She was nearly about to come.

"Yes, love?"

"Do you...?"

"What, my love?" He let out a low groan.

"Do you want to bite my arse?"

He cursed again, but the cursing was mixed with laughter. "Fuck yes, I want to bite your arse. I want to sink my fangs into it. I want to drink your blood; then I want to bite it again."

She was nearly over the edge. "And you're only telling me this now after a decade of being wed?"

"Well..." He groaned when she twisted her hips and bounced faster. "I like to keep things fresh." His voice was slightly higher pitched.

Brigid came in a bright burst of a climax, her head felt like the top had flown off, and she felt Carwyn shudder beneath her moments later.

No sooner had he come than he plucked her off his cock, tossed her to the end of the bed, and sank his fangs into the round curve of her bottom.

She gasped as another shivering orgasm fluttered through her and he drank her blood; she felt his pleasure twine with hers.

Brigid let out a gasp as Carwyn pulled at her flesh, sliding his hands under her and up her body until they gripped both her breasts, tweaking the nipples as she twisted underneath him.

"Oh God!" The third orgasm was a shock. It jolted through her, and her fangs swelled in her mouth. She bit down and sank her teeth into the down mattress pad, the fabric ripping as heat bloomed over her body.

He lapped at the wounds in her skin, then picked her up, threw her over his shoulder, and walked to the bathroom. "Someone's getting steamy again. Time for another cold shower."

She glanced at the mirror as they passed it and saw his erection was already back at full mast. "Not that cold."

His wicked laughter echoed through the room, but he yelped when she reached down and pinched his own arse.

"Remember, husband." Brigid grinned and her fangs nicked her lip. "Turnabout is fair play."

SIXTEEN

Carwyn held Brigid's hand in the car on the way to the Del Marco Casino. She had withdrawn into herself again, and he could almost see her counting off in her head.

Two nights. One day.

Approximately thirty-six hours before Zasha's game was up. If they couldn't find Lucas in that time, Carwyn had a rough idea of what was going to happen.

Rose would demand that they hand over the city to get her son back.

Agnes would resist because she knew it wasn't a logical move and Zasha was likely going to kill Lucas anyway.

The Ankers—if they were behind all this—could make an active move.

Zasha would likely kill Lucas.

The fourth move, Lucas's death, was nearly a certainty unless they could find the boy before the deadline. Whether Rose or Agnes got their way, the boy's death was nearly a given.

Brigid wasn't brooding—she was desperate.

Carwyn squeezed her hand. "Remember, Lee finally got into Lucas's computer today. That's excellent news. He'll be able to reset the boy's password and access his phone. He won't stop until he's dug all the secrets out."

Brigid nodded. "I'm hoping Miguel has a report on the cars today."

"The cars?"

"There were cars missing from Gary Preston's giant garage. Miguel was going to speak to a contact at Las Vegas PD this afternoon and get APBs put on all of them as they were nicked. He was also going to ask the casinos in town to check their surveillance footage for the vehicles and anyone seen driving them."

"He reported the Preston murders?"

"Yes. He still hasn't reported Lucas missing, but he reported the murders."

"You know why that's not a good idea," Carwyn said. "The moment Zasha realizes that Agnes and Rose have broken the rules—"

"Rules they set," Brigid snapped. "Rules they can change anytime they fuckin' want to."

"Nevertheless." He squeezed her hand. "As odd as it may be, they're playing with you. We can use that, Brigid."

She dipped her chin in a tense nod. "We should contact Gary Preston's office. His house was barely lived in. I have a feeling that he lived his life at work. He'll have an assistant or a secretary or somethin'. That could be the closest relationship in his life. He or she would probably know his movements better than anyone."

"Good idea." Carwyn watched her.

She was sinking into herself. Hiding her feelings again. It wasn't the first time, but it still pissed him off. He knew it was how she processed ideas, pulling threads of knowledge, tiny scraps of information, and instinctive observations to make the intuitive leaps that made her so good at finding the lost. She had the uncanny ability to put herself into the mind of both the monsters and their prey.

It wore on her, and yet he knew she wouldn't stop.

Carwyn knew she felt responsible for Lucas's kidnapping, as if her mere existence had tempted Zasha Sokholov into bringing their twisted games to America.

They pulled into the Del Marco Casino and walked through the delivery entrance to the private elevator where they were stopped by a guard.

"Please wait." He touched his earpiece. "I have two guests arriving. Both night crew."

Carwyn frowned. "Pardon me, but Rose and Agnes—"

"Sir." The man held up a finger. "I'll wait. Names?"

"Carwyn ap Bryn and Brigid Connor," Carwyn said.

The guard repeated their names into the microphone. He was wearing gloves, and it was still nearly ninety degrees outside.

Carwyn cocked his head and examined the human, who was covered from the turtleneck he was wearing under his dress shirt to the gloves to the long black slacks.

Brigid murmured, "There's been a breach."

"Yes." The humans were taking extra precautions against vampire influence, and the private elevator had added security when before a passcode had been enough until guests reached the vampire floors.

"Cleared." The man opened the elevator with a different passcode. "Thank you for your patience. They're expecting you in the head office."

"What happened?" Brigid asked.

"Nothing to be concerned about, ma'am. Enjoy your time at the Del Marco."

With another curt nod and a punched-in code, the elevator doors shut and the compartment began to move.

No sooner had the elevator begin to go up than Carwyn's phone rang. "It's Lee." He answered. "What's going on?"

"I'm in the panic room. Three cars showed up outside the house and set off my alarms. I'm locked in here until you tell me it's safe."

"You changed all the codes the night we moved in?"

"Already overridden, and I couldn't find a master code in the system. I'm secure for now unless they have a vampire who can rip through metal doors."

Carwyn could rip through metal doors, but he didn't tell Lee. It took a very old earth vampire with an affinity for metallic matter to rip through steel, and he doubted they would send one after a computer programmer.

"We're at the casino and there's increased security. It's likely Agnes and Rose's people, but I'll check and make sure when we get to their office." The elevator doors opened and Bernard was waiting for them. "Lee, hang on."

"I'll wait."

Carwyn put the phone on mute. "The cars at our house. Your people?"

Bernard nodded. "Increased security."

"Understood." He unmuted the phone. "Lee, they're friendly."

"Got it. Just wanted to make sure. I thought I recognized the guy who was walking to the front door."

Bernard said, "Miguel was heading up the detail. If your assistant has any questions, he can ask Miguel."

"Lee, the man you recognize is Lucas's personal guard. We've worked with him. He might be a good resource as you're going through the boy's devices."

"Oh, good call. I'll let you go."

"Call when you find anything useful."

"Already making a list, boss."

Carwyn hung up the phone and turned to Brigid. "Lee was in the panic room, so he followed protocol."

He saw the worry in her eyes ease. "Good."

"Miguel is at the house." Carwyn turned to Bernard. "It's good timing. Lee finally got past Lucas's security in his computer this afternoon. I told him Miguel might be useful going through the device."

"Good idea." Bernard led them through the first set of locked double doors and down the carpeted hallway leading to Rose's office. "I'm sure you noticed the increased security."

"Someone tried to break in?"

"Uh... not exactly. We do have a bit of a situation though."

Brigid asked, "What happened?"

"The Sokolovs—not Zasha, Oleg's people—may be on the move against us?"

Carwyn frowned. "For God's sake, why?"

"I spoke to Oleg early this week," Brigid said. "From what I could tell, he had nothing to do with this. In fact, he was quick to praise Rose and Agnes's leadership of the city. Said it made it easy to do business."

Bernard grimaced. "He may be singing a different tune today."

"Why?" Carwyn had a very bad feeling.

"Because last night, an hour before dawn, Rose ripped the head off one Sokolov soldier and nearly killed another."

Carwyn froze. "And by 'ripped the head off,' you mean—"

"Not a metaphor," Bernard said. "The roulette wheel will have to be completely replaced. I don't think anyone will be able to bet after the image of an eyeball spinning around and landing on red 19."

"AGNES IS CROSS WITH ME." Rose's lower lip trembled. "She screamed at me, Carwyn. She said that 'my little temper tantrum' might have cost Lucas his life." Pink tears welled in her eyes. "Do you think she's right? Is Lucas going to die because of me?"

"Rose." He held her hand, ignoring the smatter of arterial spray that she'd missed on her neck. "We don't know that." She'd obviously taken a bath because she was in a feather-collared housecoat and a pair of slippers. Her hair was wet and slicked back into a smooth bun at the nape of her neck. "I know Agnes is upset—"

"I love her so much." The pink tears fell. "She's the best thing in my life, Carwyn, and I know... Honey, I make her put up with so much. My tantrums. My little whims. I don't deserve her, and now I've gone and done this."

Carwyn sighed. He knew Rose wasn't the most stable of vampires, but he wouldn't have expected this. "Has Agnes contacted Oleg?"

"She said she was going to reach out when she'd made sure all our properties and people are secure." Rose pouted. "It's not like it was unprovoked. Do you know what those animals were saying?"

"I didn't hear anythin' about them."

Her fangs fell, and Carwyn was quick to squeeze her hand again. "Rose, don't tell me if you're going to get upset again." He put a heavy warning in his voice.

Her fangs stayed down, but the fire in her eyes cooled. "They were calling him a pet. Joking with each other that they should buy me a puppy and name it after Lucas so I wouldn't mind losing the human so much." Rose blinked. "As if he was just another human. As if I hadn't changed his sister's diapers and dried his tears when he missed his mother and read him stories at bedtime."

Carwyn wasn't sure he wouldn't have done the same thing in Rose's place. "Those were cruel words. They shouldn't have ever said that."

"But now it might cost Lucas his life." Rose's lip trembled again and her tears kept coming. "How will I tell Anna? How can I live without him, Carwyn? We can't lose him."

He would speak to Oleg himself if he needed to. This was not an unprovoked attack by a fickle vampire ruler. This was a reaction to a direct insult to her clan in a moment when that clan was under threat.

"Brigid and I are doing everything we can to find him. Lee got into his computer tonight. We're hoping that will give us more ideas about how—"

"Why isn't he home already?" Rose screamed and sprang to her feet. "Where is my child?"

Agnes rushed over and grabbed her mate by the neck, closing a firm hand around Rose's throat until her mate settled. "Rose, no."

Rose twisted her neck and bared her teeth at Agnes, who lifted her lip and growled at Rose. In seconds, the blond vampire's face crumpled in grief and she reached out for Agnes. "What do we do? What do we do, baby?"

Agnes's eyes immediately softened, and she pulled Rose into her arms in a swift embrace. "We're going to find him. I'll take care of Oleg."

Brigid had been speaking with Agnes and Bernard on the other side of the room, watching the dramatic burst of grief from Rose with a distanced eye.

"You can use this." Brigid's words fell like a stone in a quiet pool. "It's all in how you frame it. Emphasize that Lucas is a human under your aegis. You take care of your people and won't put up with insults against them or questions about your authority. No one can doubt that Rose is a lethal leader after this. You frame it as swift retribution for a committed wrong, not a loss of control."

Carwyn raised an eyebrow. "And you say you're not political."

Agnes had her eyes on Brigid. "You know the Russian."

"I do, and I am willing to act as an intermediary. This wasn't unprovoked," she said. "Oleg will be reasonable. He doesn't suffer fools, and it sounds like both of these men were fools."

"The more important question right now is how these two Sokolov soldiers knew about Lucas," Carwyn said. "Brigid didn't share anything with Oleg at their meeting the other night, so no one could have overheard gossip. We only know that Oleg was aware of Lucas's kidnapping because Mika Arakas met with her privately. According to Mika, Oleg wasn't keen to speak to Brigid because he didn't want to upset the apple cart as they say. He doesn't want you two out of power, so how did these two know about it?"

Agnes cocked her head. "I didn't consider that Oleg wouldn't have told his people."

Brigid said, "I suspect if he didn't bring it up at our meeting, he doesn't want his people to know. If nothing else, he would have offered polite concern if it was public knowledge. It's not. So two of his men knew about it." She looked at Carwyn. "I'll arrange a meeting with the Russian and Agnes." She looked at Rose. "Do you want to be there?"

"Is it a good idea?"

Brigid walked to her. "Can you be cool? Aloof? Cold like an avenging angel dealing out punishment? If you can't be, don't come."

"Avenging angel?" Rose smiled a little. "I can be that."

SEVENTEEN

For her second meeting at the Enclave, Brigid arrived first, her mate at her side. She had been careful to satiate her hunger with blood-wine at Agnes's office so she wouldn't appear ravenous to the Russian's people.

Oleg arrived wearing a navy-blue suit and a chocolate-brown tie that set off the cool grey of his eyes and the smattering of silver in his full beard. Mika followed behind him.

The fire vampire sat across from Agnes and Rose in a private room at the Enclave, a large conference table between them. Brigid was sitting at the table next to Rose, and Carwyn was standing at the end of the room, keeping an eye on everything.

Agnes and Rose wore impassive expressions, and while Oleg's jovial manner wasn't in evidence, he didn't look angry.

Irritated? Possibly.

Brigid was annoyed by the entire charade. Nothing about this was going to result in any additional information to help them find Lucas. This was a politically driven waste of time.

A vampire manager stood at the head of the table and greeted both parties. "Welcome to the Enclave, an exclusive membership-only property by Wallace Ventures. While you are here, please abide by the rules governing all of Mr. Wallace's properties and refrain from violence." The man nodded at Rose and Agnes, then at Oleg, and after that he left them alone.

"Before we begin," Brigid said, "I want to note that I am acting as a neutral party in this meeting, but I feel honor-bound to inform you, Oleg, that this was not an unprovoked attack."

The man's face turned to stone. "The surviving soldier informed me that they were... joking. Obviously their humor struck a nerve."

Rose stared at Oleg with unwavering focus. "Would you stand for a stranger in your own territory to call your child a pet?"

Oleg lifted an eyebrow. "I no longer have children."

Agnes sat ramrod straight, her eyes never shifting as she looked at the Russian fire vampire. "While we do not apologize for defending our territory or those under our aegis, we do regret that this matter was settled without your input."

Oleg cocked his head and sat back in his chair. "Input? How would that work?"

Agnes's lips didn't move, but Rose was quick to speak. "It wouldn't, of course. Agnes is being polite. But you and I aren't all that different, are we Oleg?" She leaned forward, and Oleg would have had to be truly dead to ignore the spill of cleavage from her dress.

Brigid was a happily married woman and even she was impressed.

"We protect what is ours," Rose whispered. "Your men didn't respect that."

"And they paid the price." Oleg kept his eyes on Rose. "How do you suggest we settle this?"

Agnes took over. "In the past, the more civilized of our kind settled disputes such as this with a simple transaction. What is your blood price for the one lost soldier and the damaged one?"

"Damaged?" Oleg looked amused again. "Your mate nearly ripped his head off."

"He suggested a beagle." Rose pursed her lips and stared at Oleg. "As a recompense for my child."

Agnes continued, "The damaged vampire will heal in time. If you have no suggestion, I would offer one million for the dispatched individual and five hundred thousand for the other man's inconvenience."

"Ludicrous," Oleg said. "The soldier was experienced. He was worth over five million in training alone."

"Two million for both, and I would also offer that these two men were not speaking with... discretion." Agnes nodded at Mika. "Your second met with Brigid Connor and informed her that you were keeping quiet about Lucas's disappearance so we could conduct our investigation and set our city in order from the threat from your extended clan, yet these two vampires were joking about the matter openly and in our own casino. Were these your men or perhaps individuals in alliance with someone else?"

Brigid could see that the thought hadn't occurred to Oleg.

He sat back in his chair, folded his hands in his lap, and considered the offer. Then he turned to Mika and murmured something in what Brigid guessed was Russian.

The two men exchanged a few quiet sentences, and then Oleg turned his attention back to Rose. "Miss Di Marco, as a father who has lost children, I deeply regret that my men's words caused you pain." He turned to Agnes. "As you set your city in order, it becomes evident that there might be some inconsistencies in my own ranks that could be seen to. I accept your offer of two million US dollars and look forward to working with you in the future. Perhaps on the new immortal development you and Rose are building next year."

"We aren't currently looking for investors, but an experienced collaborator might be a welcome consideration when these current distractions have been dealt with."

"That is acceptable to me." Oleg rose and buttoned his jacket. "Rose Di Marco, Agnes Wong, I will expect the blood price delivered in gold within the next forty-eight hours. Once that price has been paid, I will consider this matter settled."

Agnes and Rose also came to their feet, and Agnes nodded. "Very well, Oleg Sokolov. I am satisfied that we have come to an agreement." She turned to Brigid. "Brigid Connor, I thank you for your introduction tonight."

She'd hardly done anything. "You're most welcome. I'll join my mate and meet you back at the casino."

Agnes and Rose were shown the way out by the host, leaving Carwyn and Brigid with Mika and Oleg.

"Father." Oleg nodded at Carwyn. "It's never an unpleasant meeting when you are in attendance."

"I'm flattered, but I'm not a priest anymore." Carwyn put an arm around Brigid. "I'm a happily married man."

"And a full measure of blessing to you both." Oleg said something in Russian again. "I will never understand this Western insistence on priestly celibacy. In the East, we don't expect our priests to offer wisdom when their balls are like shriveled apples."

Brigid blinked. "What a poetic figure of speech."

"Maybe it sounds better in Russian." Oleg shrugged. "Either way, I got rid of two idiots and will have some gold in recompense."

Carwyn frowned. "I thought the second man survived."

"For now." Oleg's lip twisted, and Brigid got a glimpse of a thick, pure-white fang. "Agnes Wong was right. There was no reason for these two men to have known about their son's situation or Zasha's arrogance." He glanced at Mika. "We will find out what he knows. If anything interesting happens to fall out of his mouth, Mika will call you."

BRIGID AND CARWYN returned to their borrowed house to find Miguel and Lee nearly jumping up and down in front of the computers.

"There." Miguel pointed to the screen. "I saw him texting that name too."

"Texting?" Lee glanced at them. "Hey, boss. Hey, Carwyn."

Carwyn murmured, "Well, good to finally have that confirmed."

"Uh…" Miguel frowned. "Yeah, messaging. Whatever. On that Discord thing on his phone."

Lee nodded and switched to another screen. "So this is another person he was likely chatting with."

"Yes." Miguel's voice was nearly vibrating. "And you can get his phone number?"

Brigid and Carwyn kept their distance so they didn't disturb the flow.

"Miguel, my friend, I will have this guy's shoe size, social media handles, and kindergarten report card in a few minutes." Lee typed with lightning-fast speed. "How many names does that make for the list?"

"Five confirmed with real names and IDs."

"Cool."

Brigid glanced at Carwyn and shook her head. "Care to fill us in?"

Miguel lifted a small notebook she'd seen sticking out of his jacket pocket the past few nights. "Lee's found the kid's online friends, and at least three of them were not who they were pretending to be online. I'm waiting for this last name; then I'm tracking these lowlifes down."

"Lowlifes?" Carwyn asked.

"Most of the accounts belong to middle-aged men," Lee said. "One woman. The majority of them don't seem creepy; they just like acting immature online. But there are three who asked a lot of personal questions about Lucas. They could be working for Zasha."

"And if they're working for Zasha," Brigid said, "they might have a clue where Lucas is being kept." She patted Lee's shoulder. "Good thinking."

"They're keeping the kid somewhere during the day," Lee muttered, still typing. "Someone is going out to get newspapers and food and stuff for the kid to keep him happy. A hundred bucks says the errand runner is not Zasha Sokholov."

"I won't take that bet." Brigid pointed to the third screen. "What's the craic with this?"

"I have a program with pictures of the missing cars running over the downloaded footage that I've been able to access from traffic cams in the city. I'm getting a few hits, and as soon as I'm done with this, I'll start going through them." He turned to Miguel. "You ready for Wyvern24?"

"Hit me."

"Name is Clarence Johnson, forty-five years old, grew up right here in Las Vegas, Nevada. Used-boat salesman. I'm not going to lie, he does not strike me as a typical gamer, so this one may be your guy." The picture from the Nevada DMV showed a White man with an angular jaw wearing a blue polo shirt. He had a receding hairline, silver stubble, and a face that looked overly familiar with tanning beds. "I'll email you his address."

"Got it." Miguel tucked the notebook in his pocket. "I'm heading out; the rest of the detail will stick with the house for now."

"It's really not necessary," Brigid said. "Agnes and Rose made a deal with the Russian."

"That may be," Miguel said, "but until I get word directly from them, the other guys are staying." He clapped Lee on the shoulder. "Lee, my man, I'll give you a call if I need something else."

"You got it, man. I'll be looking into financials for all these guys while you pay them a visit."

Carwyn stopped Miguel before he left. "You're not going alone, are you?"

"Don't worry; I'll take some backup, but I don't want to take a whole team. We don't have a lot of time."

"You have five names there," Brigid said. "Why don't we take two of them? Bernard is trying to track down Preston's secretary. We have time."

Miguel walked over and tore off two pages. "You take these two; I'll jump on the other three." He glanced at Brigid. "You and the big guy have a driver?"

"Sure do." Brigid looked at the names. "Jessica Mathis and Wayne Song?"

Lee piped up. "I'll email both of you the entire list. Also, our boy was a pretty badass chess player, and he did not lose often."

Miguel waved his notebook. "I'm heading out to get a jump on these. Lee, keep me updated if you find anything else."

Brigid waved at the man before she walked over to Lee's desk. "What does that mean?"

"I kind of doubt it's related, but Lucas was playing in tournaments. Online chess tournaments. He was also betting on himself." Lee tapped the right side of the screen. "That's his account balance."

Brigid's eyes went wide. "That's over ten grand."

"Not bad for a fifteen-year-old kid." Lee clicked to a list of Lucas's matches. "He started about six months ago. He was playing in the online tournaments, but it looks like Wyvern24—that's the last name I gave to Miguel just now—turned him on to this site." Lee brought up another dashboard where numbers were updating in front of their eyes. "This is the betting arm of the tournament site. Technically you have to be eighteen to get in, but Lucas must have had a fake ID or something to tell them he was of age."

"Probably not a stretch for a bright young fella like him," Carwyn muttered. "So he was betting on himself?"

"Mainly, though he did place a few bets on RedRaptor. That's the screen name for Jessica Mathis, one of the names I just gave you."

Carwyn touched Brigid's shoulder. "Lucas strikes me as cautious. I don't think he would have bet on this RedRaptor player if he didn't know her."

"Agreed." Brigid held up the paper. "Why don't we go give Jessica Mathis a wake-up call?"

EIGHTEEN

Carwyn and Brigid walked away from the house in North Las Vegas, stepping gingerly over the cracked concrete on the pathway.

"Wayne Song is certainly an unusual individual."

Brigid glanced at him with one raised eyebrow. "Eccentric doesn't mean criminal."

Carwyn smiled. "He strikes me as immature more than anything."

"True." She glanced back over her shoulder. "For some reason, I assumed that the people Lucas talked to would also be playing chess."

"No, the Discord thing isn't connected to the chess site."

Brigid grimaced. "I can't keep up with it, Carwyn. The social media sites, the internet apps; they change every feckin' year. Has change always come this fast?"

"Brigid, for the first half of my life, the hot new technology was being literate." He opened the car door for her, waving away their driver, who had been waiting inside. "So no. Computers have sped everything up."

Brigid settled into the back of the car and huffed. "I feel old. And I'm not old." She scowled. "You're the oul' one, not me."

He barely managed to keep from laughing. "Have you calculated your mortal age lately?"

"Don't be soft in the head." She shot him a side-eye. "I'm in my twenties forever, don'tcha know?"

"And I'm a fresh and lively thirty-three." He narrowed his eyes. "I think. Honestly, it's been so long I don't really remember how old I was when I turned."

Their driver lowered the divider. "Mr. Bryn, where to next?"

"Jessica Mathis's address please."

"Sure thing." He turned to look at them over his shoulder. "And I couldn't help but overhear, but it's not just you. My kids are twelve and fifteen, and I don't even feel like I speak the same language."

He smiled. "You have a fifteen-year-old?"

"Oh yeah."

"So what do you know about Discord?"

"Uh... it's not Facebook?"

Brigid gave him I-told-you-so look. "It's impossible to keep track."

"I do think it's mostly popular with the video game crowd. My son loves those first-person combat games even though they drive my wife nuts."

"First-person combat?"

"Yeah, like you're playing that you're a soldier or a knight swinging a sword, you know? And the game is from your perspective."

"Of all the things I want to play at in life..." Brigid shook her head. "Lucas was playing something called *Legend Quest*."

"Oh yeah, I've heard of that one. It's really popular, but not as violent as what my son likes."

Carwyn was starting to question the man's casual attitude to his son wanting to virtually murder other humans. "Does he visit a Discord server for that?"

"No, he and his buddies just group chat in the games they play."

Carwyn looked at Brigid. "Group chat *in* the games? I didn't know that was possible."

"Sure, most of them have that option."

Brigid lowered her voice. "We'll have to ask Lee if Lucas got any messages from Angel that way. If we could find out where they were meeting..."

"Agreed." He glanced out the window and saw that the car was slowing down. "We're at Jessica Mathis's house?"

"This is the address." Their driver craned his neck. "No lights on."

"It's nearly midnight," Carwyn said. "Should we risk it?"

"Lucas doesn't have time for us to be polite." Brigid barely waited for the car to come to a stop before she was leaping out. She was halfway up the walk before Carwyn could catch up.

He followed her and waited on the narrow stoop while Brigid knocked on the door.

A few seconds later, she was about to raise her hand again when someone looked through the window. "Who are you?"

"We're private detectives, and we're looking for Jessica Mathis," Brigid answered. "We're so sorry to come so late, but there's a missing boy involved."

The face disappeared and the door opened to reveal a woman in her late fifties or early sixties who vaguely resembled Jessica Mathis's driver's license photo. "A missing boy?"

"Ms. Mathis?" Carwyn hung back and spoke softly so as not to startle the woman. "Are you Jessica Mathis?"

"I'm her mama." She pulled her robe closed at the neck. "I watch the kids on the nights Jessica works, and I got dogs and a gun inside, so don't think of tryin' anything."

"We don't mean to startle you or make you uncomfortable," Brigid said. "If Miss Mathis isn't here, would you be able to tell us where she is? Again, we wouldn't bother her, but time is very short in this case."

"That sounds awful." The woman frowned. "You said a missing boy?"

"He might be a runaway, but he might also have been taken or tricked somehow. We're hopin' that your daughter has some information about where he might've gone. They were online friends."

The woman's eyebrows went high. "I hope you don't think that my girl would be fooling around with no teenage boy. She's a good woman and she's got two kids of her own to take care of."

"There's no indication of that." Carwyn was quick to reassure her. "Their texts seemed purely friendly. We think he might have confided in her, something like that. Like a big sister maybe?"

The woman seemed to relax. "Okay, that makes sense. She's kinda the mama bird, you know? All her friends, she's always takin' care of them if you know what I mean."

"One hundred percent," Carwyn said. "We know she'd be worried about Lucas too."

"That his name?" The woman gave them a wide-eyed stare. "Poor kid." She took a deep breath. "Jessi works at the Dirty Martini lounge on weeknights. It's not too busy, and she makes real good tips 'cause it's by the airport. You should be able to talk to her there. I think her boss is sweet on her. You need directions?"

"Dirty Martini lounge by the airport?" Carwyn nodded. "I'm sure our driver will know it. Thank you, ma'am. Thank you very much. We won't take any more of your time."

They turned to go and the woman shouted after them, "I hope you find him."

Brigid turned. "Thank you. We will."

JESSICA MATHIS MIGHT HAVE ONLY BEEN in her late twenties, but she definitely had a maternal air about her. She had soft brown hair cut in shaggy waves and vivid blue eyes with a kind expression. She looked like the girl next door as she gently chastised two drunks and told them to eat something before they got sick, even as she was handing them another drink.

She took her break just before one and met Carwyn and Brigid at a back corner table in the wood-paneled bar. "You said Lucas is missing?" She shook her head. "That's horrible. I haven't heard anything on the news about that."

Brigid skirted the question. "Well, you know they don't treat teenage boys going missing the same way they treat younger kids or girls."

"I guess so." She looked worried. "I should have known something was wrong when he didn't send me a message after my match on Tuesday. I beat the pants off that guy, and usually Lucas would be the first person to message me."

"Your match?"

She nodded. "Lucas has been teaching me chess. We met playing this game called *Mystic Scrolls*. We ended up playing at a lot of the same times, I guess? Anyway, he had this funny screen name. Rookosaurus." She shrugged. "My son loves dinosaurs. I asked him about it and he just went on and on about chess. I admit, I was kind of impressed a kid that age was into chess. I always think of it as kind of an older game, you know?"

"So he was teaching you?"

She smiled. "I like talking with Lucas. He's a really sweet kid."

Carwyn returned her smile. "You became friends?"

"I guess you could say that. It was totally innocent." She held up a hand. "I don't even think he had a crush on me or anything. I think I was kind of like... a big sister maybe?"

"Makes sense." Brigid was taking notes. "Just so ya know, we don't suspect you of anything. We know who took Lucas—we're just trying to find him."

Jessica shook her head, and Carwyn saw tears pooling in her eyes. "How could anyone...?" She swallowed hard and wiped her eyes. "Yeah, whatever I can help with. His parents must be frantic." She cleared her throat. "You know Agnes and Rose, right? His biological parents died when he was young, and I think it was his two aunts were raising him or something. Him and his little sister."

"We're working for them, yes." Carwyn nodded. "What else did you talk about other than chess?"

"Um..." She sighed. "His parents obviously. He talked about his little sister a lot, but honestly? He seemed lonely. Said all the kids at school were spoiled rich kids. I got the feeling that his parents were pretty strict and expected a lot of him, but he clearly loved them. He wasn't an unhappy kid. I told him that he was going to go to college—he *needs* to go to college, the kid is brilliant—and he'd meet so many people there. I tried to give him advice about making friends and meeting girls." She shrugged. "You know, just kind of big-sister advice and stuff."

"Did he ever talk about a girl named Angel? Did he talk about meeting anyone outside of school?"

Her eyes grew wide. "'Met an angel today, Jessi.' I thought he was joking; I didn't realize that was a name. That was a couple of weeks ago, I think? Maybe a week and a half." She closed her eyes. "He met an angel at the gas station." She frowned. "I don't know why he was at a gas station—he didn't have a license, but maybe he just stopped there after school. No idea."

The video of Alina meeting Lucas in the elevator was three

days before he went missing, so clearly the initial meeting was earlier than that.

"A gas station." They could ask Miguel about that. "He met her at a gas station, and did he say anything else? Did he mention meeting her again?"

"He didn't. I think they texted more than they talked in person, you know? And she was a gamer too, he did mention that. Said she liked chess." Jessica closed her eyes. "I feel horrible."

Carwyn frowned. "Why?"

"I was so excited for him. I thought it was sweet, you know? He met a girl! And she even liked chess. Did this girl Angel have something to do with him running away?"

"We don't think he ran away. We think he was taken."

She covered her face with both hands. "You have to find him." She sniffed and looked up. "He's so sweet. Just the thought of someone hurting him..." She wasn't shy about her tears anymore. "I want to go home and hug my kids."

Carwyn reached out and touched her arm. "Would you like us to speak to your manager?"

She sniffed and shook her head. "No, I can't go home. The kids are in bed anyway, and I can't afford to miss a shift."

Brigid handed her a card. "If he texts you or messages you, will you give us a shout?"

"Oh my God, of course I will." She took the card eagerly and held it with both hands. "I wish I knew more. Do you think this has anything to do with how much money he was winning at chess?"

Carwyn hadn't even considered it. "He was winning, but by Las Vegas standards, we aren't talking about huge amounts."

Jessica huffed. "I don't know. I know guys who would beat up a priest for a hundred bucks."

"A priest, huh?" Brigid smirked. "Any of them looking for work? I'll take their cards."

"Very funny." Carwyn angled his foot and stepped on his wife's toe. "Jessica, I think that's all. Please call us if you think of anything else." Carwyn rose and waited for Jessica to walk away. "Did we learn a single new thing from that conversation?"

Brigid turned and started toward the door. "We learned that Lucas was a good chess player and that he met Angel before we thought. He was an innocent. She preyed on him; I'm certain of it." She glanced over her shoulder. "I'm finding it harder and harder to blame Oleg for taking her out."

"The only problem is that when Oleg takes out a player in this situation, that means we lose a line to where Zasha might be keeping Lucas."

Two nights. One day. And half of one night was already gone.

NINETEEN

They met Miguel at a twenty-four-hour coffee shop on Desert Inn Drive. They walked in to see a glass case full of brightly colored donuts with bizarre toppings like giant strawberries, breakfast cereal, and bacon.

There was a bearded man in drag behind the counter, waving them in while he perused a magazine. "Welcome to Night Cup. You can order at the counter or seat yourself."

Brigid couldn't stop staring at the donuts. "Why are American donuts so good?"

She wasn't really expecting an answer, but the man behind the counter muttered, "They're made from fat, sugar, and an overinflated sense of historic purpose."

The corner of her mouth turned up, and she stepped closer. "And bacon."

The man cocked a bright purple eyebrow. "Honey, that's our bourbon, bacon, and maple-glazed long john. You want heaven in your mouth, you try one of those." He glanced at Carwyn. "Is that your man?"

She looked over her shoulder. "Himself?"

"Yes."

"I'm afraid so."

The man pursed his lips. "Never mind. I bet you get heaven in your mouth anytime you damn well please." He waved her away. "You don't need a donut."

An unexpected laugh burst from her mouth.

Carwyn had been looking around the coffee shop. "What's that?"

She turned and angled his shoulders toward the booths on the right. "You don't wanna know."

"Miguel's in the booth in the far back." Carwyn glanced at the man behind the counter. "Oh, hello. How are you tonight?"

"And an accent too?" The man behind the counter winked at Brigid. "Just let me know what I can get you. Sally's your waitress, but she's on break."

Miguel was eating a simple glazed donut and drinking a cup of coffee. The man looked exhausted.

And defeated.

Brigid knew the feeling. They had just over twenty-four hours to find Lucas, and she still felt lost.

Carwyn sat down in the booth opposite Miguel, and Brigid slid in next to her husband.

"None of the people we talked to were leads." Carwyn didn't beat around the bush. "Jessica Mathis was like a big sister. All we got from her was worry."

"And Wayne Song is... unusual." Brigid couldn't deny it. "But he seems harmless and nearly as big a chess addict as Lucas. He knew the boy purely from their online tournaments."

"Same." Miguel gulped his coffee. "I've got one more lead to go look at—the Clarence Johnson guy—but I'm not optimistic. I mean, I guess I should have expected that a vampire wasn't going to go hunting for a kid online, but I thought we'd maybe get something."

"We did have one question." Carwyn glanced at Brigid, then

back at Miguel. "Jessica Mathis mentioned that Lucas told her he'd met... How did he put it?"

"An angel," Brigid said. "He told her he'd met an angel at a gas station. Would that even be possible? I can't imagine Lucas was getting his own petrol. He had a driver."

Miguel's cheeks reddened a little. "That's my fault. I mean... Okay, so Rose and Agnes were manic about keeping the kids' diets really healthy, right? But Lucas started high school and starts asking me about different snack stuff. What are Doritos? Why was everything flaming hot? I figured it was no big deal, right? He's old enough to make some of his own choices, so whenever we'd stop for gas, I'd let him go into the gas station and pick one snack. Just one. The rule was he had to eat it in the car and he had to brush his teeth before his moms woke up that night so neither of us got in trouble."

Brigid shook her head. "So you're saying that Alina was able to target Lucas was because he stopped at gas stations for crisps?"

Carwyn shrugged. "That may have been the only time she could get him alone. I'm sure they followed him, figured out his routine. Was there any particular place he liked to stop?"

Miguel nodded. "There's a Rebel convenience store not too far from his school that was near an In-N-Out Burger. A lot of kids from his school liked to hang out there. I figured since it was a familiar place, it would be safer."

"She probably blended in with the kids," Brigid said. "I doubt you'd have noticed her."

"He was never in there for more than a few minutes," Miguel said. "Hell, half the time the other guard would go in with him."

"But not all the time?" Carwyn asked.

Miguel shrugged. "I guess not. I mean, the kid was already chafing at having two guards on him all the time. If we'd tried to look over his shoulder while he was getting his after-school snack around a bunch of kids he went to school with, he would have rioted."

"So the Discord chats are likely nothin'," Brigid said. "And we know where they probably met, but that tells us bugger all about where he's being kept." She looked at Miguel. "Have you heard from Lee? Has he found anythin' about those cars missing from Preston's?"

"He sent me a text," Carwyn said. "Traffic cameras spotted two of the vehicles, and both sightings were in Henderson."

"Henderson is southeast of the city," Miguel said. "Not far. It's kind of like a suburb these days."

"So we focus the search in that area," Brigid said. "Like Lee said, someone is going out to get supplies for the boy, get water and food, buy newspapers. Two traffic cameras picking up Preston's cars in one city isn't a coincidence. We have to narrow the focus."

Normally it would be thin information to narrow a search, but Brigid was feeling desperate. They had a little over twenty-four hours and nearly nothing to go on.

Miguel looked at the table as his phone began to buzz and light up. "It's Bernard."

"He's been distracted by all this nonsense with Rose ripping off heads," Carwyn muttered. "Not a good situation. We need him focused on Lucas."

"Let me call him back." Miguel picked up the phone, and Brigid slid out of the booth.

"Where you going?" Carwyn frowned.

"I'm getting a maple-and-bacon donut," she said. "I can't stop thinkin' about it. It'll either be heaven in my mouth or utter disaster. Tell me what Bernard said when I get back."

SHE FINISHED with her maple-and-bacon donut as Bernard walked through the doors. He nodded politely at the host before he headed toward them.

The vampire lieutenant was wearing his typical uniform of a black three-piece suit, brown oxford shoes, and a demure silver tie with a ruby pin. His hair was set in immaculate waves, and Brigid would have had to be blind not to catch the café host's admiring look as Bernard walked down the narrow aisle between booths.

He looked down his nose at Brigid. "Donut?"

"Heaven in my mouth." She licked the maple glaze off her little finger. "What information do you have for me?"

He looked around the shop. "Where are Miguel and Carwyn?"

"It's two in the morning and we have leads to follow. I told them I'd wait for you here while they visited the last questionable contact in Lucas's chat history."

"Who is?"

"Man by the name of Clarence Johnson. Forty-seven, former boat dealer, and deeply in debt because of online chess tournaments."

Bernard slid into the booth, and it instantly felt fancier. "And they think waking a human up at two in the morning to ask questions is a good idea?"

She glanced at the clock. "Barely over twenty-four hours. We don't have much of a choice. We're focusing on Henderson because two of Preston's cars were spotted there, so move your people in. Sniff things out. See what the vampire rumor mill is saying. There have to be whispers, but your people are the ones who would hear them. We're new faces."

"Understood and I agree. I'll contact our informants."

"What's the mood like back at the Del Marco?"

Bernard shifted. "To the public? Business as usual."

"And privately?"

He looked reluctant to speak.

"Bernard, I'm not asking to spread gossip," Brigid said. "I need to know what kind of expectations I'm working with."

"Rose and Agnes are arguing. Rose wants to hand the city over to Zasha and whoever their allies are. Just walk away with the children."

"And Agnes knows that isn't an option."

Bernard nodded. "No one wants to lose Lucas, but handing the city over to an individual like Zasha Sokholov—any of the Sokholovs, but particularly them—would be a disaster."

"And it probably wouldn't keep Lucas safe anyway."

Bernard offered her a curt nod. "Correct."

She sat back and mulled over their options. "You send those pictures of the flooring to your daughter?"

"I have."

"Anything?"

"She's still searching images online to find anything that can narrow it down. It appears to be a man-made material. It appears woven. It's unusual but it's also black. The computer doesn't know quite what to search for."

"Woven, synthetic carpet." Brigid turned the idea over. "Wouldn't be industrial. Could it be something from a garden center? Something like that?"

He cocked his head. "That's an interesting thought. Woven vinyl perhaps? Why would you need woven vinyl flooring? What would be the purpose?"

"It wouldn't be comfort." She tapped her fork on the edge of her plate. "It wouldn't stain if it got wet."

There was something there...

Wet.

Drainage.

Then why not a slick flooring like in a garage? Something easy to spray off?

A thought was tugging at the back of Brigid's mind.

You wouldn't want to slip.

"Why would you slip?"

Bernard asked, "What's that?"

She looked up from contemplating her empty plate. "Woven vinyl flooring. It wouldn't be damaged by water. It wouldn't pool on the top like a solid flooring. Think about those outdoor carpets they make for conservatories, things like that."

"Conservatories?"

"Ah... patios." Brigid waved a hand. "Outdoor spaces."

"So you think Lucas is being kept outdoors? Not likely."

"No, it was definitely inside."

There was something she wasn't putting together, and it was sitting right on the edge of her mind. There was a connection she was missing because she was feeling stressed and desperate to find the boy.

You know what it's like to sleep in fear.

"If and when Bernice gets back to me with an answer, I'll call you immediately." Bernard craned his neck and glanced at the front of the coffee shop as the bell over the door rang. "I should get going."

"Thanks for meeting me here."

"Not a problem. I needed to clear my head anyway." Bernard slid out of the booth and stood. "I wish I had something else to give you right now, but I don't."

"This city is too damn big."

Bernard's expression was grim. "And hiding one teenage boy isn't difficult."

She nodded. "I'll call Lee. See if he's come up with any other ideas or leads. I can catch a taxi back to the house if I need to."

He pointed to the front. "My driver and I can take you if you prefer."

The thought of sitting in the back of a car with Bernard, reeking of failure, made her shake her head. "I'll wait for Carwyn and Miguel."

"Very well." Bernard started to leave.

Brigid sipped the glass of water the host had handed to her when she picked out her donut. "Bernard?"

He turned and walked back so he wouldn't have to yell. "Yes, Miss Connor?"

"What about Preston's secretary? Did you find her?"

"I have a number and address, but unlike middle-aged video game players, I do not think we'll get anything from Gayle Pickman in the middle of the night. We're going to have to wait until tomorrow evening if we want her to cooperate."

"I get it." It drove her crazy to be so limited, but she knew it was the reality she had to deal with. "Thanks."

The man walked out of the coffee shop, and she saw his driver jump out of the car to open the back door. The low-slung sedan pulled away from the entrance to Night Cup, stopped, and immediately backed up.

Bernard's door flew open and he rushed into the restaurant, not bothering with niceties at the door.

Brigid was already standing, sensing the man's urgency. "What is it?

"Come with me." He held out a hand. "We need to go to the hospital right away."

TWENTY

Miguel was an easy companion to work with, and if there wasn't a missing boy sitting in the front of his mind, Carwyn would have greatly enjoyed chatting with the man more.

"Little League." Miguel pointed at Carwyn. "I tell you, those parents get crazy. I offered to be the assistant coach—*assistant*, right? And I thought the head coach was exaggerating."

"He wasn't?"

"Nearly had fist fights between innings." Miguel shook his head. "Unbelievable. I told my wife, 'Honey, I don't think this is the right kind of influence on our boy, you know?' But he loves it. Absolutely addicted to the game."

"How old is he?"

"Just turned ten." Miguel was beaming. "And our little one, he's all about soccer. Of course they couldn't like the same sport, right?"

"Is there a lot of gear with baseball?" Carwyn knew a little about the sport, but he hadn't had young children in centuries. "There are helmets and such, yes?"

"Bats, helmets, gloves, uniforms. It's a lot."

"At least with soccer the equipment is simple."

"True, but if I have to run out one more time right before a game starts because my kid forgot his shin guards..." The human shrugged. "I can't complain. I was a shit when I was a teenager. Nearly got myself killed a few times. My dad wasn't thinking about bats or shin guards, you know? He was thinking about how to keep me alive." Miguel fell silent, a shadow falling over his face.

Carwyn could see paternal responsibility written all over the man's face. "You're very attached to Lucas."

"He was like my first kid." He swallowed hard. "I started guarding him right around the time my oldest was born. They say that a good bodyguard shouldn't get attached, but—"

"That's pure shite." Carwyn shook his head. "You're spending that much time with anyone, you're going to have feelings for them. It's impossible not to. They become like an extension of yourself, and there's nothing wrong with that. We protect those who are important to us with a ferocity that is instinctive."

"But I also allowed him freedom I probably shouldn't have." Miguel grimaced. "I just can't think of what I could have done different, you know? Not let the kid use the bathroom on his own? Not let him pick out chips at the corner store?"

"This isn't your fault." Carwyn reached over and put his hand on the man's shoulder. "Lucas ran away. You weren't supposed to keep him prisoner. That wasn't your job. You did the best you could."

Miguel swallowed hard. "I think Bernard is the only reason my kids still have a dad. I saw the look in Rose's eyes, and..."

"Parents become feral when we lose our children." Carwyn flashed back to the desperation, the raw panic, the overwhelming rage when his own son had been taken by an enemy. "I lost a child. He was centuries old, but when I looked at him..." He blinked, then refocused. "I still saw the boy he was. He was my descendant by blood and by amnis. I saw him grow up. I remember…"

In his mind, Carwyn saw a round-cheeked baby playing in the mud and laughing at farm dogs. A vibrant boy, thin as a sapling, bounding across fields at midnight. A curious young man, eager for knowledge and eternity, begging Carwyn to sire him.

"I remember every moment." His voice was rough. "We never forget our children."

Miguel pulled up to a low-slung tract house in a middle-class neighborhood that had seen better days. The grass was overgrown in the front, and an old boat sat in the driveway gathering cobwebs under the hull.

From the front window, Carwyn saw a flickering light that appeared to be the television. "Clarence Johnson looks like he might be awake."

"I'm gonna pull into the driveway with the lights on," Miguel said. "Give him a heads-up that he has company."

"Are you sure that's a good idea?"

"He's gonna be either shocked or supershocked that someone is knocking on his door at two in the morning. I'd rather give him a little advance notice if we can."

Carwyn was still staring at the boat. "Why own a boat when you live in the desert?"

Miguel looked at the boat. "Oh, there're lakes around here."

"Lake Las Vegas? I thought that was one of those artificial landscaping kind of lakes to make rich people feel like they have waterfront property."

Miguel chuckled. "It's artificial, but it's not just for landscaping. You can boat on it. Fish. But the real deal is Lake Mead. Oh man, that's some good fishing. I remember going out with my dad when I was a kid." He pointed to the boat in Johnson's driveway as he pulled up next to it. "That's a sport fisher. You can take them on the ocean, but you'll see a lot of them on Mead."

"Is that the lake with the massive dam on it?"

Miguel nodded. "Yeah, that's the one. Hoover Dam." He unclipped his seat belt and opened his car door. "I know you can't go out during the day and all that, but it's beautiful at night too. When I was younger, me and a bunch of buddies would rent a houseboat and take that out on the lake. It was a hell of a good time. And the stars out there in the middle of the desert?" Miguel shook his head. "Magical."

"Must be heaven for water vampires."

Miguel laughed. "We don't get too many of those around here."

They walked slowly up the front walkway, which was overgrown with Bermuda grass and weeds. There was a dusty set of folding chairs sitting on the small porch; one appeared to be broken. An overflowing ashtray sat in the middle of a tilting table, and a crushed silver beer can was stuck under one leg in an attempt to straighten the table's lean.

"How does this guy have over twenty grand to lose betting on chess?" Miguel muttered.

"Clearly he doesn't." Carwyn reached out and knocked on the door. He gave it a solid but not thundering rap and almost immediately heard someone stir inside the house. "Good idea with the headlights, Miguel."

"I do occasionally have—"

Cannon fire cut off Miguel's voice, and Carwyn jumped back as the wooden door of the house splintered outward. A second explosion rocketed out, and dust flew through the air. Through the ringing in his ears and the confusion, Carwyn's eyes darted from the smoke and dust at the door to the dark figure kicking in the dust.

"Get the fuck away!" a voice screamed from the house. "I don't know anything! Get the fuck away!"

He moved with preternatural speed, rushing the human who had shot through the door, grabbing the shotgun, throwing him on the ground, and punching him in the head until he was still. Then he rushed to Miguel, rolling the man to his back.

The human's chest was a mess of blood and dirt, deep red seeping through caked earth where he'd fallen forward onto the dusty front lawn.

"Help!" Carwyn's voice boomed through the night. He rolled up his sleeve and his fangs fell. He slashed a deep gash in his wrist with his own teeth and poured the blood directly onto Miguel's chest. "Anybody, help! Call an ambulance!"

Carwyn heard doors opening and a woman's sharp scream. A few moments later, he heard sirens wailing.

"Stay with me." He bit his other wrist and poured more blood into Miguel's wounds, hoping to keep him alive until the ambulance arrived.

Miguel didn't speak, but his eyes were wide and pleading.

"Stay with me." Carwyn didn't let go of his hand. "Stay with me. Your children need you. It's not your time to die. Do ya hear me?"

The man's head moved in an incremental nod.

"Good. My blood will help stop the bleeding."

Another small nod.

Carwyn calculated the spread of the shot, the velocity it must have had to blast through the door and hit the man.

A second shot in the heat of panic and fear.

Miguel was dying in front of his eyes, and Clarence Johnson lay still on the ground, blood from his nose seeping into the dry earth.

MIGUEL WAS AT THE HOSPITAL, and Clarence Johnson was in a hole in the ground.

Carwyn sat cross-legged next to the hole and the bleary-eyed man who had shot Carwyn's new friend. Clarence's head and shoulders were sticking out of the earth, but everything below that was immersed in rock; the earth vampire had complete and utter control.

He kept his voice low, hoping to hear a buzzing sound from his phone in the distance or the call from Lee that Miguel had emerged from the surgery with his heart still beating.

"The man you shot," Carwyn said quietly. "He's a good man. Has two children. He coaches baseball even though he doesn't like it. He's searching for a lost boy."

Clarence Johnson coughed, and Carwyn could see the man was confused. "What's going on?"

"You're going to explain why you shot him in the chest when all we did was knock on your door, Clarence."

The man struggled against the ground, but the earth didn't give way.

This ground knew Carwyn now. It would keep his captive.

The human was slowly waking from his stupor. "H-how did I get in this hole?"

"I opened the ground and set you in it." He dug one hand in the ground and closed his fist around the earth, which responded by compressing Clarence's chest until the man gasped.

"What are you doing?" The words burst from his mouth as if the ground had squeezed them from the man's throat. "What's happening?"

"Do you think Miguel felt pressure like this?" He clenched his hand again, then released it. "When you shot through the door. Do you think his chest felt pressure, or did it just feel like *fire*?" He pulled from his amnis and sent heat from his body into the earth, enough to make the human feel a scalding burn cover his body.

Clarence Johnson screamed into the night. "Oh God, what is happening?"

They were at Preston's ranch, an empty stretch of land with no one within yelling distance. Clarence's head swiveled around, searching the darkness, but the only figures other than Carwyn were two vampires from Agnes and Rose's guard, watching in the distance and waiting to see what information Carwyn could glean from the human who had shot Miguel.

The man was sweating and coughing. "Who are you? Where am I?"

"Those would have been very appropriate questions to ask us when we knocked on your door." Carwyn bent down to Clarence's face and let his fangs fall, slick and shining in the moonlight. "Instead, you shot blindly and now my friend might die."

"Oh fuck!" The man started to twist, but he couldn't move. "You're one of them. You're one of them!"

"So ya already know about vampires, do you? That should save us some time." Carwyn squeezed his hand again, and the twisting stopped. "You know what I can do, so you know you're going to answer all my questions, Clarence."

The man was crying and shaking his head. "I didn't know. I didn't know. I thought you were him."

"Thought I was who?"

"The Dutchman."

Dutchman. Interesting. "Is the Dutchman a vampire?"

"Yeah. I didn't know. At first I didn't know any of this stuff. I don't want to know anything about it!"

"Why would this Dutchman come to your house?"

"Because I tried to warn him."

"Tried to warn who?"

"The kid!"

Carwyn tensed and the ground tensed with him, causing Clarence to gasp.

Shit.

He released his grip on the man. "Tell me everything from the beginning."

"The Dutchman messaged me on the server. I just thought he was some punk. It was months ago. I'd lost a match to him, but he said he didn't want the money. Just said that he wanted me to start talking with this other player, Rookosaurus." Clarence shook his head. "I thought it was a scam. I thought he was a creep, so I blew him off. I didn't want to get mixed up with some asshole who wanted to know about a kid."

A hint of sympathy peeked through Carwyn's rage, but then he remembered the dozen holes in Miguel's chest. "Keep going."

"I go to work the next day" —he started to cry— "and my boss pulls me in. I worked at the boat dealership, you know? He said he got the email and I was already on thin ice and that was the last straw."

Carwyn had to sort through the mixed metaphors. "Why were you in trouble at work?"

"Because of the drinking!" The man sobbed. "But I swear I didn't send that email!"

"What email?"

"It was pictures. Naked pictures. The girls looked like they were in high school or something. It went out to everyone, even my old secretary. My boss said he'd call the police if I didn't leave." Clarence shook his head. "I was pissed, and I was so confused."

"The Dutchman had hacked your email?"

"I got another message." Clarence gulped. "He knew everything about me. My ex-wife. My daughter in school. He knew my daughter's car and where she's working and everything." He attempted a shrug. "What could I do? I'd already lost my job. I'm a shit dad; I couldn't let this creep hurt my daughter."

Carwyn knew that the manipulation and blackmail that Clarence Johnson had faced was only a hint of what the Ankers likely had in store. If they got control of the city with Sokholov, they'd have access to everything and everyone. Executives. Entrepreneurs. Digital barons. Government employees.

Clarence Johnson was only the beginning of what they could expect.

"So you started a conversation with Lucas?"

"Who?"

"The kid. Rookasaurus."

"I *had* to. Don't you see? I had to!"

"What did they want?"

"Just... dumb stuff. Where he liked to hang out. What his plans were. They wanted me to lose to him at chess, ask him for advice, make like we were friends." Clarence blinked, and tears rolled down his dusty face. "I did it. The kid... he seemed like a good kid. He just liked chess and girls and cars. Talked about going to college and how boring most high school kids were because they were immature."

"Keep going."

"He talked about this girl he met." Clarence shook his head. "And something in me... I just knew. I was going to warn him that she wasn't safe. That something about her was off, but just when I started to say something, I got locked out of my account."

"How?" Carwyn wished Lee was with him, though he knew the man would be put off by his methods. "What happened?"

He shook his head. "I don't know. I figured they had to be listening in somehow. Like they bugged my computer or something. That was about two weeks ago, and I haven't slept since." The tears were flowing now. "I thought you were them. They came to my house once in the middle of the night and they threatened my daughter. They threatened her mom. I didn't mean to hurt your friend, I promise."

Carwyn stood, leaving the man weeping in the dirt as he walked away. He motioned to one of Rose and Agnes's men who had been standing at a distance. "I'm finished with him."

"What should we do with him?"

Carwyn turned to watch the human. His face was covered in dust and the tear tracks had turned his face to a muddy mess. Snot was dripping from his nose. He looked... pathetic.

"We wait and see. If Miguel lives, we turn him over to the police. If he doesn't..."

The two guards waited.

Carwyn stepped away, leaving Miguel's shooter encased in the earth. "Let Rose deal with him."

TWENTY-ONE

This is my fault.

It echoed through her mind over and over again as she sat in a corner of the waiting room at the human hospital, counting the hours until Lucas's time was up. Dawn was a little over two hours away, and she was pushing her luck. She would have to leave soon if she wanted to make sure she was safe in her day chamber.

This is my fault.

The repeating chorus in her mind wouldn't stop.

Lucas wouldn't have been taken if Zasha Sokholov hadn't become interested in her.

Miguel wouldn't be fighting for his life.

Alina Oorzhak might still be alive.

Oleg wouldn't be missing two soldiers.

Gary Preston and two domestic workers wouldn't be dead. She didn't even know the two women's names. They were two more helpless souls taken because an obsessive had fixated on Brigid.

Why?

Maybe it didn't matter. Maybe the only way to stop this was to...

She didn't know.

"How do I stop it?"

"Brigid?"

She looked up and Bernard was staring at her. "What?"

"You're muttering."

"I do that." She rose and started to pace. "What's taking them so long?"

"It's been less than an hour, Brigid."

She knew that. Logically, she knew that. "There's something... It's right there, and I'm not seeing it. There's a connection that—"

"Carwyn is on his way here. He questioned Clarence Johnson and discovered that he'd been blackmailed by someone he called the Dutchman—"

"One of the Ankers."

"Presumably yes. He'd been coerced to become friends with Lucas. That's how they started tracking his movements. I happened over months. Alina was simply the final draw to lure him away from his guards."

"That tells us nothin' about where he is now." She stared at the glass doors and saw a black shadow approaching. Tall and broad, the shadow moved with an efficient stride that had always been one of the most attractive things about him. He knew the ground he trod upon because it had been his source of power for over a millennium.

Carwyn pushed through the glass doors, and his eyes immediately found hers. He held out his arms, and she walked to them.

"I'm sorry." She laid her head on his chest. "This is my fault."

He enfolded her in an embrace. "It's not your fault."

"But it's because of me." She took a deep breath to inhale his scent. Earth and leather and a hint of something fresh and herbal. "It's because Zasha is fixated on me."

His arms didn't loosen, but she felt him freeze when he tried to respond.

"I know, Carwyn." She lifted her head. "I just don't know how to stop it."

"It's not your fault."

She closed her eyes and shook her head. "I know I'm not responsible for Zasha's actions or all the fallout, but I can't escape that they have remained in the States because they're obsessed with me. They called me 'the Irish one.' I would have been better off facing all this in Ireland with Murphy."

"Why are you saying that?"

"Things are more tightly controlled there. We both know it." She pulled away. "Maybe I should go back to Dublin."

He growled at her. "Fuck no, you won't."

"I mean after this." She shook her head. "I can't leave now, but maybe I should go back to Dublin after we find Lucas. You don't have to come, you can stay with Lee, and I'll ask Murphy when his next boat..." She blinked. "Fuck me."

"Brigid."

"Murphy could send a boat."

Carwyn frowned. "I know that."

"I think I've seen it." She put a hand on his chest. "Carwyn, I think I know where I've seen—"

"Are you Mr. Estrada's family?"

She spun in Carwyn's arms and saw a doctor in blue scrubs standing there with a chart in his hand. "No. We're his friends."

"I'm his brother-in-law." Bernard stepped forward. "My sister is on her way. She had to find someone to watch the kids, but I can tell her—"

"Great. Come with me." The doctor waved him over to the hallway. "I have an update for you guys."

Brigid patted Carwyn's shoulder and pointed to Bernard. "You should go with him. I have something to check out."

He glanced at the clock on the wall. "We only have two hours before sunrise."

"I have just enough time. We're already halfway to Oleg's at this hospital. This will only take fifteen minutes to check. I have a question for Mika and Oleg. I'll take a cab to their house, ask the question, then find a Formula One racer to take me home." She nudged him toward the hallway. "Go check on Miguel. I'll have my phone."

Carwyn looked at Bernard, then back at Brigid. "Are you sure?"

"Positive." She patted his arm and started to walk away. "It's a quick question. I'll see you at home."

SHE TOOK a taxicab to the gate of Oleg's neighborhood and stood at the massive wrought iron gates, punched in the house number with a stick, and waited for it to ring.

"Yes?"

"This is Brigid Connor to see Mika Arakas. Is he in tonight?"

There was a pause and some muttering in Russian. "One moment."

She stood there in the middle of the road while the gates began to open.

"Brigid Connor, Mika Arakas will meet you at Oleg's gate."

"Thank you very much." She walked through the gates, trying to remember exactly how she'd gotten to Oleg's last time. She could feel three vampires in the area, but they kept their distance.

"Brigid Connor?"

She turned toward the voice in the shadows. "I'm Brigid Connor."

"Follow me please."

The vampire took off at immortal speed and Brigid followed, racing through the palm-tree-lined neighborhood on the edge of the water. She could smell it, the damp algae and creosote. A storm was coming, and the electricity in the air was invigorating.

They arrived at Oleg's house in just under a minute, and Mika was leaning against the gate. "Brigid Connor." He nodded slightly. "You didn't come with tea cakes this time."

"Is there somewhere private we can speak?"

Mika shrugged and nodded toward a corner of the garden. "There are ears everywhere."

"Noted."

They walked under an alley of trees that lined a path that ran around the gated compound.

Brigid started. "Miguel was shot tonight by a human the Ankers had blackmailed. He was paid to give them information about the boy."

"That sounds like something the Ankers would do."

"He's not dead."

"Yet?"

"Hospital. Human doctors."

Mika shrugged again. It seemed to be his favorite gesture. "The humans will save him or they won't. What request do you have for me, Brigid Connor? Does killing make you... How do they say it? Queasy?"

Right now killing something would be intensely satisfying.

The sentiment must have shown on her face because Mika laughed. "I don't think that is the problem for you. Maybe for your mate, but not for you. Murphy's little matchstick doesn't have a problem with her fire."

"I have a question, not a request." She looked over the distant lights on the water. "Can I look at Oleg's boat?"

"His boat?"

"I have a theory."

Mika was already walking toward the waterfront. "Which boat do you mean? That little putter boat or the pontoon?"

"Both."

Mika shrugged again. "Sure. Why not? You're not going to find Zasha hiding around here. That one? Even I find them distasteful."

"Zasha thinks everything is a game."

"In that, Brigid Connor, they are not wrong." Mika walked down a dock that jutted into the waters of Lake Las Vegas, and Brigid was struck by how large the lake actually was. This wasn't a landscaping pond or a pool. The lake stretched across a massive distance, and she could see lights twinkling along the far shore.

"How often do you take the boat out?"

"We have some water vampires in our employ who take it out more often than the earth vampires of course."

Rumor was, Mika Arakas was a wind vampire, and his energy matched the quick, twisting vibrance of that element.

They stepped on the deck of the small craft. "Can I take a look inside?"

"Of course." He smirked. "We haven't killed anyone belowdecks in months."

If Brigid was right, the interior would have a thick, synthetic woven mat that was easy to clean, waterproof, and nonslip. Perfect for the interior of a fishing boat.

Mika followed her below the deck, and she tensed for a moment, then remembered how quickly she could blow up the boat and Mika if she wanted to. Her fire had blasted a hole in a freighter hold years ago. A fiberglass boat like this one? It would probably melt under her hands.

"I'm not sure what you're looking for."

"I'm looking at carpet."

Mika was silent.

Brigid searched every corner of the vessel, but nothing resembled the woven mat that she'd seen in Lucas's picture.

"I am trying to understand why you want to see the carpet. I can assume it has something to do with the proof-of-life photographs you received."

"The carpet in the pictures was hard to make out, but I think it's similar to some I remember from one of Murphy's boats back in Dublin."

"This one is not woven."

"No." She looked up. "Can I see the pontoon?"

Mika lifted a lazy shoulder. "I'm curious now."

They walked back up the pathway to the massive garage next to the house.

Gary Preston had a huge garage.

Brigid was putting two and two together. "You called it a pontoon boat?"

"Yes, a party cruiser." Mika sneered. "The human guards haul it to Lake Mead and put it in the water there. It's like a little club on the water. They take girls, alcohol, whatever drugs they want to indulge in." Mika opened the door. "Oleg doesn't mind."

"Did he buy it?"

"It came with the house."

Brigid saw the long vessel as soon as she stepped inside. It was impossible to miss. This was definitely why Gary Preston had such a huge garage. It was to keep this massive boat inside to be hauled to Lake Mead during the boating season.

"It wasn't the cars."

"Sorry, what was that?"

Brigid shook her head. "You don't need a huge garage for cars around here. You need it for boats."

"And houseboats," Mika said. "Yes."

She climbed on board and immediately spotted the flooring she was thinking of. Just inside the glass-enclosed cabin, the floor was blue instead of black, but the texture was the same.

He was on a boat.

Gary Preston must have had a boat, and that's why they killed him. That's why they targeted Preston—to get his boat. She knew where to find him. She still had to search the lake, but she knew where to find him.

Brigid hopped down and walked toward the door. She felt like her amnis was going to burst from her skin. "Mika, thank you."

"Anytime." He was leaning against a wall. "Do you need a car? Do you need a light-safe room? We have guest quarters here that are more than secure."

No way was she staying at Oleg's house, and borrowing a car took time and attention. She needed to get to Lake Mead, and she needed to do it now.

She glanced at the clock on the wall. There was only an hour before dawn.

She whispered, "Fuck."

"The night is over," Mika said. "You're not going to do anything else tonight, Brigid Connor. At least let me get you a fast car to your safe house."

"You're generous." She smiled at him. "But no. I'll find my way home. Cheers." She didn't know if Oleg knew the locations of Agnes and Rose's safe houses, and she wasn't going to give them away. "I'll call for a taxi."

He spread his hands. "At least let us take you to the correct area of town. It might be difficult to find a taxi going that direction this time of night."

Mika had a point. She could have them drop her off at the corner store a mile from the house. That wouldn't be enough for them to get a location. "That'd be much appreciated." Brigid nodded. "Thank you."

LUCAS IS ON A BOAT. That's why they hadn't been able to find him. He was on a boat in Lake Mead. It might even be a house-boat they were keeping docked somewhere isolated enough to keep anyone from asking questions but close enough that they could get supplies.

Agnes and Rose couldn't find him in the water, but that didn't matter, because Brigid finally knew.

She stared out the darkened back window of the car, wishing the man would drive faster. She'd never cut things this close in a foreign city, and she was starting to regret taking the chance and not taking Mika up on his offer of a safe room.

Carwyn is going to worry.

"I can drop you off at your house, yes?" The driver was a human with a thick Russian accent.

"Just at the corner please." She leaned forward and looked out the front window. "I don't know if this is the right direction." She wasn't that familiar with the city, but it looked like they were circling around the lake, not headed back toward Las Vegas.

"Is right direction. I have map, Brigid Connor."

God save her from human men who wouldn't ask for directions even an hour before dawn. "I think we need to be heading north. We're going east."

"Road curves around. It's okay. I know. I know."

She kept her eyes on the road. He turned right, then left, past a subdivision of houses and toward a dark road that quickly led into an industrial area of town. There were warehouses on both sides and nothing that looked like they were headed into the city.

"Where are you taking me?" She frowned. "This isn't the right way."

"No? You know the city better than me?" He pulled over and brought out a map. "Come." He waved her toward him. "You show me the neighborhood, okay? You show me where to go."

She did it without thinking. He was human. He was one of Oleg's. He couldn't be a threat.

The pinch of metal at her neck and the buzzing jolt of electricity was enough to remind her that humans had weapons too.

Everything in her body lit up for a brilliant millisecond, and then her amnis reacted to the jolt of the Taser current and her fire exploded outward in a massive ring, incinerating the driver, the car, and everything around them.

Brigid's vision went black.

TWENTY-TWO

Carwyn felt a jolt of panic in his blood. "Lee!"

He'd been pacing the house, worried that Brigid was going to have to shelter somewhere else for the day. She wasn't back. She'd said that she had a question for Oleg that would only take fifteen minutes. Thirty minutes had come and gone, but he hadn't panicked. She knew her own limits. She'd be home.

It was forty minutes before dawn when he felt it.

"Lee!" He stormed out of the day chamber and banged on the human's door.

Lee opened it, rubbing his eyes. "Seriously? I finally got to sleep like five minutes—"

"Brigid isn't back."

Lee glanced at the window. "It's still dark."

"She's in trouble." He headed for the door, but the human ran after him.

"What are you doing?" Lee shouted. "You can't be out when the sun rises over that horizon! You can't get anywhere in town in a half an hour."

"I *felt* her." He turned and pounded a fist over his heart. "I felt her in my blood. Panic, then nothing. Something happened."

His expression froze. "Nothing?"

Carwyn's heart was thumping at a slow, steady rate. An ancient instinct for someone whose heart hadn't needed to churn in a thousand years. Emotion was overwhelming him. The bond to his mate hadn't severed—he knew she was still alive—but something was very, very wrong.

"There was a burst of panic, and now I can feel her but it's a low hum." He rubbed his chest. "Like she's sleeping. This is how it feels when she sleeps before me."

Carwyn was older than Brigid. He could be awake during the day if he needed it. He could feel the dawn tugging at the edge of his body, but it was easy to ignore when he was this worried.

"I need you to go to Oleg's house and find out what happened." He slapped Lee on the shoulder. "Go. Do it now. Talk to the human guards at the gate and call me."

Lee's dark eyes went wide. "You want me to go see the Russian?"

"Yes. He and Brigid are friendly. She was going over there to ask a question. If something happened, I need to know. If she didn't show up, I need to know."

"Don't you want to call Agnes and Rose or someone at the—?"

"Lee." He grabbed the man's shoulders and attempted to pull himself back from panic. "Do you understand that I am helpless right now?"

Lee's voice was tight. "You don't seem helpless to me. Honestly, you seem terrifying."

Carwyn took a deep breath and stepped back. "I am sorry. But I cannot leave this house without incinerating myself, and my reason for existence is in danger. Do you understand?"

Lee nodded.

"I will call" —he lifted a hand that he was barely keeping from curling into a fist— "*all* those people, but you are the one that I trust. And I need you to go now. Immediately."

Lee hesitated for only a few seconds. "Yeah. Of course. I'll go. I can go. I think it'll take me about forty minutes to get there. Will you still be awake?"

"Yes." If he were a wind vampire, he could fly, but not even vampire running or tunneling speed could get him to Oleg's before dawn. "Talk to the guards, tell them you work for me. You will be fine. Find out when she was there. Find out which direction she went."

"I will."

He walked out the door, and Carwyn held tightly to the thread of amnis he felt humming in his blood. Brigid was alive.

She was alive.

It was thirty-seven minutes later when Lee called. "Okay, I'm at the gate and these guys are not cooperating with me. I said I'm looking for Brigid Connor, and they're saying they don't know who that is."

"Bullshit." He spoke into the speakerphone. "Give your phone to whoever appears to be in charge."

"Okay, sure."

There was some muffled muttering, and then a voice came on the line.

The man had a thick Russian accent. "Who is this?"

"This is Carwyn ap Bryn, immortal son of Maelona of Gwynedd, daughter of Brennus the Celt. Former priest of Rome and head of my clan. Who are you?"

"Uhhh, this is Yuri."

"Nice to meet you, Yuri. Now my mate, the Irish fire vampire Brigid Connor, went to Oleg's house an hour and a half ago to ask your boss a question. They're *friends*. I need to know if she was there, and I need to know where she went when she left. If she's still there, I need confirmation. Speak to Mika or whoever is in charge right now."

It had occurred to Carwyn that Oleg would have safe quarters for guests, but that didn't explain the panic he'd felt in her amnis.

"You are vampire, yes?"

English clearly wasn't his best language.

"Yes."

"And you are awake now?"

Carwyn began to pace. "Listen, Yuri. I am very, *very* old. I can stay awake all day if I want to." A stretch, but Yuri didn't need to know that. "Now talk to your boss and find my mate. I'll wait."

The man must have handed the phone back to Lee, because the next voice he heard was his computer guy. "Okay, they're going to the guardhouse. They're all speaking Russian, but it definitely looks like you put a bug in their butt."

"What an absolutely lovely mental picture, thank you."

He waited on the phone while there was nothing but muffled voices and static in the background.

"Carwyn, they're coming back."

"Do they look worried?"

"I don't think that's an expression these guys have. He's waving for the phone."

Yuri came back on the line. "Your mate, she was here. Mika put her in car with Pyotr. Good driver."

"When?"

"Eh, plenty of time. An hour maybe."

That should have been enough time to get to their house, which was maximum forty minutes from Oleg's.

"Yuri, do you have a tracker on that car?"

"Of course. You want me to look?"

"Please." Something was wrong. Something was very wrong.

"Eh, the guard in the house, he is saying the car is only a few minutes from here but not moving. I will go with your man to check it out."

"Very well." Carwyn was trying to figure out how Lee could get Brigid back safely if she was trapped in the car for some reason. Maybe that was the panic? She'd realized that the car wasn't going to be able to get her home in time before dawn.

That was probably it.

His head began to swim. He hadn't fed in over a week, and he was starting to feel it.

"Carwyn?"

"Yes, Lee."

"I'm switching the call to the car, so it might break off. If we get cut off, I'll call you when we find the driver."

"Good idea." He was still pacing when the call cut off, just as Lee had predicted. The hands-free system in the van wasn't the best.

It was maximum ten minutes later that Lee called him back.

"Carwyn, you're not going to like this."

"What is it?" He stood and started pacing again. He felt simmering rage bubble beneath his skin.

He was helpless. Completely helpless.

"We found what was left of the car, but it's not much. Driver is bones. Looks like Brigid lost it and exploded inside."

He relaxed a little bit. "Her fire never hurts her."

"Can't say the same about this driver." Lee dropped his voice. "Yuri is shouting at someone on the phone in Russian. He seems really pissed. I saw him kick what looked like a melted Taser under a piece of metal."

Carwyn growled. "A Taser?"

"Did Brigid carry a Taser?"

"Not last night, but if someone used one on her, it would

definitely cause an explosion." He should know. He'd used one on her in a particularly extreme situation.

"Fuck around and find out?" Lee switched to video and showed Carwyn a scene of absolute chaos. It looked like the silver sedan had been taken out with a missile strike. Shrapnel and debris were scattered in a clear blast radius.

"Dear God," Carwyn muttered. "But where is she?"

"She's probably hiding nearby." Lee turned in circles. "Honestly, there's a ton of warehouses and a lot of abandoned stuff. I'd be willing to bet the guy tried something, hit her with the Taser, and she ended up finding someplace light safe around here to hole up until nightfall."

It was as good an explanation as Carwyn could think of. Lee was probably right. The panic could have been from the Taser, and the low humming buzz fit with Brigid finding an underground hideaway where she could hide from the sun.

"You're probably right." Carwyn forced his voice to be calm. "Head back to the house. If Brigid is hiding, you won't find her. Come back and get some sleep. We'll have to wait for her at nightfall."

CARWYN WOKE AT DUSK, and the first thing he did was check the blood tie that ran through his blood. Brigid wasn't awake yet, but he could feel the low, constant presence in his blood. She was alive. He didn't know where she was, but their bond hadn't been broken.

He lay in their bed, smelling her scent around him on the sheets, on her clothes hanging in the corner, even on the book she'd been reading, which was on the nightstand. It was a historical novel about the Mongol empire or something of the kind.

Moments after he woke, there was a knock at the door.

"Carwyn?" Lee was on the other side.

He rose and walked to the door, shirtless and still wearing the jeans he'd fallen into bed in the night before. They felt rough and stuck to his legs.

Carwyn opened the door and saw his computer hacker on the other side. Lee's face was a picture of dread.

"We got an email about an hour ago."

His fangs dropped. "No."

Lee stepped back, clearly sensing the growing fury. "Carwyn, I can't tell you what we know until you take a deep breath and get less scary."

He clamped down on the worst of his fear and rage, took a breath, and centered his mind.

Whatever Lee was going to tell him, he knew Brigid was alive because he could feel her.

He could feel her.

"It came to the business email account. A picture of Lucas again, same room, holding today's newspaper."

"With Brigid?"

Lee nodded. "It looks like the same location as before, but Brigid is propped up next to Lucas. She looks asleep. The message said: 'Bonus round. Twelve extra hours.'"

"They took it during the day." Someone had touched his mate when she was helpless. Only Carwyn knew just what a violation that was. Whoever had done this? They were dead. They were already dead.

"Lucas looks... He looks terrified. I'm sure he has no idea who Brigid is, so he just thinks they put a sleeping vampire in the room with him."

Zasha Sokholov was going to die. If not by Brigid's hand, then by Carwyn's.

"Call Agnes and Rose. Call Oleg. We need to figure out why she went there and what she found."

I'm going to find you.
Brigid, do you hear me?
I'm going to find you.

"THE SIMPLE FACT IS, your son is safer with Brigid there than when he was alone with Zasha." Carwyn was trying to calm Rose as Agnes paced in front of the fireplace in their desert mansion. "Rose, you have to believe me."

"She's a fire vampire!" Rose nearly screamed. "And she's barely a decade old. When was the last time she fed, Carwyn? When was the last time she expelled energy like what you described? She's awake now, and she's going to be hungry and *our son* will be the only one nearby!"

Carwyn didn't know whether to laugh or rage. "You think Brigid is going to feed on Lucas?"

Agnes looked grim. "You have to think about our perspective. She's dangerous, and I doubt they're going to provide her with blood to feed on. If they're alone too long, you and I both know that she'll revert to her instincts."

"This is because we didn't hand over the city!" Rose burst out. "Because you were too stubborn, Agnes. We hired this fire vampire, and now Zasha is going to use her to kill our child."

Carwyn's anger leached into the ground beneath him, and the house rumbled as a crack opened in the black-and-white marble-tiled floor.

"Stop it, both of you." He snarled. "We came here as a favor because of a situation you were in."

"A situation we never would have been in had you and your mate not killed Zasha Sokholov's only child." Agnes squared her shoulders and stared Carwyn down.

A deep part of Carwyn wanted to crush the woman under

his hand, toss her into the nearest wall, and leave so he could go search for his mate. "Brigid would sooner cut off her own arm than harm an innocent. Get out of my way and let me look for them both."

Agnes's angry gaze never wavered from Carwyn, but she remained silent.

"Oh God, oh God." Rose had pink tears running down her face. "Lucas. My baby. Where is Anna? Where is my Anna?"

Agnes snapped at a maid hovering near the door. "Get the girl in here. Rose needs her."

Carwyn wasn't at all sure that the best thing for Lucas's little sister was to be the emotional support for an overwrought vampire, but it wasn't his home.

"Lucas is safer with Brigid there," he repeated. "There is no one more resourceful than my wife." He stood. "I'm going to leave you and get to work finding them. Zasha Sokholov doesn't understand mating bonds. I'll know if I'm near to Brigid. I can look for both of them now. If they're keeping them together, I will find them tonight."

TWENTY-THREE

Brigid woke in confusion, fear, and anger. She didn't smell the familiar scent of her mate next to her. She didn't recognize the sounds around her or the smells.

She reared up, wincing as she hit her head on a metal railing just over the place she was resting. She hissed and her fangs fell down.

The scared heartbeat of prey filled her senses.

She rolled to the ground and crouched next to the bed, shielding her vulnerable front and sweeping her eyes around the tiny chamber.

Someone was panting, and the smell of their blood was sweet liquor to her senses.

"Please."

Her head swung in the direction of the sound. The voice came from the corner around the bed. Brigid stayed low but leaned forward and angled her head to see the prey.

Lucas was crouched in the corner, trying to make himself as small as possible. His heart was racing, and sweat bloomed on his forehead. His eyes were pressed closed, and he appeared frozen in place.

He smelled terrified and delectable.

"Lucas O'Hara?"

His eyes opened. "Who are you?"

The hunger and rage fled, leaving Brigid alone with the fifteen-year-old boy she'd spent days searching for.

Despite their circumstances, a sigh of relief escaped her. He was alive.

One night left, and he was alive.

"I'm Brigid." She swallowed hard and concentrated on calming her voice. "Sorry for the way I woke up. I don't like waking up in places that I don't know."

"I know the feeling." His voice was still small.

"I'm sorry if I scared you." She pushed up to all fours, then sat on the floor cross-legged, her fingers digging into the black woven mat that covered the floor of what she guessed was a houseboat somewhere on Lake Mead. "Your mothers hired me and my husband to find you."

"You're a... vampire detective?"

"Somethin' like that."

"And you got caught?" The corner of his mouth turned up. "Not a great recommendation."

"Not my finest hour, as they say." The boy appeared in good health. His eyes weren't traumatized. He was still showing signs of humor. Brigid added, "I let my guard down because I was running out of time. Have you ever let your guard down to the wrong person?"

Lucas blinked. "Yeah."

"So we're both stuck here." She scooted back, giving him as much room as she could in the tiny bedroom. "They keep you in here all the time? Have they ever moved you?" If Lucas was still in the original location, there would be some tie that Carwyn and Lee could find. If they'd traded vessels, they were in trouble.

Lucas shook his head. "I haven't moved. I mean, I can feel

the boat moving, but they haven't moved me from the room." He pointed at the corner. "There's a bathroom there. They bring food in when they come to take my picture." Lucas pointed to a small refrigerator. "There's chips and trail mix and sandwiches there. I think the only place they shop is a gas station, but it's more than I need. You can have whatever you want."

"Thank you, but I'm good for now."

"You looked dead when they brought you in, but I knew you were alive because Agnes and Rose look the same when they're sleeping."

The thought of being manhandled in her sleep made her toes curl and her stomach churn. "I'm sorry you were scared."

"I thought..." He shrugged. "You know, I thought Zasha had gotten bored with me or something and was going to feed me to you. I knew Agnes wouldn't give up the city. She's logical."

"Agnes loves you very much." She could see the resignation in the boy's eyes. "Zasha made a mistake bringing me here. We're stronger together, and I won't let anyone hurt you."

"Unless it's during the day."

"Vampires are sleeping then, and humans are easier to kill. I can teach you how to kill the humans if they try to hurt you," Brigid said. "Have you ever killed anyone?"

Lucas blinked. "I'm only fifteen."

Brigid shrugged. "Even so."

"No, I haven't." He swallowed hard, and a small frown formed between his eyebrows. "Miguel taught me some things, but I've been thinking about it a lot in the past few days, and I don't think I could kill anyone. Even to save myself. Maybe if I had to protect Anna or something." He looked up. "That probably sounds stupid to you."

"No, it sounds very thoughtful and honest." Brigid brought her knees to her chest. "Has Zasha come to see you?"

"A couple of times. They're weird." Lucas cocked his head. "Are you Zasha's enemy?"

"Zasha has a lot of enemies."

"No." He shook his head. "They said they wanted to spend time with an enemy who intrigues them." He pointed at Brigid. "I think that's you."

"Why?"

"Because they didn't kill you right away. Wouldn't they have killed you if they just wanted to get rid of you?"

"Maybe they wanted me to kill you first."

Lucas shook his head. "No. I think you're the vampire Zasha was talking about."

Brigid felt her heart sink. It was one thing to suspect she was the cause of all this. It was another thing to have it confirmed. "Yeah. You're probably correct."

"Why do you think you intrigue Zasha?"

Mika's words came to mind: *They see your fear, and yet somehow you have not allowed hate to consume you.* Brigid hopped to her feet, needing to move, to pace, to do something. "I don't know. Maybe because we're both fire vampires."

Lucas froze. "You're a fire vampire?"

"Yes."

Lucas frowned. "In my whole life, I've never met a single fire vampire and now I know two. I feel like that's not a good sign." The boy heaved a big sigh and knocked his head against the wall. "It doesn't matter. Zasha is in check, and they know it."

She turned to him. "What do you mean, Zasha is in check?"

"They're one move away from inevitable loss." Lucas rose and straightened his pants. "Checkmate."

"I know what checkmate is, but why do you say Zasha is in check?"

"They said they wanted to spend time with you but that their partners wanted the city from Agnes and Rose. I told them

Agnes and Rose wouldn't give up Las Vegas because they wouldn't sacrifice a whole city for one person. Checkmate. They lose."

"Why do you think Agnes and Rose wouldn't give up the city?"

Lucas shrugged. "It's not logical."

"Logic doesn't really apply to parents and children, does it?"

"They're not my real parents."

Brigid leaned against the wall, pressing her hands to the fiberglass, feeling the metal behind it. "Real parents by blood don't necessarily mean they care about you more. My adoptive parents were much better than my mother and my stepfather."

"What about your dad?"

"He died when I was a baby."

Lucas pressed his lips together. "Mine too."

She felt the aching hole in his chest as if it were her own. She had never even known her father, but she missed him keenly. "I'm sorry."

"It was a long time ago. I don't really remember him." He shrugged again. "Just pictures."

Change the subject. Don't give in to despair. "I wouldn't discount Agnes and Rose if I were you. Or me. Where do you think we are?" She started feeling around the room, reaching up to touch the low ceiling and test the walls. From her initial impression, there weren't any evident seams or vents.

"On a houseboat, I think. I went with Miguel and some guards one time. I'm pretty sure that's where we are."

"Smart lad." Brigid kept pressing her hands along the walls. "Probably Lake Mead."

"That makes sense."

"What do you say we try to find a way out of here?" She turned and put her hands on her hips. "What else are we going to do?"

"I tried to pick the lock, but I couldn't." He walked over. "Do you know about picking locks?"

"A bit." She glanced at him. "I'm very glad you already know about vampires. If I had to put up with a blubbering and confused teenager, this'd be a lot more annoyin'."

"Glad I don't annoy you." His voice betrayed dry humor. "I'd prefer to keep all my blood for my own use, thanks."

"Ya know they put us in the room together because they thought I'd kill you." Brigid bent down to examine the lock. "They don't know me very well."

Lucas pulled over a chair to watch her. "To be fair, Zasha said they wanted to know you more, not that they knew you well. Deep down, I think they want to be friends."

"That's... terrifying."

"Yeah." Lucas narrowed his eyes to peer at the lock. "I don't know you well, but I can already tell I don't want to be friends with either of you."

"Harsh." Brigid barely contained her smile. "But I appreciate the honesty."

BERNARD WAS AT THE CASINO, and Mika Arakas was in the chair across from the desk when Carwyn arrived.

"Miguel is out of surgery and still being observed." Bernard didn't wait for introductions. "Clarence Johnson has been turned over to local authorities after blubbering about a monster who tried to crush his chest in a hole in the ground."

Mika turned to Carwyn with an amused look. "What a baffling story."

"Probably drugs induced." Carwyn touched his temple. "Maybe sun damage. What did Brigid want to know?"

"She wanted to look at Oleg's boats." Mika shrugged. "She

seemed to be very interested in the carpet on the houseboat, and then she left."

Carwyn sat down next to Mika. "And one of your men put a Taser to her head."

"That was not on my orders." Mika lifted a single finger. "Do you think I would be so stupid? I know what that kind of electrical jolt would do to a fire vampire. Whoever bought Pyotr off probably wanted him dead and Brigid incapacitated but alive."

"I agree." Bernard kept his eyes on Carwyn. "Are we going to have a problem?"

"No," Carwyn said. "They're trying to point fingers at Oleg when we already know that Zasha's people have made inroads into Oleg's organization."

Mika narrowed his eyes. "I'd hardly say *inroads*."

"You killed Alina Oorzhak because she compromised multiple guards, and now one of your drivers has been incinerated because he tried to incapacitate my wife. I'd say *inroads* is exactly the right word."

"I will deal with these... inroads." Mika had lost his smile. "While you try to find your lost mate."

Carwyn wore a minute smile. "Do you think I'm worried about Brigid? I'm angry, Mika Arakas, not worried. The stupidest move Oleg's kin made was when they took my wife."

"If what I hear about Brigid Connor is correct," Bernard said, "that woman will destroy the Ankers and Zasha Sokholov from the inside."

Mika muttered, "Like trying to confine a badger in a barn."

Carwyn said, "When we have more time for the badger story, I want to hear it, but for now we have an appointment with Gary Preston's secretary, don't we?" Carwyn nodded at Mika. "Tell your boss that I want everyone in his organization with ties to the Ankers or Zasha. I want to know what they know, and so does he." He stood and started toward the door.

"Do not worry, Carwyn ap Bryn." Mika rose and turned to Carwyn. "They will be dealt with."

"No." Carwyn held up a finger. "I want them *alive*. I'll question anyone you find, Mika Arakas, but I want them alive."

Mika smiled, and two daggerlike blades gleamed in his mouth. "I'll see what I can do."

BERNARD SAT in the back of the sedan with Carwyn. "Despite your bravado, I am keenly aware you must be worried about your wife and I am very sorry for that."

"The Ankers play dirty," Carwyn said. "I can play dirtier. As long as I can feel her" —he rubbed his chest— "I'll be steady. And I worry less about Lucas knowing she's with him."

"How is it?" Bernard glanced at him. "You can feel her, but you don't know where she is."

"She's not touching ground." He looked at Bernard. "Boats, my friend. Oleg's boat? Brigid suspected Lucas was being kept on a boat. It's the easiest way to make sure no earth vampire would be able to sense him."

"Which is why we couldn't get his scent," Bernard said. "You think Preston had a boat? We checked his financials. There was no evidence of a boat."

"Maybe the secretary knows things that aren't in the official record," Carwyn said. "He did have an awfully big garage."

"And the cars were showing up in Henderson, which is on the way to Lake Las Vegas."

Their driver pulled up to a generous suburban home off Far Hills Drive in Summerlin. The master-planned community was neatly landscaped with modern desert xeriscaping and brightly lit homes. Moderately luxurious cars lined the driveways, and more than one house had a boat in the driveway.

"Looks like Preston paid his secretary well." Carwyn peered out of the window. "She knows we're coming?"

"Yes. She's expecting Miguel, and I don't know if anything has been on the news."

Carwyn looked down at his chino pants and almost subdued Hawaiian shirt. Bernard was wearing a three-piece suit even though the temperature was still in the high eighties. "Think she'll believe we're police detectives?"

"Probably not." Bernard exited the car, and Carwyn followed him. "She'll probably think we're mob. She'll still talk."

They strode up the front walk, and Bernard knocked on the door.

In the back of his mind, Carwyn felt Brigid's amusement, and it made the knot in his chest loosen just a little bit. She was fine. She was with the lad, and she was looking for solutions.

If Zasha or the Ankers started to torment either of them, he would know.

"Mrs. Pickman?" Bernard looked at the modern doorbell camera affixed to the wall. "I'm here to speak to you about Mr. Preston. You spoke to my colleague Miguel a few days ago?"

"Just a minute." The voice came through the small speaker by the doorbell.

A few moments later, the door cracked open. "Detective Estrada didn't say anyone else was coming."

There was a chain on the door. Nothing that Carwyn couldn't push through with a slight shove, but he didn't want to scare the woman.

"Detective Estrada was involved in a shooting last night," Bernard said. "I'm not sure if you saw it on the news. I'm his supervisor, Bernard Aguirre."

"Oh my God! That's horrible!" The door shut, the chain rattled, and it swung open.

The woman at the door was middle-aged with straight blond

hair, a forgettably attractive face, and an athletic figure. She was tan and wore biking shorts and a T-shirt. "First this horrible business with Gary and now Detective Estrada? I can't believe it. What is this city coming to?" She turned. "Brian! The police are here about Gary."

She waved them into the front room. "Let me get my water. I just got off my bike."

A trim man in a polo shirt wandered into the room and waved. "This about Gary's murder?"

"Yes, sir." Carwyn piped up. "We're investigating since Miguel is in the hospital."

"Was that shooting related to Gary's death?"

"Absolutely not," Carwyn said. "Unrelated and unfortunate. Miguel was in the wrong place at the wrong time." He walked over to the man and shook his hand, suffusing the human with an easy calm. "We'll try not to take up too much of Mrs. Pickman's time."

"Of course." The human smiled. "No problem."

Mrs. Pickman walked back in the room and waved her hand. "Call me Gayle. Have a seat, guys. I brought some water, unless you want coffee this time of night?"

"Not for me." Bernard sat on the couch. "Gayle, we had some questions about Gary Preston's books."

She blew out a breath. "You and me both. I worked for Gary for years, but in the last year, I gotta tell you, I was getting really uncomfortable. I'm a bookkeeper. I do human resources. General office management, you know? But after he split from Shelly—ex-Mrs. Preston. She and the kids moved to Reno to be near her folks." Gayle shook her head. "He was a changed man. I don't judge people's marriages, mind you. I knew they were having problems and I knew why."

"Why?"

"He stepped out on her. Multiple times." Gayle rolled her

eyes. "And he gambled, but who doesn't in this town? It was the affairs that did them in. He wanted to live the high-roller life, and that wasn't Shelly, you know? She liked tennis and the PTA and being a basketball mom. She wasn't into the flashy stuff he liked."

"The ranch house...?"

"New," Gayle said. "Post-divorce Gary. They were building it, but then they split up..." She shook her head. "That poor family. His kids are going to be devastated."

"Did they have a boat, Gayle?"

"A boat?" She blinked. "Okay, so that's a good question and I'm not entirely sure."

Bernard leaned forward. "What does that mean?"

"It means he had one, but I don't know how. I never saw sales records for it. I never saw a contract or a loan document. It showed up, and he said he'd won it in a bet. Well..." She huffed. "You can imagine I had questions. I asked about the registration. I asked about transfer documents. He brushed me off, said that was all getting taken care of. Seemed delighted with himself, to be honest. He had it in the garage at the house. It's not still there?"

"No, ma'am." Bernard looked grim.

"Well, he bragged about it to everyone." She shook her head. "Can you imagine if that dumb houseboat got him killed, Brian?" She turned to her husband. "That ridiculous houseboat. They probably stole it."

Carwyn tried to get the conversation back on track. "So if there was no documentation on the vessel, you don't know what type it was or the registration number or—"

"Oh, I know what type it was." Gayle's husband piped up from the back of the room. "Gorgeous thing. It had to be at least sixty-five feet. Maybe seventy? Newish. Maybe 2005 or later. Pretty sure it was a Summerland."

Carwyn and Bernard exchanged a look.

"So you saw it?" Bernard asked.

"Oh yeah. Gary had a barbecue a while back, was showing it off to everyone." The man wrinkled his forehead. "Can't remember what the name was. Dutch something. It was weird. Dutch Folly. Going Dutch." He shrugged. "Can't remember that bit."

Carwyn stood. "Mr. Pickman, I don't suppose you remember where he was going to dock it, do you?"

"I remember that part," Gayle said. "Only place around here people dock houseboats. Callville Bay on Lake Mead. He had me looking into slips there, but then he dropped it. Not sure why. You want to find that houseboat? I'm sure it'll be somewhere around Callville Bay."

TWENTY-FOUR

"Do you like being a vampire?"

It had been hours of searching the room for weaknesses, and Brigid was losing her patience.

She flexed her hands. "What kinda question is that?"

Lucas was lying on the bed, staring at the blank white ceiling overhead. "I'm just curious."

She'd been experimenting with heating her hands and directing fire to try to melt the door lock, but they'd put some kind of sensor on it. As soon as it reached a certain degree, a cold blast of air filled the room and quenched the door.

She was getting frustrated and snappy. "I'm not happy or sad. It just is."

"That's a weird answer."

"Why is that weird?" She stepped away from the door so she didn't lose her cool and explode. "I am what I am. I could moan and cry about my human life being lost or about how I miss the sun or how I hate having to drink blood, but that won't change the fact that all those things are my life now. Useless to complain about them."

"I thought blood tasted good to vampires."

Brigid considered the question. "It tastes... satisfying. Taste is different when you're immortal. All your senses are elevated, so—"

"Is that why your voice is so soft?"

"D'ya ever let people finish answers? Or d'ya just jump in and ask the next question?"

Lucas stared at the opposite wall, evidently bored with the company and the conversation. "I can usually guess what people are going to say by the way they start their sentence, so it's boring to have to listen to them spell out all the details."

Brigid turned back to the door. "You really think you're smart, don'tcha?"

"I am. I took a lot of tests when I was younger and I'm a genius. Diagnosed."

Despite his attitude, the corner of her mouth turned up. "You say *diagnosed* like it's a disease."

"It kind of is."

Brigid looked over her shoulder. Lucas had shifted on the narrow bed and drawn his knees up into his chest. He was staring at his sock-clad feet as he spoke.

"It's hard to make friends when you're smart. I used to think that being smart would mean that people would like me when I went to regular school. Like when you're really good in sports and score a goal, that's a good thing. People cheer for you."

Brigid knew where this was going. "But not when you're smart in school."

"No." Lucas shook his head. "At first that was really confusing. Then I realized why."

"Why?"

"People think having athletic ability is rare. Not everyone is tall and good at basketball, you know? Not every person *expects* to be good at sports."

"But all people expect to be smart?" Brigid turned back to

the door and started to feel around the seams. Maybe the hinges were vulnerable.

"No, but no person wants to feel dumb."

She turned to look at him again. "That's true."

"Yeah."

She started heating the bottom hinge of the door, sending heat into the joint as she applied pressure with her shoulder. Any movement would mean—

"Fuck me!" She jumped back when the trigger released again. A cloud of frost and the smell of cold air filled the room. "Lucas, you okay?"

"It's liquid nitrogen," he said. "It would take a lot more than that to poison me. You wouldn't die, obviously. Vampires can't die from asphyxiation. You just stop talking."

His clinical voice rubbed her the wrong way and she didn't know why. "Do you like being smart, Lucas?"

"What kind of question is that?"

She looked over her shoulder.

He was smiling at her. "It just is."

Brigid smiled back. "Yeah."

"Better question." He scooted to the edge of the bed. "What's your favorite thing about being a vampire?"

"Honestly?" She leaned against a wall so as not to frighten the boy. "I love being someplace empty. A field or an island or something like that. Something with lots of fuel where I can feed my fire and the energy grows and grows and consumes everything. It gives me strength. I feel powerful and alive."

His eyes narrowed. "You can't feel powerful here because if you let go of your power—your fire—you'll kill me."

She nodded.

"But if you didn't care about killing me, you could escape easily."

She pointed to the wall she was leaning against. "I could

explode. Turn myself into a bomb and blast my way out. If you weren't human, you might even survive. I've done it before."

"But I *am* human, so I'd die?" Lucas nodded. "That's probably what Zasha wanted, right? To make you feel powerless."

"I'm sure that's something they're enjoying, yeah."

"And since you're an ethical vampire, you won't kill someone you were hired to protect."

"I wouldn't kill you even if I didn't know you," Brigid said. "You're an innocent."

His cheeks reddened. "Not really."

"In my world, you're an innocent. Trust me." She smirked. "For a teenager? I don't have any idea about that." His face was still red and his blood smelled even more delectable. Brigid swallowed the heat in her throat and turned back to the wall, feeling the panel for something—anything—that could be exploited as a weakness. "What's your favorite thing about being a genius?"

"Chess."

She glanced over her shoulder. "Chess?"

He nodded. "It's a battle game. Did you know that? It originated in India as a military strategy game. The pieces we call castles or rooks were chariots. The bishops were elephants."

"I've known a couple of bishops in my life. One might be mistaken for an elephant."

It was useless. Brigid turned, let herself slide down the wall, let her arms rest on her knees.

Lucas stared at the wall in front of him, his eyes growing animated as he talked about chess. "Both the queen and the bishop were originally much weaker pieces. Now the queen is incredibly powerful and the bishop is equal in strength to a knight." He looked at Brigid. "Sometimes I think of vampires like chess pieces."

She smiled. "Really? Where do you think fire vampires fall? Are we the queens of the vampire world? Or the pawns?"

"Not pawns." He shook his head. "Humans like me are the pawns."

Brigid didn't respond. He was right. Too often, humans were the pawns in vampire games.

Lucas's eyes darted around as if he was watching a chess game on the plain white wall of the narrow bedroom. "The piece you are would depend on if you care about collateral damage."

"Like Zasha?"

"Zasha is a knight." Lucas's voice was definitive. "They don't care about collateral damage, so they're flexible. Good in close combat with a lot of different pieces on the board. If someone gets damaged in the game, they don't care."

Lucas. Miguel. Alina. All were collateral damage in Zasha's game.

"Yeah," Brigid said. "I can see that."

Lucas looked at her. "You're more like a bishop."

She snorted. Brigid a bishop? Not likely.

"I don't look much like a holy man or an elephant, kid." She stood again and started to pace the room, trying to find a way to protect Lucas so she could bust out of the ship. She'd tried simply punching through the hull with a heated hand and that did nothing.

"There's nothing holy about the bishop in chess," he said. "You have to forget the religious connotations. The bishop is a powerful piece that can move great distances as long as it has room to maneuver. A clear board." He scooted forward, clearly loving the metaphor. "Right now you're obstructed by a pawn." He pointed at his chest. "Me."

"Exactly." She was more than obstructed, she was stymied.

"But you'll figure out a way to move me out of your path. You're smarter than most vampires."

She frowned. "Thanks?"

"That's when bishops can work best, when they have a clear board. You can do a lot as long as you don't have obstacles in your way."

CALLVILLE BAY MARINA was a dot on the north side of Lake Mead, nearly an hour away from downtown Las Vegas. The marina was a sparsely populated outpost with little more than a curving building topped with red tile, a long boat launch, and rows and rows of white-and-blue houseboats bobbing quietly in the calm blue waters of the lake.

Lake Mead itself was a deep blue slash in a sea of desert brown. Unlike the California lakes Carwyn was familiar with, it wasn't surrounded by forests or meadows. It was a massive flooded canyon in an immense desert landscape. A few struggling palm trees attempted to give it some character, but the emptiness was profound. The lake was rimmed by rock walls, boulders, and narrow sandy beaches.

Carwyn looked at the lake on the map. "It's huge."

"Over five hundred miles of shoreline." Bernard had changed out of his suit and was overseeing the group of searchers.

"And the houseboats" —Carwyn glanced at the square white vessels in the marina and scanned the map— "they can go anywhere?"

"It's expansive, but we'll utilize our wind vampires to scan the area and look for possibilities. Chances are they're not far from the marina."

"They're getting papers every day."

"Exactly."

"Unless Zasha has wind vampires too."

Bernard muttered, "Yes, I had thought of that."

Carwyn suspected that even if Zasha had a flyer or two on the payroll, the boy was being guarded by humans. Zasha might have been the grand-orchestra conductor in this twisted symphony, but holding a human required twenty-four-hour awareness, which vampires didn't have.

"Do we have pictures of the houseboat?" Bernard asked.

"Lee looked online." Carwyn spread out three printed photographs. "If Gayle's husband was correct, it's a Summerland houseboat that looks something like this. We don't know the year, and nothing in the records was registered to Gary Preston, but these are the most likely possibilities."

Bernard studied the photographs. "With *Dutch* in the name."

"It's late, not many people are around, and frankly it's only the beginning of houseboat season according to what Lee could find," Carwyn said. "I think we'll do better to track activity than track the boat."

"Agreed." Bernard gave a sharp nod. "Rose and Agnes have already alerted their businesses in this area to be on the lookout for strangers. They have people in Boulder City, which is south of here, the Lake Las Vegas area, and Temple Bar Marina. They'll report any unusual vampires so we can question anyone who doesn't owe allegiance to Agnes and Rose."

Carwyn raised an eyebrow. "Is that wise?" Las Vegas had become popular in the immortal world for its hands-off, don't-ask-questions policy. It was one of the reasons they had so many vampires who came to the city for holidays.

"From a hospitality perspective? It could backfire." Bernard crossed his arms. "But I advised them that a few grumbles were preferable to a quiet takeover from the shadows. Until Brigid and Lucas are found, hospitality comes second to security. One of the patrols has already picked up a couple of Russian-speaking vampires hanging around the South Shore in Lake Las Vegas."

"And?"

"They claimed to be socializing at the country club. We're holding them for now, and we called Oleg."

Carwyn stared at the lake, feeling ill at ease. Agnes and Rose had water vampires on the payroll, but not many. He was worthless on a boat, and Brigid was apparently being housed in very small quarters with a human child she had to protect. For a young fire vampire like Brigid, it was a recipe for disaster.

"Boss!" A human came running up. "Possible lead. There's an old guy at the store, says a foreign couple come in every morning to pick up the newspaper and snacks. They're staying on a houseboat in the marina. They said they were on holiday."

"Foreign? He couldn't be more specific?"

The man shrugged. "I asked. He just said they were tall, white, and foreign."

Bernard grimaced. "Did he know which slip?"

"He's trying to call a dockhand he knows at the marina. Says the couple has been here for just over a week, keep to themselves, and don't chitchat much."

"Is there any way we can get down on those docks and just walk around?" Carwyn knew if he could get close enough to Brigid, even with her on the water, he would be able to find her. He could feel her frustration growing in his heart, and he was starting to worry she'd try something desperate to escape.

Like a badger in a barn.

Badgers could do damage. A whole hell of a lot of damage if they got desperate enough.

BRIGID HEARD FOOTSTEPS ABOVE THEM. Scurrying feet and a heavy clatter. Something that sounded an awful lot like a body dropped to the deck overhead.

"What was that?" Lucas looked up.

"I think something fell." *Something or someone.* Brigid went to stand in front of Lucas, blocking the boy from anyone who came through the door. "Stay behind me."

"Is it Zasha?"

"I think so."

Lucas sounded nonchalant. "I don't think they're going to hurt me."

You don't know Zasha.

"Zasha gave your mothers a deadline to hand over the city," Brigid said. "And that deadline passes tonight."

"What does that mean?" His voice finally sounded a little less detached.

"It means that they may have figured out what you knew days ago." She glanced over her shoulder. "Checkmate."

Lucas's dark eyes were wide. "Brigid—"

A thought sprang into her mind and she spun around. "Can you swim?"

It was a last resort, but it was better than nothing. Carwyn was not going to find them surrounded by water. She had no idea where they were, but they didn't have time to wait for help.

"Y-yes." Lucas's eyes went wide. "I can swim."

"Go to the bathroom. Get in the shower and turn the water on. Soak yourself. Your clothes, your hair, everything. Is there a fan?"

Lucas scrambled to his feet. "Yeah."

"Turn it on and leave it on." Brigid's eyes never left the door. She could hear something approaching, and the faint scent of ash that pricked her nose told her a familiar vampire was walking toward them.

"Maybe I could kill a vampire." Lucas stood in front of her, his thin body shaking. "If I had to." Lucas walked away and slammed the door to the bathroom. "I'm shutting the door, locking it, and turning on the fan and the water."

"Good lad." Brigid waited for the door to open with a crash or a bang, but a faint tap and a creaking hinge was the only warning before a familiar pale face peeped through the door.

"Brigid." Zasha Sokholov smiled. "It's been too long."

TWENTY-FIVE

Carwyn, Bernard, and three humans walked down the broad dock, the humans in front of them armed and checking to the right and the left as they made their way to the covered slip where the "foreign" couple was staying.

They passed a large warehouse and smaller boat slips on the left, and then the first row of uncovered houseboat moorings was on their left with more on the right, cozied up to the main dock closest to shore.

"How big was their houseboat?" Carwyn asked quietly.

"The old man didn't know."

They passed the second row of moorings, and in the distance, Carwyn could see a few lights dotting houseboat windows.

The third branch of the dock stretched out to the left and into the darkness of the lake at night, the moonless night made more profound by the soaring metal roofs that sheltered the watercraft on the third row of boat slips.

"Here." Bernard turned left and started down the walkway, moving at human speed as his eyes darted right and left. "Their houseboat is on the right side."

There were a few ordinary humans sitting out on the decks now that the day had cooled to night, enjoying the desert breeze and the warm, dry air off the shore.

"Three down on the right," Bernard whispered.

Carwyn heard the proclamation as if it were a bomb. "She's not here."

"We have to look."

He could feel her in his chest, her blood mingled with his. "Fine, but she's not here. I can't feel her."

Bernard stopped at the slip that the store owner had mentioned. In the darkness, the glowing white walls reflected the hint of light from the low lights that marked the walkways.

The houseboat's name was *Desert Breeze*, and it looked like a rental. There was generic furniture on the back deck, little clutter or anything personal, and two bikes were tied up to the storage box nailed to the dock.

"Hello, *Desert Breeze*," Bernard called. "Authorities from the Callville Bay harbormaster. We'd like to ask you some questions."

Carwyn heard feet moving on the deck, and a tall, thin couple came walking from the front.

Brigid was not here. He couldn't feel her, and if his mate were aboard this boat, there would be no way to fool his amnis.

"Hello?" A polite male voice came from the darkness. "Hello, we are renting this boat for the week. I'm Jan de Haag, and this is my partner Mina. Is there a problem, Officer?"

Bernard didn't correct them. In his dark clothing and vest, he looked like an officer. "I'm sorry to disturb you. We're searching the docks. There's a fifteen-year-old boy who has gone missing, and we've been given information that he may be in the area."

Carwyn could see the two people clearly. They were Dutch from their names, but he saw no sign of deception on their faces.

"That is very troubling. I am so sorry," the woman named

Mina said. "We haven't seen any boys on their own. There was a family who rented the boat in the slip over there." She pointed down the row and to the right. "But he was clearly in their family. There were three children. I didn't notice anything strange or dangerous." She looked at Jan. "Did you?"

"No." He frowned and shook his head. "They left to go upriver yesterday."

"And you've been here the whole week?" Carwyn asked. "You don't take the boat out at all?"

"Oh yah, for sure, during the day we do." Jan nodded. "But we like to tie up at night. Visit the store in the morning for coffee. All that." He waved in the direction of the harbor convenience store. "The old man there, he tells me the good fishing spots."

"I see." Bernard stepped forward and reached out a hand. "I'm going to give you my card. If you see anything out of the ordinary, please give me a call."

"We for sure will," Mina said. "His poor family." She looked at Jan. "All our kids are grown now, but I'm sure his parents must be worried."

"Thank you," Bernard said. "If you think of anything or see anything, please do call."

They turned and walked back to the shore. In his gut, Carwyn knew that Brigid wasn't in any of these boats. "So with a houseboat, you can stay out on the lake for how long?"

"If you prepare correctly, you can stay out for a week or more. People moor the boats to the beaches out on the lake. They don't need deep water because they're flat and long. But we know whoever is keeping Lucas is out getting newspapers every morning."

"Yes." Carwyn looked over and pointed to the small powerboat attached to the back of a houseboat nearby. "But what if they have one of those?"

Bernard turned to Carwyn and his eyes went wide.

"They could be moored anywhere," Carwyn said. "If they have a boat, they could access the store, buy the newspapers and whatever supplies they need, then zip back out to the house-boat." Carwyn looked into the darkness and the black depths that stretched into the distance. "How many miles of shoreline on Lake Mead?"

"Over five hundred." Bernard came to stand beside him. "I'll tell the wind vampires to hurry up."

"Tell them to get a move on," Carwyn said. "And get us a boat."

ZASHA WAS SITTING on a folding chair, their legs crossed and one foot swaying back and forth in an idle motion. Behind them, a thin vampire with a milky-white face, slightly red cheeks that indicated he'd fed recently, and sandy-brown hair and a goatee leaned against a wall. He was wearing a nondescript cream button-down shirt and linen pants, and he stared at Brigid with piercing blue eyes.

"It's good to see you," Zasha said. "I feel as if we've been able to spend more time together in these last few days."

You absolute raving monster.

Brigid glanced at Button-Down Man, but Zasha made no move to introduce him.

"You know, Zasha, if you wanted to see me, all you had to do was call." Brigid squared her shoulders to the door, never turning her back on the frightfully elegant creature in front of her or their silent companion. There was something magnetic about Zasha and there always had been. They were attractive in the same way a deadly flower or poisonous plant was beautiful. You knew it could harm you, but leaning closer was irresistible.

Zasha plucked at their pant leg. "I don't know, Brigid. I feel like you would have ignored me if I asked you for a visit." They glanced over their shoulder. "What do you think, Henrik?"

Henrik didn't move or look away from Brigid.

Zasha turned back to her. "Henrik is Dutch and he's very business-minded. Very *focused*. I admire that."

"Opposites attract?"

Zasha perked up. "See? We do know each other. Henrik would like to maim Lucas to get our point across to his mothers that this is a serious proposition, but you'll be happy to know that I have convinced him to keep the boy intact—"

"How generous of you."

"—until the official timeline lapses." Zasha glanced at the wall. "Which will be in five hours."

Brigid's mind raced with options to get Lucas off the boat. The boy was in the bathroom and the door was thin, but the shower door behind it where Lucas had the water running was made of tempered glass.

Henrik hadn't moved or looked away from Brigid, so she decided to act as if the man—likely one of the Anker clan—did not exist.

"I'd apologize for not spending more time with you, Zasha, but I don't usually befriend sociopaths."

Tempered glass would crackle on impact, not shatter, right? Lucas might get cut, but he wouldn't die. The shower turned off, and there was silence beyond the door.

"But you're friends with Tenzin." Zasha's mouth pursed into a bow. "And Tenzin is most definitely a sociopath."

Henrik smirked. Brigid narrowed her eyes. There was something else there. Henrik seemed to be in on a joke Brigid didn't know.

She turned her attention back to Zasha. "Tenzin is not a

sociopath. I admit my husband was surprised. But she took a test online, and she's missin' a fair few of the markers."

"How droll."

Brigid shook her head. "I don't even know what that means."

Lucas piped up from the bathroom. "Droll is another word for amusing."

Brigid barely kept from rolling her eyes. "Cheers, Lucas."

He added, "But in a dry, sarcastic kind of way—"

"Turn on the shower again please."

The shower turned on and the steady stream of water allowed Brigid to relax just a little.

"Really, Brigid." Zasha tutted. "You'd think you didn't trust me. We haven't harmed the boy."

"But you did kidnap him." Her fire spread outward. Always. She'd never been able to direct an explosion when she lost control. "And Henrik wants to maim him. So I think trust would be a bit of a stretch, don't ya?"

Zasha smiled. "Fair point."

She could control a stream of fire with her hands and her amnis, but an explosion with the force to break through the reinforced walls of this boat? She couldn't control that.

Zasha glanced at Henrik and said something in a language that sounded oddly familiar but not. The man nodded, then walked out the door.

They turned back to Brigid and swung their leg back and forth. "You shouldn't trust me, and you definitely shouldn't trust Henrik. The Dutch are so economical in their cruelty, don't you think?"

Definitely Dutch. Definitely Anker. "I don't know many Dutch people—I just love the cheese."

Zasha blinked. "I don't eat cheese. It tastes like spoiled milk."

No wonder you're a sociopath.

TWENTY-SIX

Bernard moved onto the triangular boat with yellow and black stripes that pulled up to the dock. He handed a phone to his human assistant and turned to Carwyn as he stepped down into the large vessel.

Ugh. Boats.

He'd never liked the things and he never would. At least this lake wasn't the ocean, with miles and miles of water keeping him away from his element.

"Rose and Agnes are on the way," Bernard said, "and they're sending more humans by helicopter."

Carwyn didn't know any vampires who wouldn't destabilize a helicopter, but many kept them just so they could move around human staff quickly. "How many humans?"

"A dozen, all who know how to drive a speedboat. They'll be dropped off at the major marinas on the lake. Agnes is already calling in favors to secure the boats we'll need."

Carwyn felt the boat pull away and the earth getting farther and farther from his touch. "How many marinas in total?"

"That will already have the kind of boats we need? Three. This one, Temple Bar on the east side of the lake, and the main boating marina near Boulder City. They've already called all their people in the area, several of whom are water vampires. Houseboats have to dock near the shore, and there are a limited number of beaches where a boat of that size could be. We're going to find them."

Carwyn sat at the far back of the cruiser as it puttered through the parking lot of lake vessels. He would keep well away from the electrical panels and instruments, but he craned his neck to look forward. "The signs back at the marina said that high-speed boating wasn't allowed at night."

As much as Carwyn loved an adrenaline rush—preferably on land—he felt that hurling a large floating vessel into the night at high speeds in the company of a dozen other boats piloted by humans was a recipe for disaster.

Bernard nodded to the front. "All the boats will have a vampire in the front to keep an eye out."

As if he'd given a signal, a blond head with long hair tied in a topknot popped up from the bow of the ship, and Carwyn realized that the front of the boat was entirely open to the air. Fascinating.

The vampire in the bow raised her hand and motioned with her fingers in a "come on" gesture. The human piloting the boat pulled the throttle down, the engine roared, and the speedboat plunged into the black darkness of the moonless night.

"IT'S BEEN fun getting to know you better, watching you run around the city at night, following your little leads and clues." Zasha was still pretending to be friendly, maybe more so since Henrik had left Lucas's room. "It's been like my own personal detective drama. You even have a tortured psyche to speculate about."

"Do I?"

"Oh yes. The combination of addiction, Catholic guilt, and obligation makes you most entertaining."

"Glad I could amuse you."

Zasha cocked their head. "Do you mean that?"

Brigid frowned. "Of course I don't. And we haven't spent any time together, Zasha. You *don't* know me; we're not friends."

"Now you're being boring again. That's your mate talking with his borrowed human morality."

"Human morality? Why don't we talk about immortal etiquette, eh? You've been terrorizing a young lad who's under the aegis of two powerful vampires. Humans under aegis are supposed to off-limits, Zasha."

"I didn't kidnap him." They put a hand to their chest. "He came to me."

"To Alina."

Zasha's eyes grew cold and distant. "I am really quite annoyed with my brother for killing that girl. She was a lovely pet."

Brigid wasn't particularly pleased with Oleg herself. "Added to all that, you're carryin' water for the Ankers, a clan of spies, blackmailers, and thieves."

"And? You're listing all the things I like about them. At least their dishonesty is honest. What do you get out of lying to yourself, Brigid Connor?"

Brigid ignored them, creeping closer to Zasha by increments. "You're more powerful and you're smarter. Why do you bother doing their bidding?"

"Money." Their eyes were alight with amusement.

"Bollocks. You don't care about money."

Zasha pouted again. "I don't care about money—you're right."

"So why?"

They smiled, propping their chin on their fisted hand. "When I first met you, you were using an alias and you had the most delightful wig. Do you remember that? It feels so long ago."

Brigid sighed. Trying to have a logical conversation with Zasha was like trying to chase a squirrel. "Are you talkin' about Claire?"

She'd been infiltrating the human hunts of Ivan Sokholov, Zasha's direct immortal descendant. She wasn't sure if Ivan was a child or a grandchild, but there was a blood connection for sure.

Zasha clapped. "Yes! Lovely, innocent Claire."

"I remember riding across from you in the car from Eureka."

"Hmmm." Zasha laughed a little bit. "Claire McKee. So quaint and Irish of you. That was my first clue."

"That my name was too Irish? Brigid Connor isn't any less Irish."

"I know, but there was something *there*. You were good, but you just didn't look like a Claire."

"I didn't know who you were; I thought you were beautiful."

"Thank you." Zasha cocked their head. "I'm flattered. That means a lot to me."

Keep the focus on them. If there was one thing she knew would kill time, it was Zasha talking about themself. Narcissists loved to talk about themselves.

"And powerful," Brigid continued. "I couldn't tell anything about your amnis or your element. You were like an elemental black hole."

"It's a talent I've perfected over the years." They plucked at their pant leg again. "I don't like to advertise."

Even now, knowing Zasha as Brigid did, she couldn't feel their fire. The faint hint of smoke was the only tell. "What about me? How am I doin'?"

"Smoke is practically coming out of your pores." Zasha's smile was flirtatious. "You've never been very good at hiding what you are, Brigid Connor."

"You're probably right. I was shite at undercover with anyone but humans."

"And yet here you are, successful despite all that."

Successful? Was Zasha jealous of her? That didn't make sense. They were far more feared in the vampire world. Brigid was a blunt instrument that Murphy pulled out to bully people, and Zasha was a clever, seductive scalpel.

"Why are you doin' this?" Brigid asked. "Why d'ya care about the Ankers gaining control of the city? You're more powerful than any of them lot. All they have is money and information. What good is any of that to you?"

"There's very little I want in the world, Brigid Connor." A hint of Zasha's Russian accent crept into their speech. "I want to be amused. I want to hunt and have my way. I would say I like to kill humans, but in reality I find them boring. It's really been a very long time since I had any worthy adversary."

"I don't know, but I can imagine. Are you calling me a worthy adversary?"

Zasha ignored the question, and their eyes drifted to the wall behind her. "I am older than your mate. My own mate was older than me. Far older."

Wait, what? Brigid tried to not let the shock show, but Zasha must have sensed it.

"You didn't know I had a mate?" They smiled. "I did. They loved me, the only creature who ever did. Their blood still lives in me. That is the gift of mating." They leaned forward and their fangs fell, cutting their bottom lip. "They survive. They *persist*. No matter how long they are gone, their amnis is with you. Their memories are yours. They live on in you, and their vengeance becomes your own."

"Their vengeance?"

Zasha sat back. "There are things I want to know, and you... Stumbling, stupid little girl. You fell into power because you were a heroin addict. A drug addict who had the good timing to kill herself in front of a sentimental vampire."

How did Zasha know so much about her? Why did they care? Their words stung no matter how many times Brigid had repeated them to herself over the years. "Correction. I *am* a heroin addict." Her voice was rough. "I just can't get high anymore."

"Except with your fire." Zasha's eyes lit up, and their accent grew stronger. "Does it feel the same? Does it take you away? I never experienced drugs in my lifetime. Describe it to me."

"No."

Zasha rolled their eyes. "You're boring, Brigid Connor. Weak and boring. You ended your human life and landed in one with power and potential. So I suppose you're weak, boring, and *lucky*."

A sour taste gathered at the back of Brigid's throat. "So leave me alone then."

"No." Zasha stared at her with unblinking eyes. "Do you know how long it took me to become a vampire? Fifteen years. Fifteen years of servanthood and abuse. Fifteen years fucking whoever came into my sire's household if they wanted me. Fifteen years of being a blood slave for a monster."

"That's terrible and should have never happened to you." If there was a life that would produce a sociopathic vampire, that was it. "You've been a captive, Zasha. Let Lucas go. This is between the two of us. You want to fight me? You want a duel? What?"

"Boring," Zasha spat out. "You irritate me, Brigid Connor. I fought and bled and suffered for my immortality. I groveled before my hateful sire to gain this power, and you? You trip into it and land in roses. You don't even want it."

"I do want it." Brigid said it without thinking and blinked when she realized she was telling the truth. "If for no other reason than to protect the innocent from monsters like you."

"Monsters like *me*?" Zasha stared at the bathroom door over Brigid's shoulder. "You want to protect the boy? Take him away from those two vampires who will turn him as soon as he reaches maturity. *That* would be protecting him."

"A grand idea. Why don't you let us go and I'll take him away."

Zasha sighed. "But I made a promise, Brigid Connor."

"To who?" Brigid's mind was racing. Lucas had turned the shower off again. He was listening to their conversation, and all Brigid could think about was getting the lad away from Zasha. The vampire had no tells. For all Brigid knew, they could explode at any time, consuming Brigid, Lucas, and the entire boat without a hair on their head being singed. "You promised me to the Ankers? You promised to hand over the boy? The city? Like you care about promises. Let the boy go and we'll keep things interesting."

"I think it's interesting right now." Zasha leaned back. "Don't you?" They twirled their finger in Brigid's direction. "I can see your little mind whirling, trying to think of a way out, but there isn't one. We customized this houseboat especially for you, Brigid. And the boy, but mostly you. You can't get out of here without killing him."

"Are you sure about that?"

"Fairly sure, yes."

She needed to call her fire, set off an explosion, and get Lucas off the boat.

How?

Her blood began to boil, and her fire whispered to her in the back of her mind.

Let me go.

Let me burn.

You know I won't hurt you.

Her amnis caressed her mind, rising to the surface and stroking the deep part of her gut where the hunger lived.

The hunger was her constant friend. Her own familiar monster.

"Fuck the Ankers." Brigid curled her lip. "And fuck you too."

Zasha sat up straight. "Well, well. Now you're becoming interesting again."

Brigid moved closer, and inside her, the fire sat at the ready. "Fuck the Ankers and *fuck you too*. I thought you were powerful, Zasha, but you're nothing but a rich man's servant again."

They narrowed their black eyes. "I am no man's servant."

"But they bought you all the same." The amnis licked at her skin, and she felt the fire in her palms. It sat just below the surface, ready to snap. "The Ankers *bought* you. What was your price this time? They couldn't buy you with immortality. What did they give you?"

"It's what they *will* give me," Zasha said. "When the time is right."

"You think they'll keep their promises?"

"I will make them."

"They'll put a knife in yer spine the first chance they get. You think they have plans to let you survive after the takeover?"

Zasha smiled. "You're deluding yourself that they could kill me."

"Maybe not them, but Oleg could."

Zasha blinked, and it was everything Brigid was hoping for.

"Think about it." She stepped closer. "I know you think I'm a stupid, stumbling girl, but think about what they'll gain by picking you off for a more powerful friend."

Zasha narrowed their eyes. "Oleg and I share blood."

"So? Oleg is already making moves," Brigid whispered. "You think your kin will care if the Ankers get rid of ya? He'll be *thankin'* them. You're a nuisance in his eyes. How do you think I figured out you were on a houseboat? Mika is the one who told me. Oleg's people are already counting you out."

Zasha stood and forced Brigid to look up. They were much taller. "I know what you're doing."

"What?"

"You're trying to start a fight, but I have other plans for you, Brigid Connor, and I'm going to use the mate you love to bring me what I want." They leaned down and ran a finger down Brigid's fevered skin.

"Carwyn has no part in this." She felt the fire leaping to get out. It bit against her skin and made her heart race.

Zasha had to hear it. There was no chance that Brigid was hiding her anger.

"He'll justify it in the end." Zasha smiled. "He'll bring me what I want because he won't be able to stand to see you hurt. It will kill part of his pure conscience, but that's not my problem, Brigid Connor. It will be up to him."

It was all it took. The thought of Carwyn sacrificing any part of his bone-deep honor to give Zasha what they wanted in exchange for Brigid's safety was enough to make the fire burst out of her skin in an explosion of rage.

The last thought in her mind was a desperate plea to her amnis.

Not the boy!

Then Brigid heard a pop as the room split apart and shattering glass in the bathroom before everything went red.

TWENTY-SEVEN

Carwyn stood when he heard it, nearly falling over in the buffeting wind. "There!"

Bernard was already shouting. "Where was it? Get me the pilots in the helicopter, damn it. Get them on the phone now!"

Carwyn nearly jumped into the water before he stopped and bellowed in rage and frustration. "Zasha!"

"Carwyn, sit down!" Bernard pulled at his shoulder. "There are two people in the air—they'll be there in moments."

And looking for the boy, not his wife.

For the first time in a long time, Carwyn desperately wished his old ally Tenzin were around. She was the strongest wind vampire he knew, and she'd have been able to fly into any wreckage and pick up his mate.

He felt helpless on the water. There was no element for him to pull power from, and his raw human strength wasn't enough.

There was another explosion in the distance and he closed his eyes, sending a silent prayer to the heavens.

Don't let us be too late.

In that moment, Carwyn knew he should care about the child, but all he could think about was Brigid in the middle of an explosion that Zasha had directed at her, burning in the element that gave her life.

He reached into the darkness for their bond, but all he felt was emptiness.

EVERYTHING WAS BLACK.

Brigid woke in cold blackness, her body curled into the fetal position and her feet touching the muddy bottom of the lake as pieces of metal sank slowly in the barely perceptible light.

What happened?

Boat. Explosion.

She had caused the explosion.

Lucas!

Brigid pushed off from the bottom of the lake, surfaced, and coughed out the water that had flooded her lungs when she blacked out. She immediately looked around, puking water and blood as her eyes scanned the white-capped chop. "Lucas."

Her voice was barely audible to her own ears.

She coughed again. "Lucas!"

The wreckage of the houseboat was burning, allowing light to touch the black surface of the lake. Pieces of doors and walls floated. Bits of foam drifted in the air, and the remains of the houseboat rocked violently in the wake.

"Lucas!"

Brigid didn't see Zasha, but there was a body floating in the distance. It was too big to be Lucas. Henrik?

Brigid turned to the sound of splashing and saw a familiar dark head surface and cough.

"Lucas!" She swam toward him, pulling through the water to reach the boy. "Are you hurt?"

He turned toward her, face a mask of shock and confusion. "You blew up the boat."

"Oh thank God." Brigid reached him and grabbed him around the chest. She could smell blood and felt a chunk of glass under her arm, embedded in the boy's chest. "Tell me what hurts." She didn't wait for his answer but began to swim toward the beach in the distance.

The houseboat had been moored near a sandy inlet at the base of a sheer red rock wall. Boulders curved out into the water, creating a small, crescent-moon beach, but the entire spit of land was no more than a dozen feet deep and maybe only thirty feet long. Scrubby bushes grew in the cracks of the rock, and the waves lapped at the red stone walls as the water around the burning houseboat tossed its remains against the shore.

"I can't hear you." Lucas tried to turn toward her as they swam. "I can't hear you."

"Dammit." The blood she smelled wasn't enough to be life threatening, but she'd have to wait and see when she took him out of the water. "You might have burst eardrums."

Even as she swam for shore, she scanned the water around her, waiting for Zasha to emerge. It was too much to hope that they were dead. According to Zasha, fire didn't hurt them, though Brigid only had the other vampire's word on that.

She could feel cool water against her nape and knew that much of her hair had probably burned off again. As she passed the houseboat, she blinked and paused, trying to understand what she was seeing.

The back of the houseboat, where she saw the remnants of pipes and walls, was relatively intact, with the metal shower doorframe still dangling from a single standing wall.

The front of the houseboat, on the other hand, was demolished.

Brigid blinked and the corner of her mouth turned up. "I directed it."

For the first time in her immortal life, the fire had listened to her. She'd pleaded with it not to hurt Lucas and it had listened. The blast had touched the bathroom where he'd been sheltering, but not badly. Most of the force of her fire had been directed at Zasha.

"Brigid, I can't hear you. I can't hear anything."

She patted his shoulder and leaned in to his ear. "Can you hear that?"

He nodded, and she felt some of the tension leave his shoulders.

"Your ears are damaged, but it's probably not permanent."

Brigid struggled to the shore, spitting out lake water as it rushed into her mouth. Once her feet touched the sandy bottom of the beach, she helped Lucas find his footing. He limped a little bit, but otherwise, he was fine.

That was until he realized she was naked.

"Oh." He swiftly turned and showed her his back. "Sorry."

"It's fine." Brigid looked around the water for anything that might cover her body. No use embarrassing the poor boy more than he already was. She saw a torn blue-and-white-striped towel floating in the distance and walked over to grab it, wrapping it around her body before she turned Lucas around. "Look at me."

She could hear motors in the distance, and Lucas was looking at his feet. Were the motors Zasha's people? Carwyn? The Ankers? Anything was possible. "Look at me, Lucas." She tilted his chin up to get a good look at his injuries.

His face had cuts and a few bruises starting to bloom, but his eyes were undamaged. One ear was bleeding, and his lip was cut. He'd already plucked the piece of glass from his chest, and the wound was shallow.

His pants were hanging around his waist, relatively intact. His shirt was torn, and there were other small glass pieces scattered over his chest and shoulders, but none of the cuts appeared to be very deep.

You did it. You kept the fire away from the boy.

Thank you.

She let out a sigh of relief. "Lucas?"

He stared at her and narrowed his eyes. "I can hear you a little bit."

She turned and looked in the distance; there were lights coming toward them. She turned back to the kid. "We need to find a place for you to hide."

He looked around and shook his head. "There's no place here. Didn't that kill Zasha?"

"Probably not."

She picked her way through the debris on the shore, heading to an outcropping of sandstone boulders that jutted out into the water. "Get to the top of this and see if there's some place on the other side where you can hide." She boosted him up the first boulder. "Climb over and hide. I'll get you when it's safe."

"Brigid." His eyes went wide. "Don't leave me."

"I'm not leaving you." She mouthed the words clearly and pointed at the distant lights. "I need to make sure—"

"Brigid Connor!" Zasha's voice cut through the darkness.

"Go," she hissed. "Get out of sight."

Lucas scrambled over the red boulder, and Brigid turned to see Zasha walking out of the water like some enraged sea creature striding onto land. They were soaking wet, dragging a piece of metal that had sheared off from the side of the boat and embedded in their thigh.

Brigid realized that this was the first time she'd faced Zasha when they'd both been rendered powerless to use their fire.

I really wish I had a gun right now.

"Zasha." She tucked the towel around her and walked toward them. "Sorry to see you're still alive."

Not a flowing red hair on Zasha's head had been singed, but had their eyebrows always been gone? Maybe it was true. Maybe something about the vampire's amnis repelled fire and heat. They were still wearing the loose white linen clothes they'd worn on the boat, though the edges of those were torn from the force of the blast.

It couldn't repel objects though. There was a gaping wound in their gut and cuts all over their face, along with the deep puncture wound on their thigh, all of them quickly healing from the vampire's own blood.

"Clever, clever," Zasha muttered. "I see the boy lives. You've grown more skilled since I nearly incinerated you in Louisiana."

"Leave, Zasha." She could feel Carwyn now. His amnis leaped in her blood. "My mate is coming, and unlike me, he won't be unarmed."

Zasha's lip curled. "I'm not ready to let you go yet, Brigid Connor." They lunged toward Brigid with vampire speed, aiming the improvised metal spear at Brigid's throat.

She dodged to the right, falling to the sand and closing her hand around a rock she flung at Zasha's head.

The rock nearly found its mark, glancing off Zasha's temple and leaving another bloody gash. Zasha fell on her, their larger body covering Brigid's as they punched her face and tried to wrench her neck.

"You. Have. Irritated. Me." Zasha tried to grasp Brigid's head between their hands, but she struggled away, the towel falling away from her body. She was naked in the sand, struggling with sheer will against a larger opponent.

But Brigid's skin was drying out.

And Zasha's clothes were still soaking wet.

CARWYN COULD SEE two figures fighting on the beach, the lights from the burning houseboat flickering and smoke rising from the wreckage. He could see Brigid now, her small silhouette powerful and quick against a larger enemy. He could see growing sparks in the darkness, two fire vampires battling near the water, reaching to find their element in the desert night.

What he didn't see was the boy.

Please let him be alive.

Carwyn knew that if Brigid's fire had killed an innocent, she would blame herself for an eternity. He watched the two vampires struggle and felt Brigid's amnis wake, roused by the explosion and the violence. The air was dry, and warm wind swept over the water. Though water surrounded them, they were still in the middle of the desert.

And a fire vampire in the desert was dangerous.

"He's going to pull up as close as we can get to the beach," Bernard said. "We can't damage the boat if we're going to make it back."

"Understood." Carwyn was waiting until it was close enough to leap. "Come on, darling girl. It's waiting for you."

He could feel her amnis in his blood, the fear and the invigoration. She was afraid, but she was utterly and thoroughly alive.

Carwyn's fangs fell as the air around his mate ignited.

"That's a lass." He grinned as he watched her spread her arms and fling a wall of flame toward Zasha Sokholov.

The wind took the fire and swirled it around, catching the brush with its heat and raking the red rock walls of Lake Mead. He felt the hot wind against his face as he squinted and saw Zasha's own fire ignite in response to Brigid's.

Dammit.

"Where are the water vampires?" Bernard shouted. "We have to put them out!"

Zasha would burn anything and everything in their path. They would melt the walls of the canyon before they would surrender.

Carwyn stood. "Brigid, get in the water!"

"Wait!" the human driver yelled. "I'm gonna try something."

He headed straight toward the shore, the boat not slowing as Carwyn had expected.

"Bernard?" The last thing Carwyn wanted was a shattered boat this close to dawn.

"I know what he's doing," Bernard shouted. "Trust him and hold on."

At the last minute before it looked like they would crash, the driver wrenched the wheel of the powerboat, flipping the boat into a curve so tight it angled the vessel nearly on its side and sent a voluminous rooster tail of water crashing onto the narrow beach, soaking the fire vampires and dousing both their flames.

"Jump!" Bernard leaped into the water and Carwyn followed after.

BRIGID WAS SOAKED AGAIN, and Zasha looked like a wet cat looking for escape. They could see Bernard and Carwyn heading for the shore.

"Looking for your exit?" Brigid spat water from her mouth. "There's nowhere to go, Zasha."

"What are you talking about?" Their voice was nonchalant, but their black eyes swept the night like a panicked animal. "I always find a way out."

"Your allies are gone," Brigid said. "And mine are near." She felt the ground tremble when Carwyn's foot touched the shore.

"We're on land now, and that driver can keep turning in circles, dousing our fire. Tell me what the Ankers promised you."

"No." Zasha turned to the two approaching vampires and looked up. "Someone is coming."

Brigid scanned the darkness but saw nothing. Her eyes searched for Carwyn in the water, and she saw the massive outline of her mate lumbering toward the beach. "Tell me what you want with me. Tell me why you're doing this."

"His blood still calls...," Zasha mumbled, their eyes searching the sky.

"Whose blood? Your mate's?" Brigid reached down, picked up a rock, and threw it at Zasha's back. "Tell me what you want!"

Zasha turned to her and spread their arms. "For they shall visit the iniquity of the fathers upon the children and their children's children."

It was a verse Brigid had heard before. "Who shall visit iniquity? God? You're telling me you believe in God now?" Brigid shook her head. "That's not who you are, Zasha."

They smiled. "I don't believe in God, but I do believe in vengeance, Brigid Connor. And the blood of Temur remembers what she has done."

Brigid yelled, "Who the fuck is Temur?"

Zasha was silent and utterly still, their shoulders relaxed as they watched the sky. A small smile touched their lips, and they raised their arms like a child looking for succor.

Carwyn and Bernard were closing in, their speed picking up as they reached the shallows.

"Sokholov, raise your hands!" Bernard was pointing a gun at Zasha.

Brigid saw it when it was too late.

Carwyn reached down and touched the ground, ready to capture Zasha with the red sandstone on the beach, but as the ground opened up beneath their feet, a wind vampire dressed entirely in black swooped down, lifting Zasha with massive arms, snatching them away from the yawning earth as shots rang out.

Within seconds, both the vampires had disappeared from sight.

TWENTY-EIGHT

Lucas was wrapped in a silver emergency blanket as they sped back to shore, and Brigid was wearing Carwyn's shirt, its length enough to cover her nearly to her knees.

They sat in the bow of the powerboat, Carwyn sat behind her, his arms wrapped around her body.

She was in his arms, and he was satisfied. He could breathe again; his heart was calm. His heart lived in her now; the great beast that had been silent for a millennium belonged to the tiny fey creature who fought monsters and protected the innocent.

Carwyn kissed the top of her burned head. "You scared me."

She wrapped an arm around the leg he had propped up on the bench. "I didn't mean to."

"Don't go off on your own, darling girl. You know it makes me crazy."

She said nothing, but she pressed her leg against his and let her head fall back against his chest as she looked up at the stars. "It's nice out here."

He kissed the top of her head again.

"Is it a horror?"

"Not too bad." He ran a hand over the silky black hair and

the burned edges. "You can buzz it again. It's a great look on you, and you'll barely notice the burned bits."

She was silent. Carwyn could feel her amnis bouncing around, dissatisfied with not being able to find vengeance what with Zasha escaping again.

"We found a vampire on the beach with no head. Several human bodies floating."

"Was the vampire dressed in a white button-down shirt?"

"No clothes left."

"Brown hair and beard?"

"We didn't find the head. He was tall."

Brigid nodded. "It could have been a vampire called Henrik Anker. He was on the boat with us."

"Any other Ankers?"

She shook her head. "Not that I know of."

"Lee found evidence of a very sneaky virus in Agnes and Rose's servers. It looks like the Ankers weren't prepared to let Zasha take the reins after all."

"They can't work out in the open because no one trusts them and vampire tourism to the city would dry up," Brigid said. "But they need a more reliable ally. They're going to pick someone more respectable next time. Someone the rest of the world sees as legitimate."

"I have a couple of ideas." Carwyn took a breath. "Oleg."

"Oleg." Brigid looked over her shoulder. "He's my first thought."

"For right now, he's playing well with others." Carwyn had seen the fire vampire's morals come and go with the trends of the moment. "We'll have to watch and see what happens."

Brigid wiggled down farther, turning her face to his chest. "I want to get out of this city. I found the boy. Agnes and Rose can clean up their own messes here; I have the equivalent of a vampire hangover."

Carwyn smiled and ran his hand over her head again. "You saved the boy."

Brigid turned her head to look at the teenager wrapped in a silver blanket. "He's a good lad."

"I'm glad he had you protecting him."

"I didn't do much other than get caught." Her voice dropped. "I won't be trusting humans blindly again."

"Probably a good policy." He pictured the wreckage of the boat in his mind. "You directed your fire."

"Yeah." She sounded pleased. "I did."

The lights of the marina glowed in the distance, and a helicopter *thwupped* overhead. "We have plenty of time to get back to the city. Are you ready to be alone?"

"Yes, but I wanna get Lucas home first."

Carwyn nodded. He'd expected that answer, so he didn't argue even though he wanted to get Brigid back to a room with locks, steel doors, and him guarding those doors as soon as possible.

The roar of the motor was dull as the wind whipped around them. Carwyn saw several other boats with their red and blue running lights blinking in the distance.

"Did you know Zasha Sokholov had a mate?"

Carwyn's arm tightened around her. "No."

They slowed and pulled into the harbor. There were humans on the dock, and a long black car had pulled up close to the water. Agnes and Rose stood on the end of the dock, waving at the boat as Lucas stood and waved back, a huge smile on his face.

Brigid asked, "How old is Oleg?"

"Probably around my age," Carwyn asked. "Why are you asking about Oleg?"

"Zasha and Oleg had the same sire, right? Was their sire as old as Tenzin?"

"Not nearly. He was a hateful old earth vampire from antiquity, but not as old as Tenzin. A Slav, maybe part Hun. I'm not sure. Roamed around Central Asia and Eastern Europe wreaking havoc. He was awful, but he wasn't as powerful as Tenzin, though it's possible she knew of him during the period when they were both in Central Asia."

"Oleg killed him."

"Yes." Carwyn sat up, and Brigid swung her legs over the side of the bench. "What is this? What are you thinking?"

Brigid cast her eyes to Bernard and the human driver, shaking her head.

Carwyn got her meaning. "It takes force of will to kill your own sire," he said, "even if you hate them. It's not something our instincts usually allow."

"I think Zasha is playing a very long game," Brigid murmured. "And I think the Ankers are a very small part of it."

BRIGID SAT IN the living room of the mansion in Las Vegas, Lucas freshly washed and dressed in comfortable sweatpants and a T-shirt, a doctor giving him a quick checkup as his little sister jumped around. Rose and Agnes sat close to each other, watching the boy like the mother hens they were.

You want to protect the boy? Take him away from those two vampires who will turn him as soon as he reaches maturity. That would be protecting him.

She tried to rid her mind of Zasha's voice. The vampire had been messing with her head, trying to play on her fears for the child and her own mixed feelings about being turned by a loving but distraught sire.

Rose and Agnes clearly adored him. They would protect

him. Agnes almost had to handcuff her mate to keep Rose from hovering over Lucas while the doctor checked his ears.

"Excuse me?"

She turned to see Lucas's little sister, Anna, standing at her side.

Brigid hadn't even noticed the girl approaching. She was either a stealth master or Brigid was exhausted and not thinking straight.

"Hello, Anna."

"You found my brother."

Brigid smiled. "Not just me. Bernard, Miguel, and Carwyn all helped. Lots of people helped."

"But you got him away from the bad vampires?"

Brigid hesitated. "I... helped."

Anna's eyes were fixed on her face. "Did you kill them?"

Lying would be pointless. "Some of them. Not all."

"Are you going to kill the rest when you can?"

Brigid nodded. "Yes. I surely am."

"Good." Anne looked at her brother, then back at Brigid. "I can help you if you want."

"It's quite dangerous, so no. But thanks. I can tell you love your brother a lot."

The little girl's bow-mouth wrinkled. "I'm going to be a vampire as soon as I'm big. Then I'll protect Lucas. He doesn't want to be, but I do, and Rose said that she can make me one if I want."

Well that was... a lot.

"That's a very grown-up choice, Anna. I think you need to wait a long time to make that decision."

"That's what Agnes said, but I know what I want and so does Rose." Anna looked at Lucas again. "No one will ever take me from Agnes and Rose. I wouldn't let them."

I suspect they would regret trying.

"Be kind to Lucas." It was the only thing Brigid could think so say. "He missed home a lot, and he lost a friend."

"Miguel?" Anna frowned. "Rose said Miguel was going to live even though he probably should die for losing Lucas."

"No, I'm not talking about Miguel." She was glad to hear the man would live. Less glad to know that Rose blamed the man for Lucas's kidnapping. "Your brother lost a friend named Angel. He'll probably be very sad about that."

She'd seen how the news had already affected the boy when Bernard casually mentioned Alina Oorzhak's death in the car. They might have known Alina as Zasha's conspirator, but Lucas still knew her as Angel, the girl who'd flirted with and befriended him.

"I'll be nice to him." Anna picked up the large white cat that curled around her legs. "I'll even play chess with him if he wants."

Brigid smiled. "I'm sure he'd love that."

Carwyn walked over from talking to Agnes. "Hello, Anna. How are you?"

"I am doing fine." Her expression was remote. "Are you ready to go? I want Lucas to myself please."

He patted her head, not noticing that the little girl rolled her eyes. "Of course you do, dove. You've been missing your brother, haven't you? We'll get out of your hair, won't we?" He held his hand out for Brigid. "You ready?"

"Yes." Brigid rose, took Carwyn's hand, and nodded at Anna. "Anna, don't forget what I said."

"I won't." Her clear brown eyes blinked at Brigid. "You too."

"If I need your help, I'll call."

"Good." She turned, walked over to the sofa where Lucas was sitting, and climbed up next to him, placing the fluffy white cat in his lap.

Carwyn and Brigid were nearly out the door when she heard Lucas calling her name.

She turned to Carwyn. "Give me a moment?"

"Of course." He smiled. "I'll wait for you in the car."

Brigid walked over to Lucas. "Hey, how are you—?"

"Can we talk in the garden?"

She narrowed her eyes. "Sure thing."

They walked out the door, and Lucas guided her toward a winding path that led under an arbor to a quiet corner of the rose garden on the side of the house. "There aren't any microphones here. I heard Agnes say it once. That's why she has meetings here sometimes."

"I see." How much of Lucas's house was under surveillance? "It's gonna get worse now, isn't it?"

He shrugged. "For a while. Is Miguel going to be okay? Are they going to kill him?"

"I don't think so. I can make sure he has our information though. Would that make you feel better? Carwyn will check on him before we leave the city."

He nodded. "I told Agnes that it wasn't his fault a bunch of times, but Rose..." He shrugged.

"Rose loves you. Make sure she knows how much you love Miguel."

Lucas opened his mouth, then closed it and nodded.

"Good chap."

He glanced at the glowing windows of the house. "Was Zasha right?"

Probably.

"About what?" Brigid asked.

"Will Agnes and Rose turn me as soon as I grow up?"

Brigid didn't know how to answer him. "I think if that's something you want to avoid, you should make it very clear when you are young that there are *human* things you want to do as a *human* that you could not do as a vampire and you would be extremely heartbroken if you couldn't do those things *as a human.* Do ya understand what I'm saying?"

He nodded. "Yeah. Got it."

"Sometimes we hold on to things we love even when we know that it might not be the best thing or might not be the thing that's best for us." She smiled a little. "All love can be a little unhinged, Sir Lucas."

The corner of his mouth turned up. "Sir Lucas?"

"I think you're a knight too." She reached out and tapped his shoulder with her fist. "You're no pawn. You were very smart in close gameplay."

Lucas smiled. "You listened."

"Course I did. You're a smart young fella and a good strategist."

Lucas's smile fell. "Zasha isn't dead, are they?"

Brigid shook her head.

"Then you know what you need to do."

She frowned. "Maybe I did miss something."

Lucas stepped back and waved his arm as if he was wiping a table. "Clear the board, remember? Bishops are most powerful when they clear the board."

TWENTY-NINE

Lee was packing up the house the next evening. "I never thought I'd be relieved to be going back to an old house in the middle of the woods where every other tree looks like Bigfoot is hiding behind it."

Carwyn was already packed. It didn't take that much time to throw three shirts and two pairs of pants in a duffel bag. "Do you really think we need a Winnebago?"

"Fuck yes, you do." Lee's eyes lit up and he pulled out his phone. "Have you seen those things?"

Lee paused to direct two moving people toward the office and all the equipment they were shipping back to the Del Marco Casino. "Over there, guys. I already disconnected my hard drive, so all the rest is yours."

"Thanks, Lee."

"No, thank you. Good working with you guys."

Lee walked over to the kitchen counter in the rental house and picked up a tablet. "Look at this one I found. It's vintage but completely redone, and it would be easy to make light safe. Full bathroom, full bedroom, eating area."

"I feel like you want a Winnebago, not me."

"No, I want your old van, remember?" He pulled up a picture of a boxy and colorful motorhome with red stripes and a pair of bright orange hibiscus painted on the side.

Carwyn saw the flowers. "I'm intrigued."

"I thought you would be, so I put a watch on it. It's an eBay auction, and it's already met the reserve. Less than a hundred thousand miles on it and the engine was recently rebuilt."

Carwyn sat down, staring as Lee flipped through the pictures of the motor home. "It has Hawaiian-print interior?"

"Oh yeah."

He needed it. He had to have it. "Brigid!"

"She went out a little bit ago." Lee clicked through the pictures, one after another. "Look at the way they redid the kitchen."

Carwyn was confused. "What?"

"The kitchen. They painted everything—"

"Not the bloody kitchen, Lee. Where did Brigid go?"

Lee shrugged. "I don't know. She said she was going out; that's all."

Carwyn reached for her, but the feelings he was getting from her amnis were... confusing. Determination. Focus. He felt like there was a buffer around her feelings; she was confused or hiding or both.

Regret?

They'd made love at dusk and there had been something violent and a little desperate about her. She'd fed before dawn the night before, but far from the peaceful mate he'd expected to wake to, she'd been troubled and she wouldn't tell him why.

What are you doing, darling girl?

He'd put it down to her losing Zasha again even though Carwyn had told her they'd go on the offensive before the vampire could wreak more havoc. Carwyn had already called his friend Giovanni and his daughter Carla. Both had experience finding people who didn't want to be found and eliminating them if necessary.

He didn't ask questions of his daughter, but he knew.

Carwyn walked to the bedroom and grabbed his phone, dialing Brigid's number, unsurprised when it went to voice mail.

He stared at the phone with irritation, then turned it off and tossed it on the bed. "What are you doing, Brigid Connor?"

He walked back out to the kitchen. "Lee, can you track her phone?"

"No." Lee's eyes were wide. "We disabled that feature, remember? You and Brigid were worried that the Nocht software would enable Murphy to find her wherever she was, so you both asked me to disable the—"

"Fuck!" Carwyn stormed back into the bedroom and grabbed his phone again. "Brigid, what are you doing?"

Lee was in the hallway. "What's going on?"

She felt... remote. Distant.

Did you know Zasha Sokholov had a mate?

She'd been asking about Oleg. About their sire. He should have seen the signs, but he'd been so relieved to have her back with the boy in tow he hadn't realized what she was feeling.

The job wasn't finished. Not nearly finished.

Brigid was still working.

Carwyn dialed her number again, and this time when it went to voice mail, he didn't hang up. "Brigid? I know what you're doing and it's a bad idea..."

"...WE *can do this together. We* need *to do this together. I've already called Giovanni. I've called Carla. I'll explain why when you get home because you need to come home, love."* Her husband sighed. *"You need to come home. Don't... don't do this without me."* He cursed under his breath. *"Don't try to do this without me."*

The message finished, and Brigid tossed her phone on the passenger seat in the back of the hired car before she ran a hand over her freshly shaven head. Carwyn had clipped it at nightfall, right after they'd made love.

It felt clean. Fresh.

Battle ready.

She knew why her husband had called Carla. Enough quiet hints had been dropped over the years for Brigid to have figured out what Carla could do. And he was right—bringing a tracker on would be helpful. Bringing an experienced fire vampire on would be helpful too.

But this wasn't their fight; it wasn't hers either. But Brigid was pretty sure she knew whose fight it was, and the difference between her and Carwyn was that Brigid would be willing to do what it took to bring the fight to Zasha Sokholov.

"Hey, you wanted me to bring you here, I did it. I can't get in that gate, lady." The cabdriver looked at her in the rearview mirror. "You getting out or you want me to take you someplace else?"

She grabbed her phone and her backpack. "Here is fine. Thank you for being quiet."

"No problem." He looked over his shoulder. "For what it's worth, I agree with your man. You got a problem, it's never good to try to go it alone. Strong people aren't afraid to ask for help, you hear me?"

Brigid smiled. "I hear you. And don't worry—I'm going to ask for help."

"Good." He winked at her. "Good kid. Take care of you, okay?"

"Thanks." She got out of the car and paused at the gate of Oleg's housing development to wait for his guards to sense her.

She took out her phone and used a stylus to punch in a message to Carwyn.

The bishop is clearing the board.

Brigid waited in the darkness, remembering another night filled with fire and wind.

The blood of Temur remembers who you were!

Zasha had shouted it at Tenzin over a year ago, and the previous night Zasha had mentioned Temur again. Had Temur been Zasha's mate?

For they shall visit the iniquity of the fathers upon the children and their children's children.

This wasn't about the Ankers; that was a distraction. This wasn't about Agnes and Rose. It wasn't about Ivan. It wasn't about New Orleans. This wasn't even really about Brigid. This was about the life she'd fallen into, the company she kept, and the connections she'd made.

So it was maybe a little bit about Brigid.

Mika Arakas met her at the iron gate, triggering the exit to allow her into the neighborhood. "Brigid Connor."

"Mika Arakas."

"I like the hair."

"I don't." She slung her backpack over her shoulder and walked under the arching trees that lined the streets leading to Oleg's house. "I need to speak to Oleg."

"Then I'm assuming that Zasha isn't dead yet?"

"No, but they will be soon." She glanced at Mika. "And your boss is going to help me."

CARWYN SHOWED up at Agnes and Rose's house just before midnight. Lee and he had packed the van, and Carwyn had noticed what was missing.

A backpack. Her documents. Her favorite pistol.

His woman did know how to pack light.

He nodded to Bernard when the man answered the door. "I need to speak to Lucas."

The vampire frowned. "The boy is sleeping."

"It's important or I wouldn't ask." He glanced over his shoulder. "We're leaving tonight. Since we're subcontracting under Katya, I'll let Agnes and her work out whatever business arrangement they agreed to about our fee."

"Very well, but Lucas is still sleeping."

Carwyn's mood must have been evident in his expression.

Bernard cleared his throat. "I'll see if he might be able to wake up. The doctor did say his rest was important right now..."

Carwyn remained silent.

"But I'm sure he'd like to say goodbye before you leave the city."

"I'm sure he would. Good idea, Bernard."

Rose came the door moments later. "You and your mate are finished here. You have no need to speak to Lucas."

"I do." He stared at Rose Di Marco, as immovable as a stone in front of her door.

Rose didn't move either. She arched her eyebrow and cocked her head. "Do you think you scare me?"

Carwyn let a low, dangerous rumble color his voice. "I should."

She bared her fangs. "And you think I'm going to let you see my—"

"Mom."

Rose turned when she heard Lucas's voice.

"It's fine." He walked to the door and put a hand on Rose's arm. It was only then that Carwyn realized the boy was taller than Rose and nearly taller than Agnes.

He wasn't a boy; he was a young man.

"It's okay." He put his arm around Rose's shoulder. "I wanted to talk to them before they left. To say thank you."

Rose's eyes immediately softened. "Don't be long. You need your sleep."

He leaned over and kissed her cheek. "I won't. I promise." He slid on a pair of sandals and walked out the front door, rolling his eyes a little as he glanced at Carwyn.

"Rose." Carwyn inclined his head.

"Carwyn."

He followed Lucas along the path that ran around the side of the house to a small arbor that was planted with roses and night-blooming jasmine.

Carwyn didn't wait to tell Lucas. "Brigid is gone."

The boy blinked. "What?"

"She left tonight. Just after dusk. She sent me a message that the bishop was clearing the board."

Lucas's eyes went wide, and Carwyn knew he'd guessed correctly.

"She's talking about chess, isn't she?"

His voice was small. "I think so."

Carwyn huffed out a harsh breath. "I think Brigid is going after Zasha on her own, and I need you to tell me everything that happened on that boat."

"What?"

"She left, Lucas. And I think it was because of something Zasha said, so I need your help."

Lucas walked over and sat down on a stone bench. "I'll tell you everything I remember, but I didn't hear everything because she made me go in the shower and keep the water running."

"Because of the fire."

"Yeah," he said. "But I'll tell you what I did hear. And what we talked about."

Which was, Carwyn discovered over the following half an hour, quite a lot.

Carwyn stared at the boy, annoyed, frustrated, and reluctantly impressed. "You called her a bishop?"

Lucas nodded. "Because of the way she fights. Most vampires are chess pieces."

And bishops are more effective when pawns are out of the way.

"Fuck me," Carwyn muttered. The boy wasn't wrong.

"Didn't you used to be a priest?"

"But not a bishop." Carwyn raised an eyebrow. "My street-smart wife is rubbing off on my language. You should be so lucky someday."

Lucas smiled a little. "I think Brigid cares more about protecting people than anyone I've ever met. And pawns get in the way."

"You're not wrong." He took a deep breath and sat across from Lucas on the opposite bench. "A bishop."

"You're not a bishop," Lucas said. "I can tell."

"In this situation, I'm feeling more like a pawn." Carwyn crossed his arms over his chest and barely kept from shouting a stream of curses at his loving, impetuous, and stupidly brave wife.

"You're definitely not a pawn," Lucas said. "I don't know you very well, but I think you're a rook."

"I'm a bird?" The black crow was the first thing that popped into his mind.

Lucas shook his head. "The rook is the castle."

"Oh right." Everything was chess to this boy. "Why am I a rook? Because I'm big like a castle?"

"A rook only looks like a castle in Western chess. It was originally meant to represent a chariot. The chariot drivers had fortified compartments that looked a little like castles." Lucas shrugged. "You're not a bird or a castle, you're a chariot."

"Why?"

Lucas smiled a little. "Rooks are placed in the corners of the board. Sometimes people overlook them. *Often* they're forgotten. But they're actually more powerful than bishops or knights. After the queen, they're the most powerful piece on the board because a chariot can go anywhere. Bishops can only go on black or white. Never both. Knights have very closely prescribed movements. But for the rook? All the squares are accessible. Black, white. They can go a few squares or all the way across the board."

"Is that so?" The corner of his mouth turned up. Brigid was right. The boy was very perceptive.

"I think people don't remember how powerful you are sometimes," Lucas continued, "but in the end, a rook can win the whole game. He can capture the king. Checkmate."

"Checkmate." Carwyn stood, walked over to Lucas O'Hara, and patted him on the shoulder. "Good lad."

EPILOGUE

New York City

She didn't want to go to their house, so she broke into the building on the opposite side of the street and made her way to the roof that overlooked their lavish greenhouse garden and waited for the wind vampire to find her.

Brigid sat in an old folding chair that looked out over the glittering night streets of Manhattan and thought of home. She was a city girl. She was born in the city, went to school in the city, and worked in the city. She wasn't a creature of the wasteland but one keenly connected to community. As antisocial as she could be, she knew she drew energy from life around her.

But for this job she needed a creature of the wasteland.

Tenzin found her within the hour.

The wind vampire landed on the roof of the building across the street and walked toward Brigid. "You didn't come to the house."

"No."

She stopped a few feet away, sensing that this wasn't a friendly visit. "Your hair is gone."

"I burned a good portion of it off when I was fighting with Zasha Sokholov last week."

Tenzin's stare revealed nothing. "Where?"

"Lake Mead, Nevada. Just outside Las Vegas. They took a child, held him captive, and tried to take over a city."

"Why?"

"That's an excellent question." Brigid leaned forward in the chair and rested her elbows on her knees.

Tenzin glanced over her shoulder. "Ben will want to see you."

"I'm not here to see Ben."

Tenzin looked back at Brigid. "I know you're not."

"For they shall visit the iniquity of the fathers upon the children and their children's children."

Tenzin frowned. "I do not follow your Christian faith, Brigid Connor. I have little respect for human morality."

"I didn't read that in the Bible—I heard it from Zasha Sokholov."

Tenzin shifted her eyes so she was staring over the city lights. "Zasha Sokholov, who once followed an Eastern Christian faith."

"So you know Zasha?"

Tenzin blinked. "I know of them."

Brigid rose from her seat. "You know more than that."

The other vampire said nothing, but she turned her eyes back to Brigid.

"We may try to run from our past, but it finds us," Brigid said. "I know I've tried to outrun it. I know I've done my best to leave it behind. We can put continents—even millennia—between us, but in the end, the sins of the fathers will come back to visit."

Tenzin lifted her chin. "I am not responsible for my father's sins."

"I'm not here to talk about your father's sins, Tenzin." Brigid sat down again and folded her hands. "I want you to tell me about Temur."

Read the conclusion of the Elemental Covenant series, TIN GOD, coming Summer 2024.

COMING SUMMER 2024: TIN GOD

Everything comes to an end.

Brigid Connor is a vampire familiar with ghosts. The ghosts of her past, the ghosts of her victims, and the ghosts of those she couldn't save. Now in the wilds of America's most remote frontier, she'll face a specter who has haunted her steps, a fire vampire with a baffling connection to Brigid's mate, her clan, and those she holds most dear.

Tenzin is an immortal who has lived a hundred lives. She's been a daughter, a sister, a villain, and a hero. With every millennium, she has evolved, cutting ties with the past and moving forward with relentless focus, a survivor among the fiercest predators in history.

But history has a way of finding those who flee from it.

Tin God is a crossover novel between the Elemental Covenant and the Elemental Legacy series. It is the final book in the Elemental Covenant by eleven-time USA Today bestselling author Elizabeth Hunter.

Available to preorder in ebook from all major retailers.

THANK YOU FOR READING

Thank you for taking the time to read BISHOP'S FLIGHT. I sincerely hope you enjoyed reading it as much as I enjoyed writing it. But if you didn't, that's fair too. Some people have an irrational hatred of ginger vampires in Hawaiian shirts, and I am forced to respect that.

Reviews on Goodreads, BookBub, or wherever you bought the book are always appreciated and will help other readers find books they love. Or want to avoid. Or even want to hate-read! Different stroke for different folks and all that jazz.

The fifth and final book in the Elemental Covenant series will be TIN GOD, coming Summer 2024. It will be a crossover book between the Elemental Covenant and the Elemental Legacy series.

TIN GOD is available to preorder in ebook from all major retailers.

THANK YOU FOR READING

For more information about Elizabeth Hunter's work, please visit her website at ElizabethHunter.com.

LOOKING FOR MORE?

Whether you're a fan of contemporary fantasy, time travel, fantasy romance, or paranormal women's fiction, Elizabeth Hunter has a series for you.

THE ELEMENTAL UNIVERSE

Discover the series that has millions of vampire fans raving!

Immortal book dealer Giovanni Vecchio thought he'd left the bloody world of vampire politics behind when he retired as an assassin, but a chance meeting at a university pulls student librarian Beatrice De Novo into his orbit. Now temptation lurks behind every dark corner as Vecchio's growing attachment to Beatrice competes with a series of clues that could lead to a library lost in time, and a powerful secret that could reshape the immortal world.

Ebook/Audiobook/Paperback/Hardcover

THE SEBA SEGEL SERIES

From eleven-time USA Today Bestselling author Elizabeth Hunter, a unique world of fantasy, magic, and time travel.

Born into a powerful mage family, she's a time traveler whose life is constantly in flux. When one of the highest laws of magic is broken in the thirteenth month, Narine, her friends, and one unsuspecting professor must scour the past and set the timeline right.

Ebook/Paperback

THE IRIN CHRONICLES

Destiny brought them together; heaven will tear them apart.

Hidden at the crossroads of the world, an ancient race battles to protect humanity, even as it dies from within. A photo-journalist tumbles into a world of supernatural guardians protecting humanity from the predatory sons of fallen angels, but will Ava and Malachi's attraction to each other be their salvation or their undoing?

Ebook/Audiobook/Paperback

THE CAMBIO SPRINGS MYSTERIES

Welcome to the desert town of Cambio Springs where the water is cool, the summers sizzle, and all the residents wear fur, feathers, or snakeskin on full moon nights. In a world of cookie-cutter shifter romance, discover a series that has reviewers raving. Five friends find themselves at a crossroads in life; will the tangled ties of community and shared secrets be their salvation or their end?

Ebook/Audiobook/Paperback

Glimmer Lake

Delightfully different paranormal women's fiction! Robin, Val, and Monica were average forty-something moms when a sudden accident leaves all three of them with psychic abilities they never could have predicted! Now all three are seeing things that belong in a fantasy novel, not their small mountain town. Ghosts, visions, omens of doom. These friends need to stick together if they're going to solve the mystery at the heart of Glimmer Lake.

Ebook/Audiobook/Paperback

ABOUT THE AUTHOR

ELIZABETH HUNTER is an eleven-time *USA Today* and international best-selling author of romance, contemporary fantasy, and paranormal mystery. Based in Central California and Addis Ababa, she travels extensively to write fantasy fiction exploring world mythologies, history, and the universal bonds of love, friendship, and family. She has published over forty works of fiction and sold over a million books worldwide. She is the author of the Glimmer Lake series, Love Stories on 7th and Main, the Elemental Legacy series, the Irin Chronicles, the Cambio Springs Mysteries, and other works of fiction.

ELIZABETHHUNTER.COM

ALSO BY ELIZABETH HUNTER

<u>The Elemental Mysteries</u>

A Hidden Fire

This Same Earth

The Force of Wind

A Fall of Water

The Stars Afire

<u>The Elemental World</u>

Building From Ashes

Waterlocked

Blood and Sand

The Bronze Blade

The Scarlet Deep

A Very Proper Monster

A Stone-Kissed Sea

Valley of the Shadow

<u>The Elemental Legacy</u>

Shadows and Gold

Imitation and Alchemy

Omens and Artifacts

Midnight Labyrinth

Blood Apprentice

The Devil and the Dancer

Night's Reckoning

Dawn Caravan

The Bone Scroll

Pearl Sky

<u>The Elemental Covenant</u>

Saint's Passage

Martyr's Promise

Paladin's Kiss

Bishop's Flight

Tin God

(Summer 2024)

<u>The Irin Chronicles</u>

The Scribe

The Singer

The Secret

The Staff and the Blade

The Silent

The Storm

The Seeker

<u>The Seba Segel Series</u>

The Thirteenth Month

Child of Ashes (Summer 2024)

The Gold Flower (Summer 2025)

<u>The Cambio Springs Series</u>

Strange Dreams (anthology)

Shifting Dreams

Desert Bound

Waking Hearts

Dust Born

Vista de Lirio

Double Vision

Mirror Obscure

Trouble Play

Glimmer Lake

Suddenly Psychic

Semi-Psychic Life

Psychic Dreams

Moonstone Cove

Runaway Fate

Fate Actually

Fate Interrupted

Linx & Bogie Mysteries

A Ghost in the Glamour

A Bogie in the Boat

Contemporary Romance

The Genius and the Muse

7th and Main

Ink

Hooked

Grit

Sweet